This Mother's Day,
discover how three daughters cope with their
meddlesome moms in this delightful collection
featuring

BRENDA NOVAK

What a Girl Wants

"This is an author destined for stardom."
–*Romantic Times*

JILL SHALVIS

The Road Home

"Get ready for laughs, passion,
and toe-curling romance."
–*Rendezvous*

ALISON KENT

Upstairs, Downstairs

"Alison Kent delivers a knockout read."
–*Romantic Times*

Brenda Novak is a two-time Golden Heart finalist. Her first book, *Of Noble Birth,* was published in 1999 and she has since sold nine books to the Superromance line. She and her husband, the parents of five children, make their home in Sacramento, California, where Brenda juggles her busy writing career with the demands of field trips and softball games.

Jill Shalvis has been making up stories since she could hold a pencil. Now, thankfully, she gets to do it for a living, and doesn't plan to ever stop. Jill is a bestselling, award-winning author of over two-dozen novels and is a 2000 RITA® Award nominee, and a two-time National Reader's Choice Award winner. Her first single title, *The Street Where She Lives,* appeared in October 2003 and a new one will appear later this year.

Alison Kent was a born reader, but it wasn't until the age of thirty that she decided she wanted to be a writer when she grew up. Five years and a mental library of industry knowledge later, she had the most basic grasp of "how-to" and her first book in print. Alison lives in a Houston, Texas suburb with her hero, three teenagers and a dog named Smith. And she actually manages to write in the midst of all the madness.

Mother, Please!

BRENDA NOVAK
JILL SHALVIS
ALISON KENT

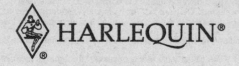

HARLEQUIN®

TORONTO • NEW YORK • LONDON
AMSTERDAM • PARIS • SYDNEY • HAMBURG
STOCKHOLM • ATHENS • TOKYO • MILAN • MADRID
PRAGUE • WARSAW • BUDAPEST • AUCKLAND

ISBN 0-373-83605-8

MOTHER, PLEASE!

Copyright © 2004 by Harlequin Books S.A.

The publisher acknowledges the copyright holders of the individual works as follows:

WHAT A GIRL WANTS
Copyright © 2004 by Brenda Novak

THE ROAD HOME
Copyright © 2004 by Jill Shalvis

UPSTAIRS, DOWNSTAIRS
Copyright © 2004 by Mica Stone

CONTENTS

WHAT A GIRL WANTS

Brenda Novak

For Kendra DeSantolo,
who came along just when I was giving up on finding
the right critique partner. Kendra, thanks for reading
this story when it was only in manuscript form,
for doing it in a week, and for being
as good a friend as you are a critique partner.

CHAPTER ONE

SOME THINGS WERE never meant for a daughter to see. April Ashton was fairly certain that watching her mother stride into her father's company Christmas party on the arm of a man clearly half her age was one of them. The bright red, skintight, sequin-covered dress Claire Ashton was wearing would have embarrassed April enough—it had a neckline that plunged almost to her navel. But her mother was also flaunting a companion who looked barely twenty-five and had the body of a Chippendale dancer.

What was Claire thinking? Pushing her tortoise-shell glasses up to the bridge of her nose, April straightened her own simple black calf-length dress and backed into a corner while she searched the crowded ballroom for her father. Walt Ashton might have launched her mother's midlife crisis, but he was not a subtle man and he wasn't going to take this well. As the owner of Ashton Automotive, he was too accustomed to being in charge. He'd built his L.A.-based company with his own two hands. Now, nearly twenty-seven years later, it was one of the most successful chains of auto-parts stores in the western United States.

A hush rolled through the room. Evidently everyone was beginning to recognize the woman in red. It had taken them a few seconds; April understood why. Claire hardly resembled the woman she used to be. Since April's mother and father had split up four months ago, her mother had lost thirty-five pounds, bleached her hair platinum-blond, acquired a tan even though it was winter, and cast aside her matronly wardrobe for…well, for something better suited to an actress on *Sex and the City*.

Not that April considered herself a fashion expert. She'd long known her brain was her best asset and didn't bother much with fancy clothes or beauty aids. She'd never possessed the kind of curves that would turn a man's head. Which was just as well. She'd learned that few men had egos that could tolerate dating a woman with an IQ above 160. Even the gold diggers her father warned her about had never materialized. She'd gone out with some of the physicists where she worked, but nothing romantic had ever developed. She and the men she dated invariably fell to discussing theories and models, and soon became nothing more than mutually respectful peers.

Suddenly, Rita Schmidt, from Accounting, who

was standing not far away, seemed to notice the whispering that had replaced the initial hush. Craning her head, she stood on tiptoe to see what was happening. "Hey, isn't that..."

Les Burrows, at Rita's elbow, followed her gaze. "Oh, my God—that's the boss's wife!"

This comment elicited a whole storm of response from others in the same group.

"You mean his *ex*-wife...."

"They're not divorced yet...."

"Believe me, that's a mere technicality...."

"It's no secret that Mr. Ashton's been diddling his massage therapist for the past six months."

A few chuckles resounded at the diddling comment, and April briefly considered slipping out the back. She didn't know what was happening to her parents, why her father had strayed after so many years. But she had a lot of work to do at the lab and didn't want to be here. Parties weren't her thing. Give her a good book on the Heisenberg Uncertainty Principle, challenge her to a heated debate on quantum physics, but please don't ask her to dance....

She couldn't leave, though. She'd promised her father she'd stay for the entire evening. He'd told her that Keith Bodine, the local plant manager, was looking forward to seeing her; she didn't return Keith's interest, but her father hoped someday she would. Besides, April was the only one who could keep some semblance of peace between her parents.

Sometimes she hated being an only child.

"I guess we're going to be treated to another family fight," someone else in the crowd whispered loudly, obviously unaware that April was standing so close.

April leaned to the left in time to see her father turn his head in her mother's direction—at which point his eyes nearly popped out of his head. His girlfriend, Regina Parks, stood beside him, but that didn't seem to matter. His face darkened to an unhealthy shade of maroon, and he started tearing through the crowd as if he'd strangle his estranged wife.

April abandoned the safety of her dark corner and intercepted her father before he could reach Claire and her muscle-bound date.

"Dad! Wait!" Bringing him to a stop by clutching his arm, she continued to hold on to him, just in case getting his hands around Claire's neck had really occurred to him. Since her mother had moved in with her several weeks ago, violence had certainly crossed April's mind once or twice. Like yesterday, when she'd come home to her small house at Redondo Beach to find that her mother had rearranged all her furniture.

Her father looked at her, but April wasn't sure

he *saw* her. He was too intent on yanking free, muttering, "How dare she!"

April struggled to retain her hold. "Hang on, Dad. You two have been going through a lot of changes lately," she said, trying to stave off the worst of his anger. "You've barely started divorce proceedings. She'll settle down soon." At least April hoped she would. Her mother's recent talk about getting breast implants wasn't a *good* sign, but April was trying to be optimistic. "Let's not make a scene, okay, Daddy?"

"Not make a scene?" he bellowed. Everyone within twenty feet turned to stare. "She's already made a scene! My God, there's not a man here who isn't stepping on his tongue! Who invited her, anyway?"

"She owns half the company, remember?" April said softly.

"Like hell she does!"

Walt's booming voice finally reached Claire. As she glanced their way, a hurt expression flitted through her eyes. But she blinked, raised her chin and pulled her young date onto the dance floor.

April's father watched with a menacing scowl. "Whether or not she owns part of my company isn't decided yet," he said. "I've got ways to avoid that. Look how she's behaving! I won't risk some gigolo like…like *that* someday staking claim to Ashton Automotive.''

In April's opinion, her father hadn't behaved much better lately. He'd chosen someone a little closer to his own age to date. Commendable. And his barrel chest was, thankfully, well covered. Also commendable. But as her mother was so fond of pointing out, *he* was the one who'd had the affair that started the whole thing.

Regina, the woman who'd tempted her father away, smiled patiently at April while patting her father's other arm. ''Calm down, Wally Woo,'' she said. ''You know you have to be careful about your blood pressure. I'm going to have a heck of a time working the stress out of your poor muscles tonight.''

Wally Woo? Judging by Regina's tone, she was offering much more than a standard massage. April grimaced as a mental picture she did not want to see flashed across her mind, and she thought longingly of her lab and the clear logic and predictability of all that prevailed there.

''She's making a fool out of me,'' her father replied. ''She—''

April never found out what he was going to say next because a tall man approached, effectively interrupting his tirade. April immediately recognized the newcomer. Quincy ''Gunner'' Stevens was a famous race-car driver who'd retired from NASCAR, at the top of his game, just a year or so earlier. She'd met him once before, at a charity auction.

"You made it." His anger temporarily forgotten, her father stuck out his hand and rigorously pumped Gunner's.

Gunner offered the poster-perfect smile April had seen on everything from cereal boxes to motor oil commercials. "Looks like a great party. I'm happy to be here," he said, but April could tell he didn't mean a word of it. His body language screamed *bored*.

Her father drew them all off to one side, and everyone else slowly went back to mingling and chatting, although April noticed several people still throwing covert, disbelieving glances at her mother.

"This is my, um, good friend, Regina Parks," Walt said, turning to Regina, who smiled and nodded. "And my daughter, April."

April didn't bother pointing out that they'd met before. She knew someone as famous as Gunner probably wouldn't remember.

"Nice to meet you," he said, immediately proving her right. As he shook April's hand, his fingers were strong and warm but, like three years ago, he looked straight through her.

His nod to courtesy over, he immediately turned

back to her father. "So, will you have time to meet with me tomorrow, as we discussed?"

"You're certainly ambitious," her father said, chuckling. "But this is a party. Eat. Talk. *Dance.*"

At the suggestion that he dance, her father gave April a little shove. She jerked back to avoid colliding with Gunner and finally got his full attention. But only long enough for him to steady her with a hand to the elbow.

"April here is a quantum physicist," her father announced proudly.

"A what?" Gunner regarded her lazily over the top of his glass as he took a drink. His eyes, April noticed, were as blue-green as the ocean, just the way they appeared on television. But his lashes were quite a bit lighter than she remembered and were tipped with blonde, like his hair. Obviously the gods had smiled on him far more generously than on most men. Not only was he a skilled driver, he was at least five foot eleven and movie-star handsome.

From the rumors that had always circulated about Gunner, and the tabloid photos of him with a variety of women, all of them blond and absolutely perfect, April figured he must possess the complete "famous, shallow, womanizer" mentality. For a moment, she pitied those women not wise enough to see through him. No doubt Gunner Stevens had broken his share of hearts.

"Let's not talk about what I do, Father," she said. "We wouldn't want to bore your guest."

Gunner slowly lowered his drink, and his eyes narrowed as he recognized something missing in her tone—probably the hero-worship he was used to hearing. "Actually, I'm quite interested—April is it?"

"It has little practical application to racing," she said, fairly certain that a man like Gunner couldn't truly be interested in anything that didn't feature him as the main topic.

"So, are you going to be joining us for the company vacation after Christmas, Gunner?" her father asked, oblivious to April's instant dislike, his mind moving on quickly, as it always did.

Gunner's eyes remained riveted on April's face, but he spoke to her father. "I'm afraid not. I have business to attend to back East."

Her father's lips turned down. "That's too bad."

"Are you thinking of using Mr. Stevens for a commercial spot, Dad?" April asked, forgetting Gunner and focusing on her father.

"Actually, I'm thinking of retiring," he said. "And Gunner's made me an offer on the business."

"*What?*" April couldn't believe her ears. Her father had long begged her to work for him so she could take over when he retired, but her heart wasn't in selling car parts. She wanted to further the work of Danish physicist Lene Vestergaard Hau and figure out how to slow the speed of light to ten miles per hour using the Bose-Einstein condensate. But that didn't mean she wanted to see Ashton Automotive go to someone else.

Walt swiveled his head in the direction they'd last seen her mother. "I won't watch what I built go to the dogs," he said. "I'd rather sell out. But I won't turn my company over to just anyone, either."

This last statement had been spoken for Gunner's benefit, April knew. Her father was fiercely protective of both his company and everyone who worked for him.

"You don't want to sell Ashton Automotive, Dad," she said. "I—"

"April, would you care to dance?" Gunner interrupted.

Surprised, April glanced over at him before returning her attention to her father. "No, thank you. Dad, listen to me—"

"I shouldn't have started with business talk," Gunner cut in again. His sensuous mouth formed a charming smile. "We could be having fun."

Her father returned the smile, took Gunner's empty glass and gave it to Regina. "Exactly. Gunner's right. Don't you worry about anything, April. You two dance and have a good time. Nothing's going to happen for a while.'' He put her hand in Gunner's as if his was the last word on the subject. And before she could object, April found herself in the arms of one of the most famous race-car drivers in the world.

CHAPTER TWO

GUNNER STEVENS DIDN'T LIKE being manipulated. He normally didn't allow it. Especially since he'd gotten out of racing. He no longer had to please anyone—not his corporate sponsors, his pit crew, or the rather inflexible officials of NASCAR.

But he was being manipulated now, and he knew it. Walt Ashton was dangling Ashton Automotive in front of him like a carrot while inviting him to this or that event, purposely putting him in contact with Ashton employees to see how he'd fit in and get along with them. It wasn't any secret that Walt wanted to feel good about letting his precious company go, which was admirable—and tolerable because it was so admirable. But, considering the way Walt had shoved April into his arms, Gunner wondered if the manipulation ended there. Maybe Walt was hoping Gunner would take an interest in his plain daughter....

Gunner lowered his gaze to April's face as they moved, rather jerkily on her part, to a Luther Vandross ballad. She had creamy, soft-looking skin with a few freckles across the nose, brown, intelligent eyes and white, straight teeth. But her lips were too thin and certainly didn't curve into an inviting smile. Her thick-framed glasses reminded him of a schoolteacher who'd once banished him from class. And he couldn't remember ever dating a woman who wore her hair in such a no-nonsense bun. Loose and messy, maybe. Sexy. But not pulled back so tight it nearly slanted her eyes.

She took her hand off his shoulder long enough to adjust her glasses. "You're staring," she pointed out, meeting his gaze without flinching.

Gunner cocked an eyebrow at her as he considered the defiant glint in those dark eyes, and purposely let his attention move lower. Skinny. Too skinny. And mostly flat. Not a good combination with a plain face and a sharp tongue.

"Do you mind?" she said.

He grinned at the annoyance in her voice. Walt wasn't playing matchmaker. Anyone could see that an intellectual like April Ashton wasn't Gunner's type. And from the stiff way she danced, and the significant distance she insisted on keeping between them, he doubted she had men standing in line.

"This is supposed to be a slow dance," he murmured when she resisted his attempt to pull her closer.

"I'm aware of that, thank you."

"So maybe you should relax." Once again he tried to maneuver her into a more natural embrace, but her eyebrows gathered above her glasses, and her arms stiffened, holding him right where he was.

"I typically don't dance."

"That comes as quite a surprise."

He knew she'd picked up on his sarcasm when she stumbled and barely missed landing on his foot. He thought she might pull away then, but, for some reason, he was glad she didn't. He wasn't quite ready to let her go. Maybe her cool indifference was a refreshing change.

Or maybe he simply didn't want to face the idea of turning his back on the whole Ashton Automotive deal, because then he'd have nothing to do but head home to the opposite coast. These days his penthouse in New York seemed empty and faraway even when he was just down the street. And the parties and people he'd associated with over the past few years appealed to him even less. Ever since his mother had died eighteen months ago, he didn't want to do anything anymore—not even visit his father, who still lived in upstate New York where Gunner had grown up. Quincy Senior had walked out on Gunner's mother when Gunner was only two. They'd barely heard from him—until Gunner started seeing some real success with racing. Then Quincy Senior began to show significant interest, and now all he could talk about was when Gunner won Rookie of the Year, the Busch Clash, the Coca Cola 600, his first Winston Cup, his last Winston Cup, his other Winston Cups, or his statistics for any given year.

Glory days. Gunner didn't like discussing the past with his father or anyone else. Recounting the achievements of his racing career made him feel as though the best part of his life was over. No one wanted to be a has-been at thirty-five.

"Your father mentioned you're a physicist," he said, preferring conversation to his thoughts.

"Yes."

"Which means you spend your days where?"

"Working in a laboratory for Lenox-Moltinger."

"What kind of company is Lenox-Moltinger?"

She twisted slightly to study the crowd at the edge of the dance floor, and he saw a blush creep up her neck. Following her gaze, he noticed a fif-tyish woman smiling into the face of a young man, both of them unnaturally tanned for Christmastime. They were standing by the silver and white tree, holding hands in a way that suggested to Gunner they weren't mother and son. "Someone you know?" he asked.

April jerked her attention back to him and flushed even more brightly. "Lenox-Moltinger builds com-puter processors," she said, reverting to his earlier question. "You see, light travels extremely fast under normal circumstances, Mr. Stevens—"

"Gunner," he broke in with a smile. He'd heard the respect and pride in Walt's voice when he'd introduced April and knew it couldn't hurt to win her over.

"Um...okay. Gunner, then," she said, obviously flustered and still preoccupied with the couple she was surreptitiously watching. "Anyway, light is a very efficient way to move data."

"Hence the use of fiber-optic cables."

"Exactly. But I'm trying to do the opposite. I'm trying to slow the speed of light."

Her eyes were now fixed on a point past his shoulder. Never had he received less of a woman's attention. When he glanced back, he saw that it was the same couple who held her interest. "Slow it?" he said, bending his head to fall within her range of vision.

"As much as possible," she murmured.

"Why? When it comes to computers, I thought speed was the name of the game."

"It is when you want to *move* data." She tilted her head to look around him and he finally turned so she couldn't see anything.

She blinked and focused on him. "It's much less desirable when you want to *store* data."

"So that's what you're trying to do? Store data using light instead of the usual hard drive?"

"Simply put, yes. In a few years, the Bose-Einstein condensate will enable us to revolutionize the whole computer industry."

Gunner noticed the older woman with the younger man leaving the tree. "Ashton Automotive employees seem pretty close," he said, turning her and nodding toward the couple.

Her lips tightened, but she didn't reveal the reason for her acute interest. "Is that why you want to purchase the company?" she asked. "Because of the camaraderie?"

"Partly." Ashton Automotive had several elements that appealed to Gunner—it was the right size, sold the right product, had the right image. But he was mostly interested in owning a business he could continue to build. Since he'd retired a year ago, he'd been living the rich bachelor's life, spending millions on houses and cars and boats, and hanging a new supermodel on his arm for every charity function he attended. He'd been trying so hard to prove he'd moved on after his mother's death—when he quit racing—that it had taken him several months to realize it wasn't working. The media and the rest of the world seemed fooled, but he'd never felt more out of touch with the self-respect that really mattered to him. So, he'd recently thrown himself into business. And now he did nothing but work.

"I'm sure one chain of auto-parts stores is as good as another to you," she said. "Why don't you start your own? Gunner Stevens Automotive has a nice ring to it. You've already got the name recognition to pull it off."

"Are you drumming up competition for your father?"

"Trying to protect him from doing something he's bound to regret."

"Why would I want to start from scratch when your father's put his company on the block?"

"I can't see my father selling Ashton Automotive," she said. "He's just going through a difficult time. It won't last long enough for him to complete the sale."

Gunner opened his mouth to argue, to tell her that he and Walt had been discussing terms. But the music was ending and a slender hand with rings on almost every finger clasped April's shoulder just as he let her go.

It was the older woman April had been watching so intently, minus her young lover. "There you are," she said. "I've been looking all over for you. The dance floor was the last place I thought to check." She glanced Gunner's way, then her mouth dropped open. "But now I see why you're here.

Isn't this Gunner Stevens? The *race-car driver,* Gunner Stevens?''

April pushed her glasses closer to her face, giving Gunner the impression she tended to hide behind them. "Yes."

"Aren't you going to introduce us?"

The muscular young man approached with two glasses of champagne, and April winced visibly at the sight of him.

"Rod, dear, we're about to be introduced to Gunner Stevens," the woman said excitedly. "You know who he is, don't you?"

"I do." Rod looked impressed, but April looked as though she wanted to die.

"Mr. Stevens." April's tone grew formal again. "Please meet my mother, Claire Ashton—" she cleared her throat "—and her, um, date."

Gunner's jaw dropped. *This* was her *mother?* From what Walt had told him, Gunner had gotten a completely different idea of Claire Ashton. He'd certainly never expected to find her at the same party as Walt and Regina. It was his understanding that the divorce wasn't going well. But now that he could see Claire's face more clearly, he saw the resemblance between her and April. Although April's hair was darker, nearly coffee-colored, she definitely favored her mother more than her father. "It's a pleasure to meet you," he said.

"Likewise." Claire beamed. "What brings someone like you to our little party?"

He couldn't exactly say that Walt was trying to sell off the company, so he kept his answer vague. "Walt and I met through some business dealings. He invited me."

"Dad's thinking of selling Ashton Automotive to Gunner," April said, instantly giving him away.

Gunner frowned. So much for winning her over.

Claire brought a hand to her chest as shock, hurt, then anger passed over her face. "Why? So he can spend more time with that...that incense-burning *floozy?* I begged him for years to take life easier, to let us go away on our own sometimes, to come home for dinner at night, to simply *relax* a little and be a husband and father. Would he do it? No! That business was too damned important to him. Now, after all the years I shared him with his beloved company, he's going to sell, just like that?" She snapped her fingers.

Gunner sent April a dark look, thanking her for putting him in such an awkward position, and she smiled in a self-satisfied way. "I tried to tell Gunner he was probably wasting his time here. Dad doesn't have the right to sell the business without your permission."

"He doesn't?" her mother said.

"Of course not," April replied. "The business is

community property. You own half of it, remember?"

"That's right." Claire's gaze remained fastened on her daughter's for a moment, then she threw her shoulders back and turned to Gunner. "We won't let him sell."

"*You* won't let him sell," April amended.

Claire stood taller still. "*I* won't let him sell."

"Even if it means you'll walk away from your divorce with several million dollars in your pocket?" Gunner replied coolly.

Claire seemed to waver. "Why does it always come down to money? We were married *thirty-three* years," she said to no one in particular. "This wasn't supposed to happen."

April bolstered her by stepping closer. "Actually, we're still hoping my father will come around and there won't be a divorce," she said.

Gunner glanced at Rod, who seemed completely unaffected by this statement. Walt was across the room, talking to Regina and a man Gunner had never met. In his view, April and her mother were hanging on to a relationship that was long gone. As painful as it was for them, he thought they'd be better off to face the truth and take what cash they could. But thirty-three years was a long time. Gunner could understand why they'd fight to save their family. He just hadn't realized the situation was quite so messy. He didn't want to be dragged into something that could possibly become even more complicated and might not end well.

Taking a deep breath, he made a decision. "If you change your mind, you've got my number." He handed his card to April, who was obviously calling the shots—on her mother's part, anyway. Then he turned on his heel and walked out, into the brisk night air—Los Angeles's mild version of winter—and hailed a cab. He was going back to New York whether there was anything waiting for him or not.

CHAPTER THREE

"WHAT THE HELL did you and your mother *say* to him last night?"

April pulled the phone away from her ear so her father couldn't blast out her eardrum while she tried to rouse herself from sleep. She'd known he wouldn't be happy with her defection where Gunner Stevens was concerned, but she hadn't expected Walt to call her at—she fumbled for her glasses and shoved them on so she could see the numerals on the alarm clock—six in the morning. On Sunday, six was early even for her. "Dad, I don't think this is the time to sell Ashton Automotive," she said.

"I didn't ask you," he thundered. "In case you haven't noticed, I've been running this company on my own for twenty-seven years and I've managed to do a damn good job."

"This is different."

"Like hell it is. This is *my* company. I built it. As long as I give your mother half of everything when the divorce is final, I've done my duty."

Since her parents had split up, April had tried to

remain as neutral as possible. She'd known her father was hurting her mother, and hated that. But her father had a right to live his own life—no matter how hard it was to sit back and watch what was happening.

"Dad, Regina's a nice woman, but surely you can see that—"

"What?" he broke in. "What can I see?"

"That she's…" What could she say? *Regina is a little strange?* It was true, but her father wouldn't accept it, and starting an argument wouldn't make things any easier. Catching herself, April tried a different tack. "Are you sure the direction your life is taking will make you happy? You spent thirty-three years with Mom. How can you throw that away?"

"Your mother and I fell out of love years ago," he said.

April winced, knowing that tears would fill Claire's eyes if she ever heard Walt make a statement that absolute. Claire had been a good wife, had stuck loyally by her man even when they were poor. Now that Walt was abandoning her, she was hurt and humiliated. Her self-esteem had plummeted and, as a result, she was doing some stupid things. But April knew Claire didn't want the divorce, although there were times she said she could never go back to him after such a betrayal.

"Mom's a wonderful person," April said.

"She's acting like an idiot."

April didn't challenge that statement for fear of the accusations that might come out of her own mouth. "What about counseling?" she asked for the millionth time. Her mother was willing, but Walt had so far resisted. If there was something wrong with him, he obviously didn't want to hear about it.

"Most counselors don't know any more than I do."

April sighed. "So, are you going to contact Gunner Stevens and try to repair the deal?"

"I haven't decided," he said, some of the anger and irritation draining out of his voice. "Maybe I'll wait until after the company trip. It's coming up fast and I still have a lot to do. Which reminds me. Keith said he couldn't find you at the party last night."

"Oh, really?" She laced her words with surprise, playing the innocent even though she'd dodged their plant manager at every turn. Her father had indicated that Keith might have a present for her, and she definitely hadn't wanted to be put in the unpleasant position of refusing a gift. "I wonder how we managed to miss each other."

"So do I."

Judging by his tone, she wasn't fooling anyone. "You know, you're not getting any younger,

April,'' he said. ''If you want a family, you need
to do something about it.''

Oh, boy. Here it was. Advice from her overbear-
ing, workaholic father who struggled with anger
management, had strained relationships with almost
everyone he knew, and was currently divorcing the
one person who wanted him for more than his
money. ''Dad, I'm afraid we'll have to talk later.''

''I'm telling you that you don't want to spend
the rest of your life alone.''

''Because I have so much reason to believe in
the institution of marriage?''

''Divorce can happen to anyone. But I wouldn't
have missed having you for anything.''

That took her aback. Just when she started blam-
ing her father, he'd say something sweet, something
that reminded her how much she loved him. But
where did that leave her poor mother?

''I know, Daddy,'' she said. ''I want a family.
It's just that…'' How did she explain to her father,
who thought his little girl was the catch of the cen-
tury, that she wasn't very good at attracting male
attention? By jumping several grades in school,
graduating from high school at fifteen and moving
right on to college, she'd never fit in with her peers.
And because she'd never fit in, she had difficulty
relating in social situations. It was much easier to

immerse herself in work twenty-four hours a day than fight her natural reluctance to meet people.

"It's just that *what?*" he prompted.

"I'll start getting out more," she promised, knowing she should.

"Keith's a good guy, April."

"I'm not interested in Keith, Dad."

"If you'd spend some time with him, I think you might change your mind. You'll see. You'll have the chance to get to know him better on the company trip."

"Dad, about Cabo…" April took a deep breath, scrambling to come up with an acceptable excuse to miss going to Mexico in the second week of January. "I've got to work" was no longer good enough. Her father knew she received three weeks of paid vacation a year and used barely one of them. "I don't know if I can get away," she said, falling back on the same old line because there simply wasn't anything in her life to stop her from going.

"I gave you plenty of notice about this, April. I e-mailed you the itinerary three months ago."

"Are you bringing Regina?"

"No."

"Still…"

"Still what?"

"Our situation has changed, Dad. You know that. Now I have Mom living with me, and I can't leave her alone. She might decide to redecorate my house." April was sure he'd assume she was joking, but she was at least half-serious. She'd moved all her furniture back and didn't want to come home to another surprise like the last one.

"April…"

Her father's tone and subsequent silence caught her attention more quickly than if he'd shouted.

"What?"

"I've been having some pains in my chest."

She shoved herself into a sitting position. "As in *heart* trouble?" Was that why her father wanted to sell Ashton Automotive? Was the pressure of running such a large business more than he could handle these days?

"Don't make a big deal out of it and for God's sake don't tell your mother, but I've got a few clogged arteries. Doctor wants to do a triple bypass as soon as I get back. So—" she heard him sigh "—it would mean a lot to me if you'd come to Cabo, honey."

A triple bypass? But Walt had always been so strong, so healthy. April wished he'd told her about the chest pains *before* she'd chased Gunner Stevens away. "Dad, are you sure you should even *go* to Cabo?"

"Of course. The doctor's given me some nitro pills. I'll be fine. I'd just like you there with me."

April thought of her mother. They'd always attended the company trip as a family. Claire was going to feel completely abandoned and would, no doubt, interpret April's actions as choosing sides, a betrayal that would be almost as painful to her as Walt's initial affair. Especially if he wouldn't let April tell Claire about the triple bypass. "Why keep it from Mom?" April asked.

"Because it's none of her business. I don't want her rubbing her hands in anticipation, hoping I'll keel over any minute."

"Mom would never do that."

"Just keep it to yourself, okay? I'll tell her when I'm ready."

Hating how this enmity between her parents threatened to tear her in two, April removed her glasses and rubbed her eyes.

"So, what do you say?" he pressed.

Bottom line, she couldn't refuse her father. He could have a heart attack at any time. What if she lost him? "Okay, I'll go," she told him. But she was cringing inside even as he thanked her. She wasn't sure how to deal with Keith and his unrequited feelings for her, knew it was going to be miserable with her father constantly forcing them together.

And she had no idea how she'd break the news about this trip to her mother....

"WHO WAS ON THE PHONE?" Claire asked five minutes later, standing at April's bedroom door with the antiaging, gel-filled mask she wore to bed these days resting on top of her head.

April swallowed a groan and opened her eyes. "Dad."

"This early?"

"He's unhappy about the fact that we ran Gunner Stevens off last night." And so was April—*now*.

"Of course he is. He's used to me playing by the rules, doing nothing against his wishes, while he does as he damn well pleases."

"I'd say last night hardly reflects your more passive side," April said, throwing an arm and a leg over her extra pillow.

"Isn't Rod handsome?" Her mother grinned in appreciation.

He wasn't to April. Gunner Stevens was her kind of handsome—naturally golden and rugged-looking. He had a cowlick that pushed his hair off his forehead and laugh lines around his eyes and mouth that made his face interesting on a deeper level than young and perfect. Most of America agreed with her.

But looks didn't make the man, she quickly reminded herself.

"Tell me Rod was a hired escort," she said to Claire.

Her mother bristled. "Why would he have to be a hired escort?"

April arched her eyebrows. "My guess is he's younger than *me*."

"Phooey. Oh, all right, he's a friend of my hairdresser's. He needed a few bucks, and I wanted to show Walt that I'm no doormat."

"You showed him," April said. "Along with everyone else. Ashton Automotive will be talking about that Christmas party for a very long time."

"Walt deserved every minute of last night."

April couldn't argue with her there.

"Is that *all* your father wanted?" Claire asked.

"Pretty much." April retrieved her glasses and pretended to adjust her alarm clock. From the corner of her eye, she saw her mother tighten the belt of her silk robe.

"I thought I heard something about the Cabo trip."

April bit back a curse. She wasn't prepared to deal with Claire's emotional reaction right now. "He just wanted to know if I was coming this year."

"What did you tell him?"

She hoped her mother had only picked up on the gist of the conversation and not the specifics. "That I'm not sure."

"I think you *should* go," Claire said.

April tucked her hair behind her ears. "You do?"

"Of course. And I think you should take me with you. We could share a room."

"What?"

"Why should I miss out on all the fun just because of Walt?"

The fact that they were getting *divorced* wasn't reason enough?

"Like you said last night," her mother went on, "I own half the company. I have every right to be there, don't I?"

"Um...I guess you do, Mom." God, her father was going to kill her....

CHAPTER FOUR

APRIL SPENT much of the next few days on automatic pilot, going to work and shopping for Christmas, which was only a week away. It was difficult to feel any holiday cheer, however, when all she could think about was her parents. She couldn't let things go on as they were. Her mother had gotten a tattoo yesterday, a rose on her hip, then cried all afternoon, refusing to say why she was so upset. Her father's temper was shorter than ever, and he was having chest pains. Chest pains!

April had never seen either of them so unhappy. Clearly they needed to stop slinging blame, figure out why they fell in love in the first place and find that again. There was no other way to put an end to the emotional turmoil, no other way to stop the fighting over assets, which promised to go on for months.

From her home office, April heard her mother banging around in the kitchen. Because Claire was still trying to lose weight, she was broiling fish for dinner. She made fish almost every night, which meant the house always smelled of it.

As much as April loved her mother, she missed the old peace and quiet, the absence of fish odor, the privacy. She longed for the holidays as she used to know them—filled with eggnog and ham and her mother's fudge. But more than anything, she wanted control of her own home again. She had to do *something* before she became desperate enough to let her father set her up with Keith as her only escape.

"Are you going to join me, April?" her mother called.

April felt nauseated by the smell alone. "No thanks, I'm fine."

"You need to eat some of this fish. It has vitamins that are difficult to get anywhere else."

"I'm not hungry, Mom."

"I ate a lot of fish when I was pregnant with you. That's why you're so smart. Have just a small portion, and a little spinach."

Maybe life with a man she didn't love wouldn't be so bad. "I ate on the way home from work," she lied, and opened the window to ventilate the room, even though the breeze coming in off the ocean was a chill one.

"I'll make you a plate, just in case you get hungry later," her mother called.

April used her finger to smooth away an eye twitch and sat down again. How could she convince her parents that they were better off together than apart?

Opening her desk drawer, she withdrew Gunner Stevens's business card and ran her thumb over the smooth embossing. April hated to see Ashton Automotive leave the family, but nothing was more important than keeping her father well. If she could talk Gunner into coming to Cabo, Walt would have a good chance of saving the deal. Better yet, Walt and Claire would be thrown together on a number of occasions while he was on his best behavior, in a setting that just might rekindle what they felt when they became engaged thirty-four years ago.

It was a long shot, but since her parents were both going to be in Cabo anyway, it was the best plan April could come up with. Getting her parents back together was all she wanted for Christmas. Besides, her mother's association with Rod had suggested a way Gunner could help her—if he would.

"April, do you mind if I paint the living room?" her mother asked loudly. "White's so drab. I was thinking a light pink would brighten things up. And maybe I could put up a few of my paintings. I've done six now, you know."

Pink in the living room? Together with her mother's artwork? Claire had started taking watercolor classes two months ago and had yet to create anything April wanted hanging in her closet, let alone anyplace more public. Why couldn't Claire concentrate on decorating the tree?

That was it. April called Gunner.

"Hello?"

He'd answered his own telephone. "Mr. Stevens?"

"Don't tell me, it's April Ashton."

She gave a little laugh, suddenly grateful she'd fought the impulse to hang up as soon as she'd recognized his voice. "Caller ID?"

"Yes. What can I do for you?"

"I have a business proposal you might be interested in hearing," she said, deciding to be as forthright as possible.

A startled silence followed this announcement.

"Mr. Stevens?"

"It's Gunner, remember?"

"Right, Gunner."

"What kind of business proposal?" he asked, and she pictured him narrowing his eyes.

"At the Christmas party, you told my father you have commitments back East this January, but if you could possibly arrange it, I'd like you to come to Cabo with Ashton Automotive."

"Why?"

"I've changed my mind. I think it probably *is* time for my father to sell the business."

Her words met with a weighty pause. "To what do I owe this reversal?"

"My father's getting older and—well, anything could happen to a man his age, right?" She purposely didn't mention Walt's heart trouble for fear Gunner would think this had suddenly become a fire sale.

"I'm not sure what you're offering, Miss Ashton."

"April. I'm saying my mother and I will support your efforts to purchase the business, if you want."

"If I want," he echoed.

"That's what I said."

"And what do *you* get out of it?"

This was where her plan became a bit questionable. "I'm looking for a temporary—" she swallowed tightly and squeezed out the last word "—escort."

"A *what?*"

"An escort, um, of sorts."

"Where would we be going?" He sounded justifiably leery.

"Just to Cabo."

"You want me to be your escort the whole week we're in Mexico?"

"A week's not that long, Mr. Ste—Gunner."

Gathering her nerve, she rushed on. "And don't worry, you won't have to do anything special. When you see or speak to my father, just go along with the story that we started communicating on the telephone and e-mailing each other after the Christmas party and that our relationship has evolved into a friendship with some...romantic hope."

"You mean it?"

A pause.

"Yes."

Nothing.

"Are you still there?" she asked.

"Explain romantic hope," he said.

April tried to forget the pleasant feeling of his muscular arms around her while they danced so she could make "romantic hope" sound as clinical as possible. She might not agree with Gunner Stevens's mentality, but she sure couldn't complain about any of his physical characteristics. "I need you to act as though you're interested in me, just for a few days. You should probably hold my hand occasionally, or put your arm around me. But we'll never even have to kiss. We'll become disenchanted with each other toward the end of the trip. Then you'll be off the hook—but before that, my mother and I will be your biggest advocates and we won't do anything to stand in your way afterward."

"You seem to have it all figured out, April."

Was that skepticism she heard? "I do," she said.

"Except you still haven't told me your purpose in creating this charade."

"I'm hoping to convince my father that I can find a man on my own. Otherwise he's going to try and force me into the arms of his balding, middle-aged, soft-spoken plant manager."

"I see. But why me?"

"If you still want to buy Ashton Automotive, you have business in Cabo, which gives you good reason to be there. And from what I know about you, I can safely say there's no danger either one of us will get hurt by this...well-intentioned deception."

"You're sure of that."

She sat up taller. Maybe he didn't seem excited by the idea, but she took heart from the fact that he hadn't refused her yet. "Of course. Even my parents won't be surprised when it blows up."

"Because..."

She knew he was baiting her, but she wanted to voice her honest opinion. "Can I be frank?"

"Please do."

"Because you and I both know I'll just be one more in a long line of women who've passed through your life. Easy come, easy go. No problem."

"You're saying I'm too shallow for a girl like you, an *intellectual* to take seriously."

She sensed a dangerous undertone to his words and changed tactics. "There's no need to interpret it that way. You're too busy with better candidates to spend much time with me. That's all."

Surely Gunner would be happy with *that* response, April thought with a smug smile. It was exactly the kind of thing a man with a huge ego would relish.

Silence stretched between them once again, and she supposed he was thinking it over. "This is a pretty crazy scheme for someone as logical as a physicist," he said at last.

April couldn't restrain her desperation any longer. "It's all about chaos, Gunner. Not logic. I haven't been able to work. I haven't been able to sleep. I *have* to get my mother out of my house."

"I suppose there's a connection in your mind between me being your escort in Mexico and your mother moving out?"

"Oh, there is. My mother's coming to Cabo, too."

"And Rod and Regina?"

"They're staying behind."

"So this is a matchmaking ploy. You're trying to get your parents back together."

"God, am I ever."

He surprised her by chuckling. "Okay. I'm in."

Relieved, April tossed his card back into her drawer. *"Really?"*

"You bet. If I'm hearing you correctly, you're going to foil your father's matchmaking plans while advancing your own. Sounds like it should work."

"Exactly!" She smiled, trying to be positive. She'd convinced him; Gunner was coming to Mexico. But there was something about his attitude that made her nervous....

GUNNER HAD RACED CARS since he was old enough to drive. He'd reached speeds in excess of two hundred miles an hour, facing mortality without a moment's fear. But he hated flying. Probably because he had to trust someone else at the controls. In any case, his stomach tensed as he took off from JFK Airport and stayed that way during the entire miserable ten-hour trip, which included two layovers, one in Houston and one in Phoenix.

Feeling rumpled and tired but relieved, he stepped off the plane into the dazzling Mexican sun and slipped on his sunglasses to survey, for the first time, Baja California. He had one week to spend in Cabo, one week of playing boyfriend for April Ashton, and after suffering through the holidays alone, he was actually looking forward to the distraction.

There were a few exotic flowering plants here

and there at the airport, but the surrounding area was basically flat and desertlike. The customs officer mentioned, in heavily accented English, that Cabo San Lucas received only a few inches of rain each year, which explained the cactus and sand. But Gunner didn't mind the dryness. It was bitterly cold and snowing in New York when he left, and he'd heard that the golfing in Cabo was surpassed only by the fishing.

Besides, his father had called yesterday and asked him to visit—since Gunner had claimed to be unavailable for Christmas. As much as he knew he should spend some time with Quincy Sr., that he should forgive his father as his mother had always encouraged him to do, this trip had given Gunner a good excuse to postpone the reunion yet again.

Finally beginning to relax, he saw the porter holding a placard with his name and let the man take his bag and load it into the limousine that Walt had sent to collect him. Then Gunner slid into the dark, air-conditioned interior to find April Ashton waiting for him.

"Thanks for coming," she said as soon as he spotted her sitting quietly in the far corner.

He was rather surprised to see her wearing a short skirt. Somehow he hadn't expected April Ashton to possess such pretty legs. But it was her tight-fitting T-shirt, which advertised a local bar called the Wiggling Marlin, that really tempted his eye. April was skinny, but not without shape, he conceded as he took in her small but firm-looking breasts. "I'm sure it'll prove interesting," he said. "I've never pretended to be anyone's lover before."

"Lover?" She glanced at him as if she didn't know how to take his comment, and he hid a smile. She thought she could dangle Ashton Automotive in front of him the way her father did, and that he'd simply perform the role she'd chosen for him. But he was determined to control everything that went on down here.

"Isn't that what you said on the phone?" he asked, playing innocent. "That you wanted me to come down here and pretend we're having a torrid affair?"

"I didn't say anything about *torrid,* and you know it."

"Oh." He rubbed his chin thoughtfully. "Then perhaps I should have mentioned that my idea of a relationship 'with romantic interest' is a little different than yours."

The chauffeur started the car and they moved away from the airport. "You're joking, right?" she said, beginning to squirm.

He watched her for several seconds, struggling to hold back a grin. "What do you think?"

"I think you're joking."

"Of course I'm joking," he said. "I know *torrid* is well beyond someone like you."

"Someone like me?" she echoed.

"An intellectual, remember? Someone who's prim. Someone who looks down her nose at a womanizer like me."

"You say 'intellectual' and…and 'prim' as if you really mean 'uptight virgin.'"

He could only keep a straight face by biting the inside of his cheek. *"Really?"*

She folded her arms beneath those firm breasts he'd noticed earlier and crossed her legs. "You're jumping to some pretty big conclusions, Mr. Stevens."

"I am? I didn't realize."

"For starters, I'm not a virgin."

He rumpled his brow as if seriously considering her words. For someone so smart, she was amazingly easy to bait. "You're not?"

"Of course not. I might not get out much, but I'm not completely naive." She frowned at the closed window separating them from the chauffeur and lowered her voice as though she was still worried about being overheard. "I was only eighteen when I lost my virginity."

He coughed to keep from laughing. "Is that so? Who was the lucky guy?"

"Bill Sossaman. He used to be one of my father's attorneys."

"An older man?"

"Not that much older. Maybe seven years. He was just starting his practice and I was on break from school."

"Were the two of you in love?"

"*I* was in love," she said.

Of course. He couldn't see April Ashton peeling off her clothes for any other reason. "But he wasn't."

She grimaced and glanced at her watch as if suddenly regretting the fact that they'd be cooped up together during the entire forty-minute drive to Cabo del Sol, a resort area eight miles north of Cabo San Lucas. "He said he was in love with me," she went on, "but a few days after the big event, I found out he had a steady girlfriend with whom he already had a child."

Ouch. Gunner could easily imagine how deeply that must have affected someone so young, serious and sensitive—at least, he guessed April was sensitive underneath all that starch. "Your first heartbreak," he said and felt a twinge of pity despite the fact that he was still angry at her for judging him so quickly—and basing that judgement solely on what the media had provided.

She didn't bother trying to act nonchalant about

her affair with the young lawyer. "That experience taught me a good lesson."

"That you can't trust love?"

"That you can't trust a man who won't give you his home phone number."

He smiled at her candid response and draped the jacket he'd brought over one knee, grateful he'd prepared for the perfect weather by wearing a golf shirt and chinos. "I'm glad it hasn't made you bitter."

"I prefer to let it make me wiser."

"And since then?"

"Since then I've been more careful."

He knew it was none of his business, but he couldn't help asking, "So that time you lost your virginity is the extent of your sexual experience?"

"I think I've already shared more information than I should have," she said with an unmistakable blush.

"You don't *have* to answer," he said, chuckling. "I can read it in your face."

She scowled at him. "Go ahead and laugh, Mr. Stevens. I know it doesn't seem like much to someone who probably has more notches in his bedpost than he's capable of counting—"

"Whoa!" He put a hand to his chest as though she'd mortally wounded him. "Did you just insult my intelligence?"

Her dark eyes snapped beneath those thick-framed glasses. "To say nothing of your character."

"My character is fair game," he said. "But rest assured that I can definitely count the notches on my bedpost. At least to fifteen hundred or so."

She looked suitably disgusted.

"Don't worry," he said, unable to resist the impulse to keep teasing her. "We've got seven full days in paradise. Maybe we'll add another notch to *your* bedpost. Good sex is probably nothing like you remember."

"I'm sure I remember...well, maybe not *good* sex. I mean, I hope that's not as good as it gets. But—" she shook her head, obviously flustered "—never mind. You're taking way too much for granted."

"Really? No, wait." He held up a hand to stall her, marveling at how easily she entertained him. And to think he'd almost refused to join her. "Let me guess. You don't want to sleep with *me*."

She looked down her dainty nose at him, just as he'd accused her of doing earlier. "Exactly."

Sobering, he purposefully dropped his focus to her lips until she began to fidget uncomfortably. Then he grinned. "This is going to be even better than I thought."

CHAPTER FIVE

APRIL'S HEART POUNDED in her ears for the rest of the ride to the Hacienda Del Mar. What had she done? Here was a man who'd cut his teeth on challenges, and she'd offered him the most irresistible challenge of all. She had to be a complete fool. Except that she really believed she could outwit a person who'd spent twenty years putting himself in mortal danger again and again and again. A man like that couldn't be *too* smart. Besides, Gunner Stevens didn't realize there was a woman out there who might be impervious to his charm.

She was that woman, April told herself—although she could feel her breasts tingling from the way he'd looked at her.

Okay, maybe she wasn't *completely* impervious to him, but she did understand her own limitations. A man like Gunner Stevens would never be genuinely interested in a woman like her. He ran with the fast and the loose. A relationship with him would be very much like her first experience with

Bill Sossaman. As soon as they went to bed, it would be all over.

The limo turned left into the cobbled driveway of the resort and wove through burnt-orange-, coffee- and bone-colored buildings, all with Mexican tile roofs and neatly tended grounds. The azure water of the ocean sparkled beneath the warm sun as April looked through the open-air reception area, beyond the massive decorative pools and palm trees, toward a white, absolutely pristine beach. Cabo *was* paradise. But April couldn't relax. Not as long as Gunner Stevens was sitting so close to her. And not as long as so much depended on this trip.

"Has your mother arrived?" Gunner asked when they'd circled the water fountain and came to a stop at the curb.

"She flew in with me this morning."

"So your father knows she's here?"

"Not yet. He sent a driver to pick me up because he was in meetings with management all day. He wanted to come with me to get you, but I convinced him, in deference to our *relationship,* to let us have some time alone."

"When will your parents meet?"

"Tonight at dinner."

"I can hardly wait," he said sarcastically.

April felt the same way.

The driver opened the door, but Gunner hesitated. "What have you told them about us?"

"I mentioned that you've called me occasionally."

"Wouldn't your mother know better? Doesn't she live with you?"

"I said this has been going on at work, where I spend most of my time, anyway."

"That's *all* you told them?"

"That's all it took to get them excited."

"Then this will be a piece of cake," he said, getting out.

April followed him and spotted her father striding through the lobby doors to meet them. Judging by his smile, she was right in what she'd just told Gunner—he still didn't know that Claire was anywhere in the vicinity.

"Gunner." Her father shook his hand as eagerly as he had at the Christmas party.

"Good to see you again, Walt," Gunner replied.

"I feel the same. Especially now that I know you're seeing my little girl." Her father grinned proudly at her, and it was all April could do not to immediately confess the truth.

"She's something else," Gunner said, and April wondered if she was the only one who could see the laughter in his eyes.

Her father winked at her. "You bet she is. But

you'd probably like to shower and change, so I won't hold you up. I just wanted to welcome you to Cabo and tell you we'll be having dinner on the beach tonight, at seven.''

"Sounds great." Gunner turned toward April. She thought he was going to say something polite in parting. Instead, he took her by the shoulders, gave her a devilish grin and swept his mouth lightly across her lips. The scent of his aftershave raced to her head, along with the smell of orange on his breath. His fingers seemed to burn through her T-shirt, sending sensation in the other direction.

"See you at dinner," he murmured.

April couldn't answer. She was too busy telling her knees not to buckle.

An HOUR LATER, when April stood in front of the mirror, a stranger stared back at her. She was wearing huarache sandals with a sarong-style skirt that rested low on her hips and a strappy turquoise T-shirt that revealed her arms, shoulders and a thin slice of midriff.

After Gunner's kiss, April felt a little too exposed. She certainly didn't want to do anything to encourage him. But her mother had just bought the entire outfit at the gift shop downstairs and wouldn't hear of her wearing anything else. Claire was on one of her "don't let life pass you by" tirades. And, knowing what they were about to face with her father, April didn't want to upset her mother ahead of time.

"You look gorgeous," her mother gushed.

April discounted the compliment as coming from someone who was blind to her faults, and examined her arms. "Are you sure that self-tanning stuff you made me try isn't going to turn my skin orange?"

"I'm sure. The good lotions don't do that anymore."

Adjusting her sarong, April considered her reflection once again. "I don't know, Mom. I can't wear a bra with this shirt."

"You're not big enough to *need* a bra. But..." Her mother folded her arms and tapped her toe, considering April's chest. April instantly regretted drawing attention to one of her most private imperfections. But she didn't need to say or do much to attract Claire's attention these days. Ever since her mother had learned that Gunner was joining them in Cabo, Claire had gone into emergency makeover mode. "Maybe you should get a boob job when I do," she said. "Men love big-breasted women, and with your flat stomach and lean hips, some size up top would have a very dramatic effect."

"No, thanks," April said, and slid her glasses into place.

"Won't you wear your contacts? Just for tonight?" her mother asked.

April shook her head. Her glasses went far toward killing the sexy effect of the new clothes, but they were familiar and she needed that reassurance. Especially because she *still* felt shivery when she remembered her brief encounter with Gunner's warm mouth. She was beginning to worry about what he might have in store for her later. She doubted he was going to behave.

She started scraping her hair into a bun, but her mother stopped her. "Not tonight," she said. "We're in Mexico. Let your hair fall free."

"Why?"

"Because it looks better that way. Come here." Claire motioned for April to join her in the bathroom. "I want to style it a bit. You need to make more of what you have. Live a little—it won't hurt you."

A few minutes later, April had a bunch of dark curls tumbling down her back. "Are we about finished?" she asked.

Claire tilted her head in an assessing manner. "Are you sure I can't talk you out of those ugly glasses?"

"Yes."

"Will you try some eye shadow or lip gloss?"

"No."

"Then I guess we're finished." Her mother twirled around in an orange-and-red, softly flowing sundress she'd accessorized with gold hoop earrings and lots of bangles. "How do I look?"

"Beautiful," April said, and it was true. Her mother's tan seemed much more natural in Mexico, where almost everyone else was tanned, too. And the weight she'd lost had taken her from frumpy and lumpy to sleek and sophisticated. "Are you nervous about seeing Dad?"

Her mother paused from fiddling with her hair, which she'd swept up in an elegant dramatic fashion. "Of course not. Why should I be nervous about that?" she asked. Still, April could tell that her mother was self-conscious. Claire cared about Walt. She was hurting over what had happened to their marriage.

April prayed her father still felt something, too.

GUNNER WAS STANDING near one of the two bars set up on the sand when April came down the temporary pathway from the hotel. He'd been marveling at how quickly hotel employees had managed to transform the beach into an outdoor restaurant, complete with two long buffets, more than thirty linen-covered tables and a mariachi band. He hadn't expected to see April quite so soon, but he turned when he heard her voice—and caught his breath.

She looked slender and exotic in the flickering lamplight, and was showing far more skin than he'd ever believed she would. Her hips and hair swayed slowly as she walked toward him, and the nervous little glance she shot him made something in his stomach tighten. April was still plain, still wearing those homely glasses. But there was also a sweet innocence about her, a down-to-the-bone honesty and such clear intelligence that Gunner could no longer call her unattractive.

It's the magic of paradise, he quickly told himself. The waves pounded the beach only twenty feet away. A perfect seventy-degree breeze stirred the palm trees. Shadows darted and moved with the lamps, concealing and distorting.

Marginally reassured, he put down his margarita and strode over to meet her—and couldn't help bending close to press a quick kiss to the hollow beneath her earlobe. Her skin, soft as a baby's, smelled of cucumbers and melon.

She stiffened in surprise, but he knew she wouldn't pull away because her mother was watching.

"You're gorgeous tonight," he told her.

"Thank you." She gave him a meaningful look, one that told him he was overacting, and he hid a smile at the knowledge that he wasn't acting at all.

"Hello, Claire," he said. "And Happy New Year."

"I'm glad you could be here with us," April's mother returned. "It's wonderful to see my daughter so excited about a man."

April hid a cough.

"I'm looking forward to our time together, too," he said. In more ways than one. Who would have thought a skinny, sexually repressed intellectual like April would be able to capture his attention when all the fabulously beautiful, and sometimes extremely talented, women he'd been dating over the past few years had left him cold?

"Shall we sit over here?" he asked, leading them to a table on the far right.

April allowed him to take her hand but, at the first opportunity, she leaned into him and whispered, "You don't have to overdo it."

He didn't have a chance to respond because Walt had spotted them and was on his way over. "There you are," he said jovially. "I've already got a table for us. It's up front." Then his eyes fell on Claire, whom he'd obviously not recognized until that moment, and he made a choking noise. "What are *you* doing here?"

April's thin fingers, still threaded through Gunner's, tightened in a death grip as a vulnerable expression flashed across Claire's face. Gunner opened his mouth, feeling he needed to protect them both, but Claire threw back her shoulders and spoke before he could.

"I have every right to be here, Walt." Her voice was as pleasant as though she'd just addressed a total stranger. Only the tightness of her smile gave away the underlying tension.

Walt harrumphed and shoved his hands into the pockets of his chinos, scowling as if they'd all double-crossed him. But Gunner looked at him expectantly and finally Walt seemed to make a decision. "Oh, all right," he told her. "You can join us."

APRIL COULD FEEL Gunner's eyes on her all through dinner. She had to hand it to him—he *could* act. His interest in her almost seemed authentic. Especially when the temperature grew cooler and he removed his jacket and slipped it over her shoulders without asking if she wanted it.

Gunner's residual body heat, which clung to his coat along with the scent of his cologne, quickly became a distraction, conjuring up visions of his kiss near the limo. It wasn't an entirely unpleasant association. Having a boyfriend—even a pretend one—had excellent benefits, April decided, although Gunner probably wasn't too comfortable sitting there without his coat.

She looked over at him, wondering if he felt cold.

But the other people at their table—Wayne Smith, the District Sales Manager for California, Wayne's wife, Christie, and Tom Corcoran, Advertising Director for the whole company, as well as her parents—had just begun a conversation about Gunner's background.

"I've never been to upstate New York," Tom said, "but someone once told me it's nothing like New York City."

Gunner waved away the waiter circulating with testers of tequila. "It's mostly rural. Lots of green rolling hills, dairy farms and small towns."

"Did you grow up on a dairy farm?" April's mother asked.

"No. My mother was the lunch lady at school. The job didn't pay much, but she wanted to be home with me and my older sisters in the afternoons." He grinned ruefully before taking another bite of his steamed vegetables. "And we weren't the easiest kids in the world to raise, so that was probably a good decision."

"What did your father do?" Tom asked.

Gunner took a sip of his margarita. "I've heard he was a truck driver, but he's done a lot of things during his life, so I'm not really sure. My parents separated when I was only two, and my dad didn't bother coming around much until I hit my teens."

April watched her mother throw a surreptitious

glance at Walt, who was sitting across from her. He happened to meet her eyes, then they both looked hurriedly away. "Do you have contact with him now?" Claire asked Gunner.

Gunner shrugged. "He calls occasionally."

"Where does he live?" Walt asked.

"He's still in New York."

Christie, Wayne's wife, set her fork down, leaned away from the table and folded her arms. "Is that where your mother is, too?"

Wayne cleared his throat and answered before Gunner could. "Gunner's mother passed away over a year ago, honey," he said gently.

"Oh." She blushed. "I'm sorry, Mr. Stevens. I hadn't heard."

"Don't be sorry." Gunner smiled and Christie relaxed visibly. But April could tell they'd touched upon a difficult subject and that Gunner was only being courteous in appearing to shrug it off.

Walt must have sensed the same tension in Gunner because he seemed eager to steer the conversation in a different direction. "Sounds like you come from pretty humble beginnings."

Gunner cut off another bite of steak. "We were definitely poor, but my mother was an incredible woman. She made sure she provided everything we needed, even though my father didn't help out much."

"Racing takes a lot of money," Walt said. "Considering your circumstances, how did you get into the sport?"

Too full to eat any more but intrigued by the conversation, April pushed the rice around on her place and listened.

"My grandfather on my mother's side sponsored me until I had enough wins under my belt to attract corporate support."

"I'll bet you could buy yourself half a dozen cars then," Christie said, obviously trying to make up for her earlier gaffe.

"Not for a while," Gunner said. "Most of the money I earned went to help with rent and the other household bills."

April pulled Gunner's jacket more tightly around her. He'd stated it so matter-of-factly she got the impression he thought nothing of giving his mother his earnings. "That was nice of you," she said.

"We all contributed what we could," he replied.

Wayne accepted a refill of his margarita. "You won early on, if I remember correctly. How old were you when you started racing?"

"I raced quarter midgets at nine."

Tom whistled. "Jeez, that's young."

"Not really. A lot of kids start that young."

"Did you go into racing full-time right out of high school?" Claire asked.

"He first got a Bachelor of Science in Vehicle Structure Engineering from Purdue," Wayne said, then smiled when everyone looked surprised that he'd know this information. "I'm a big fan."

"So am I," her father said. "You had quite a career, Gunner. I was checking your stats on a fan Web site the other day. Said you've won over fifty-four million dollars. And your last year was your biggest ever, wasn't it?"

"Yes."

A muscle in Gunner's cheek twitched and his smile seemed strained—signs that he wasn't enjoying himself. But April couldn't imagine why. They weren't talking about his mother anymore. The conversation had veered toward his impressive racing career.

Wayne and her father asked him several more questions about racing, which he answered as succinctly as possible, and April finally stepped in.

"I think Gunner's probably tired," she said. "We should let him finish his dessert so he can head up to bed. He's been on a plane all day and must be feeling some jet lag."

Gunner put down his napkin, even though he was only half finished with his flan. "Actually, I was hoping I could talk you into taking a walk with me before I turn in."

April had been ready to relinquish his jacket so

she could go to bed, too. But suddenly finding herself the center of attention, she hesitated. "Of course," she said, knowing she'd get another lecture from her mother if she refused.

The tension she'd felt in Gunner a moment earlier seemed to evaporate, and the corners of his lips twitched as he stood and pulled out her chair. Evidently he liked using their pretense to back her into a corner.

"Good night," he said to the others.

She let him take her hand and lead her away. She had to make *some* concessions. With Gunner at her elbow, her father had actually invited her mother to dine with them and, while Walt had generally avoided speaking to Claire, he did order her favorite wine. And Keith hadn't dared so much as approach April.

All in all, she thought her plan was working out nicely—until she found herself alone on a deserted beach with Gunner.

CHAPTER SIX

THE WIND had picked up considerably but April didn't mind because the stars overhead seemed larger than any she'd seen before.

"You warm enough?" Gunner asked.

"I'm fine." She hugged his sport jacket closer to her body. "But you've got to be freezing." The waves crashing only a few feet away mesmerized her, but she pulled her attention from the churning, moonlit crests to glance behind them. They'd gone far enough that the hotel appeared only as a dark shape in the distance. "I'm sure we can go back now," she said. "No one will notice us slip off to our rooms."

"What's the matter? Nervous?"

She tried to make out his expression, hoping for some clue as to why he'd bothered bringing her out here. "Of course not. I'm perfectly relaxed. I just don't see the point of continuing to act our parts when no one can see us."

"I think you can use the practice," he said flatly.

April stopped to kick off her sandals. It was getting downright cold, but she liked the soft, grainy feel of the sand between her toes, enjoyed the smell of the salt air. She didn't travel enough, she realized. This was truly beautiful. "What do you mean?"

"No one's going to believe you even *like* me if you jump every time I brush your arm," he said. "Or slide over to the opposite side of your seat when I sit down next to you. People who are falling in love move *toward* each other. They touch at every opportunity because they crave the physical contact. They have trouble even looking at anyone else in the room."

April swallowed a dreamy sigh. That was the kind of love she longed for, the kind of love she was beginning to believe would never exist. Not for her, anyway. "I admit you're doing a much better job of pretending than I am," she said. "But intimacy isn't my strong suit. And I don't lie well. Plus we already know that you have a lot more experience with, uh, relationships than I do."

He pulled her to a stop and faced her, standing only a few inches away. "You're a scientist, April."

"So?"

"So experiment."

April was halfway convinced he was joking. But he didn't smile.

"You need to get comfortable with me," he said, and he had a point. Surely if she could relax, the next few days would pass much more quickly and easily.

Taking a deep breath, she tilted her head expectantly. "Okay, go ahead and kiss me." She squeezed her eyes shut and puckered up.

She waited, but nothing happened. When she opened her eyes, she found him watching her with a quizzical expression. "Aren't you going to kiss me?"

"No."

"Why not?"

"Because *you're* going to kiss *me*."

Her heart jumped into her throat. "I am?"

"*I'm* already experienced at this, remember?"

"But the guy is supposed to be the initiator."

He shook his head. "And I thought you were a feminist."

"I am, but—" She felt her nails curl into her palms.

"I'd imagine an accomplished physicist at the ripe old age of…what? Twenty-eight—?"

"Thirty," she corrected.

"—thirty years old could handle kissing a guy."

"I didn't say I couldn't handle it."

"Then prove to me that you can," he said, but he didn't reach out to take her into his arms, which made the whole thing very awkward as far as April was concerned. How did she get close enough? Where did she put her hands?

"You're purposely making this difficult because of what I said earlier about not wanting to sleep with you, right?" she muttered.

"I'm just letting you call the shots."

"Or maybe you think that once I kiss you, I'll turn into a puddle of desire and let you have your way with me."

He grimaced. "That's pretty dated terminology, April. If you want to turn someone on, you'd better not use it. And I'm not trying to take advantage of you. I'm doing you a *favor*. I'm offering to give you…intimacy lessons."

"*Intimacy* lessons?" she repeated.

"Who can say when you might need to know more than you do?"

April wasn't fooled that he'd be doing her any kind of service. He obviously thought he was getting the better of her in some way. But if he was really offering to teach her a few basics, no strings attached, she might actually be the one to come out ahead. At least she'd be able to make up for all the years she'd spent studying while everyone else her age was dragging Main Street and learning about the birds and the bees at Pinnacle Peak.

"Are you serious?" she said.

"Absolutely. Only…"

"What?"

"You've got to get rid of these." He pushed her glasses up so they sat on top of her head.

She almost pulled them down again, for the security they provided. But he seemed resolute, and she was beginning to think that kissing him might be easier if she couldn't see him so well.

"All set?" he said.

A shaky sensation traveled through her as April placed her hands on his chest. She could feel the thickness of his pectoral muscles through his golf shirt, which seemed *too* personal considering he was only her tutor. So she slipped her arms around his neck, going for the more traditional pose of a man and woman about to kiss and, closing her eyes at the last second, lifted her lips to his.

APRIL'S LIPS PASSED quickly over Gunner's and were gone before he could even get a taste. "You call that a kiss?" he complained.

She opened her eyes, which were wide and clear, even pretty without those ugly glasses, and wrinkled her nose. "Was it that bad?"

"It was okay," he said, although, on a scale of one to ten, it was about a zero. "It just wasn't very…convincing. The best kisses have some intent, some passion behind them. The best kisses aren't stifled with inhibitions."

She released him. "You think I'm *that* inhibited?"

"I don't think I've ever met anyone *more* inhibited."

"I can overcome my inhibitions."

So he wasn't the only one who liked a challenge. "I have to tell you I'm not very optimistic about that. You seem naturally uptight. But I'll let you try that kiss again if you want," he said, as though he was the most magnanimous soul who'd ever existed.

"Maybe you could help me," she said. "I mean, you're just *standing* there."

He bit his cheek, trying not to smile. She was playing right into his hands. "What would you like me to do?"

"You could act as though you're not made of wood. Maybe you should take some of your own advice and let yourself feel something."

He *was* feeling something. Certainly more than he wanted to. Her kiss was about the most artless he'd ever received. Yet his body was ripcord tight, and his nerves thrummed with the hope that the soft mouth he'd *almost* had the chance to taste would soon come back, would linger a moment....

When was the last time such a simple thing had

excited him so much? How long since he'd burned for a woman the way he was burning for this rather peculiar intellectual?

"Would it help if I put my hands here?" He slipped his arms around her slim waist.

"That's better, I think."

Gunner wanted to take the lead and guide her swiftly and surely through what was very familiar territory for him. But he knew that if he pushed April too fast, she'd bolt. So he kept every movement subtle and understated, waiting for her to lead the way. She'd eventually figure it out; she'd just drive him crazy first.

"On second thought, maybe you should move your hands a little higher," she said, her forehead creased in concentration.

"April…"

"What?"

"There's nothing analytical about this," he said. Then he slowly and deliberately slid his hands up, massaging the muscles on each side of her spine as he pressed her fully against him.

Her eyes flew wide open as her breasts flattened against his chest. "There's plenty to analyze here," she argued. "I mean, look at us. We're complete opposites—a bookworm and a jock. Yet we've been able to find some common ground and work together to—"

"Whatever you're saying, forget it."

"Hmm?"

"Now would be a good time to quit talking."

"Oh, right. But I was about to tell you that you're an exceptional actor. If I didn't know better, I might even think—"

He bent his head and silenced her with his mouth. She stiffened in his arms, and her lips remained tightly closed, but only for a moment. When he curled one hand around her bottom and used his mouth to gently coax her to relax, she suddenly let go of all restraint and started responding to him instinctively. And he had to admit she had very good instincts.

"There you go," he murmured against her mouth, kissing her again, this time softly, gently biting her lip and pulling it into his mouth before kissing her again. "See? It's easy."

Her hand clenched in his hair, guiding him back to her mouth, and his blood began to rush through his body at triple speed.

Gunner let his tongue slide over her straight teeth, surprised that she wasn't nearly as tentative as he'd expected. Her hands moved over him, touching his face, his hair, his chest as if she wanted to absorb absolutely every detail.

He found her curiosity incredibly erotic. He started to slip his hand beneath her strappy T-shirt so he could start some exploring of his own, but she broke away.

"How was that?" she asked, sounding breathless. "Better?"

"You still need practice," he lied. "Lots of practice."

Skepticism darkened her expression. "I'm usually not a slow learner."

"You'll get it," he promised. "The good news is I'm willing to work with you until you do."

When her lips curved into a smile, he knew she was on to him.

She removed his coat and handed it back. "I appreciate your willingness to make the sacrifice, but you've given me enough to think about for one night. I'm tired. And I need to check on my mother. With my father and her in the same hotel, there could be bloodshed."

He took his jacket, frustrated that she was finished when he felt they were just getting started. "I'm in room three forty-four if you change your mind."

"I'll remember that." Laughing softly, she grabbed her sandals, which she'd dropped in the sand, and headed back to the hotel.

Gunner slung his coat over his shoulder, welcoming the cool breeze, hoping it would clear his head.

"Have a good night," she called.

He watched her go, listening to the growl of the sea and trying to remember the last time a woman had walked out on him before he was ready to see her go.

CHAPTER SEVEN

APRIL HESITATED outside her room, her key at the ready. Claire was crying. She could hear her mother's weeping even out in the hall.

Had something happened? Or was her mother crying over the same old problems?

Closing her eyes, April slid down the wall to sit on the Spanish tile floor, wondering what she should do. She knew if she went inside, her mother would choke back her tears and suffer in silence. Claire wouldn't open up and talk, wouldn't admit she was upset. She hadn't in the past four months. So how could April help her?

April sat listening for a few minutes. Then, feeling guilty for shirking her duty as a good daughter, she let her breath out decisively and stood up. She had to go inside, just in case her mother needed her. It wasn't as if she had siblings who could take on any of this responsibility.

But as soon as entered the room, her mother fell silent, just as April had known she would.

"Mom, are you asleep?" April whispered, giving her the opportunity to talk if she wanted to.

Her mother didn't answer. Obviously Claire wouldn't or couldn't share her grief. As usual. She'd probably go out tomorrow and get her navel pierced instead. Or maybe she'd have a fling with the young man who handed out pool towels.

April set her shoes quietly inside the wardrobe as if she was fooled by her mother's silence. But she couldn't bring herself to go to bed. Suddenly the room felt too small for both of them. April didn't want to be here, knowing her mother was crying only a few feet away, didn't want to pretend she didn't know.

Leaving her shoes and glasses, she slipped out of the room and hurried down the hall, putting some distance between her and Claire. When she'd been out on the beach with Gunner, she'd momentarily forgotten about her parents' divorce. She'd even forgotten about work.

Maybe it was simply too soon to return to reality.

I'm in room three forty-four if you change your mind.

His words tempted her. She had no intention of sleeping with him, but she knew that just being in the same vicinity would provide the escape she needed so badly.

It wasn't until she'd spent the next hour dangling

her feet in the Jacuzzi, however, that she seriously considered knocking on Gunner's door. If his suite was anything like hers, he had two double beds. They could talk. Or sleep...

Telling herself this was the modern world and she shouldn't think twice about it, she took the elevator to the third floor. For a short distance, the corridor was more of a bridge, so she could see the pool where she'd sat for so long reflecting the stars overhead. The serene, beautiful sight helped to calm her, but she still didn't want to go back to her own room.

Her knock on Gunner's door was far more timid than she'd meant it to be. Good manners made it difficult to disturb him when he was probably asleep. But, leaning closer, she heard the television even though the volume had been turned low, so she knocked louder.

When he came to the door, he was wearing nothing but a pair of khaki shorts, and his chest looked every bit as good as she'd imagined when she'd felt his muscles earlier. "Hi," he said, his face registering surprise.

April struggled to keep her eyes from wandering below his neck. "Any chance you've got an extra bed?"

He took in the fact that she wasn't wearing any shoes. Maybe he noticed that she'd left her glasses behind, too. He didn't seem to miss much. "I do," he said. "Come on in."

She stepped inside and immediately recognized the scent of his aftershave. Almost equally appealing, and far safer, was the box of Godiva chocolates lying open on the desk.

"A welcome gift from your father," he said when he noticed her interest.

"I didn't get a welcome gift."

His teeth flashed as he smiled. "Help yourself."

She crossed the room, slumped down in one of the chairs beside the desk and settled the box in her lap. One chocolate led to another until she'd eaten most of the top layer. Somehow there didn't seem to be enough chocolate in the world to dispel her sudden depression.

Gunner had folded his arms and was leaning against the wall, watching her. "Are you trying to make yourself sick?" he asked at last.

She squinted at a chocolate she'd pulled from the lower layer. "Do you know if this one has a cherry in it?"

"I have no idea," he said. "I pretty much stick with traditional candy bars. But they've got a vending machine downstairs, in case you're running low there."

She put the chocolate back. "I hate cherries. What's in the vending machine?"

"Are you planning to tell me what's going on?"

She licked her fingers and scowled. "Being an only child sucks."

His eyebrows drew together. "Are physicists even allowed to say 'sucks'?"

"I use words like that occasionally with people who don't know me well. It makes me come off a little less stiff."

"I don't think it's working for you."

"Figures." She grimaced. "Well, I'm getting tired. I think I'll go to bed."

His eyebrows rose. "That's it?"

"What's it?"

"You really came here because you want to *sleep?*"

"My mother was crying when I got to my room. Would you want to spend the night with a woman sniffling into her pillow, refusing to tell you what's wrong?"

"Now you know why I never married," he said, straightening. "I'll get some change for the vending machine."

AN HOUR LATER, Gunner propped the pillows behind his back as he watched April study her cards. They were sitting on his bed, playing Texas Hold'em, and she'd beaten him three hands already. But he was pretty sure that was beginner's luck. At least he hoped it was. The ace of spades, ten of diamonds and king of clubs were turned faceup between them—not bad flop cards. He should be able to make something out of *this* hand. "I can't believe you've never played poker before," he said while he waited for her.

She was obviously preoccupied with the decision-making process. "Gambling hasn't been very high on my list of priorities."

"But you didn't know how to play *any* of the games I mentioned."

"Most people learn to play games like this while they're young, or maybe in college."

"But you didn't?"

"I was fifteen when I started college, so I wasn't invited out much."

He scratched his chest. What an odd childhood. He couldn't help feeling sorry for her, thinking of all the fun she'd missed. "You were old enough to associate with college-age people when you were working on your Master's and Doctorate."

"True, but behavioral patterns are learned very young. I was shy and reclusive at that point, and there weren't a lot of men in school who seemed to feel comfortable with me."

"So you've never been to Vegas for spring break?"

"No."

"Never been anywhere just to party and have fun?"

"I'm here in Cabo, aren't I?"

"A company trip with your parents is your idea of a party?"

"I'm having fun. Aren't you?"

"I guess." He chuckled. What a life.

She stretched out across the foot of the bed, the flop cards and the pot between them. "I'll match your Twix bar and raise you a bag of Doritos."

"You must have quite a hand," he said, trying to bait her into giving herself away.

It didn't work. She arched her eyebrows coyly. "Maybe I'm a good bluffer."

"Somehow I doubt that."

"I've won three hands already."

That was a slightly sore subject. Anyway, Gunner had an excuse. "Anybody would've won with the hands you were dealt. It's beginner's luck. And the game's not over yet."

"You're overconfident. About a *lot* of things. That'll get you in trouble."

He could tell from her tone and expression that she was talking about their relationship.

"It remains to be seen which of us is overconfident about the other," he said.

"You must be *pretty* self-assured where I'm concerned. You tried to talk me into playing strip poker a few minutes ago," she told him.

He shrugged. "I didn't want to disappoint you. I have a reputation to uphold, remember?"

April glanced eagerly at the candy bars and other snacks in the middle of the bed. "So do you have the guts to call my bet? Or are you going to fold?"

"That depends on the next flop card." He turned over another ace. "Interesting." He had an ace of his own, which gave him three of a kind. He could possibly get a full house on the next round. Tossing in a roll of Life Savers and a Snickers bar, he considered what he had left to bet with and added a bag of pork rinds.

"Sorry," she said. "Pork rinds don't count."

"Why not?"

"I hate them."

"You're not going to win."

"Oh, yes, I am."

"How do you know?"

She smiled sweetly.

Damn. Maybe she *was* a good bluffer. No...April Ashton couldn't lie or cheat. She was so straitlaced and prim that she hadn't even known how to kiss properly—although she did now, thanks to him. She must have four of a kind or better.

Just for the heck of it, he leaned forward to see if he couldn't get a peek at her cards, but she immediately drew them close to her chest. "Uh-uh," she said. "No cheating."

Gunner's betting reserves were running low. He was down to a $100 Grand bar, his favorite, and some wintergreen Life Savers he liked to carry with him. If he lost anything more than he'd already bet, he'd be out of the game. So he gave up on the pork rinds and simply called her bet, only to have her throw four more candy bars into the pile.

"I'll match your two and raise you two," she said. "Your turn."

He flipped over the last flop card, hoping for a seven, or even another ten or a king. But it was a two of hearts. He didn't have his full house, and considering how cocky she was, she had to have something pretty spectacular.

Taking a deep breath, he decided to cut his losses now and try to take her on the next hand. "I fold."

"Really? You?" She sounded surprised and inordinately pleased with herself.

"Really," he said with some irritation. He hated folding, even though it kept him alive for another hand. He'd never had a lot of practice at losing.

Setting her cards carefully in front of her, facedown, she started to rake in the pot. He reached out to see her hand, but she stopped him. "Sorry."

"What do you mean, sorry?"

"You don't get to see what I was holding."

"Why not?"

"Because you'll just use the information to try and figure out what my facial expressions mean. Why should I give up that information?"

"Fine." He pretended to accept her refusal and began reshuffling. But the moment she shifted her attention to her snacks, he grabbed her cards and turned them over to reveal a three and a four.

He blinked in stunned dismay. "You've got to be kidding me. You had nothing."

"I told you I was a good bluffer."

He'd underestimated her. Probably because she was so damn appealing with her honest smile and wide dark eyes.

He made a mental note never to do *that* again.

"I have enough junk food to keep me busy for a while." She sorted through her snacks. "If you want to switch to strip poker now, I think I'm up for it."

Only because she thought she'd win. "No way," he said.

"Why not? It was your suggestion."

"That was *before* you kicked my ass. I'm not going to be sitting here butt naked with you fully clothed. A man can only take so much."

She laughed, so freely and sincerely it was almost childlike. "You've lost your nerve?"

"I'm trying to learn from my mistakes."

Standing, she stretched, and he tried not to notice how her shirt lifted to reveal a smooth, flat stomach. "Well, if you're not going to strip, the game's over." She eyed his pork rinds with disdain. "There's nothing else here I want."

"Except to see me naked?" Ordinarily he wouldn't have been surprised. The women he dated were generally pretty warm to that idea. But this was April....

"If you lose, you lose," she said.

"Or we could forget about the game and take off our clothes together. Then we both win."

"No, thanks." She peeled open a Butterfinger. "Too bad you didn't win one of these." Closing her eyes in appreciation, she took a bite and moaned, acting as though it was food for the gods.

He narrowed his eyes and gazed meaningfully at her mouth. But instead of getting nervous, as he'd expected, she licked her lips in a slow, seductive manner.

"I could take it away easily enough," he warned, standing up and moving closer—in case she didn't realize she was starting a whole new game, one with higher stakes than the last.

"There's that overconfidence again."

She was flirting with him. April, who'd only just learned to kiss. Moving more quickly, he swept her off her feet and pinned her beneath him on the bed.

"What were you saying?" He fit one leg snugly between hers and purposely applied pressure where he knew she'd like it most.

Her eyes widened as she stared up at him, and he offered her a challenging smile. "I think you're in over your head. Are you sure you want to provoke me?"

"Maybe not entirely," she admitted breathlessly.

He chuckled. Then, bending his head, he trailed kisses up her neck and used his tongue to outline the firm ridge of her ear. "What about now?" he murmured.

She shivered. "I...like that."

He lowered himself between her legs, so she could feel his arousal. "And now?"

Placing her hands on his cheeks, she held his face as she looked into his eyes. He wasn't sure what she was thinking, but he knew it couldn't be anything bad when she gave him the softest, sweetest kiss he'd ever had.

"You taste like heaven," he told her, and meant every word. He wasn't prepared for her response.

"I think *Crimson Tide* is on pay-per-view."

GUNNER WOKE to the sound of running water. Pulling the pillow off his head, he blinked, looked around the room and remembered that he'd had a sleepover. With a woman. And she hadn't spent the night in his bed.

He supposed there was a first time for everything.

"April?" he said, throwing off the covers.

She opened the shutter-style doors that separated the in-room Jacuzzi and the rest of the bath area from the beds, and smiled brightly at him, wearing the boxer briefs and T-shirt he'd lent her to sleep in. "I was hoping you'd wake up soon."

He glanced at the clock. Six forty-seven. "Last I heard we were on vacation."

"I had trouble sleeping after all that chocolate. Must've been the caffeine."

The empty Godiva box sat on the nightstand, along with the pile of other wrappers from the candy bars she'd polished off while they were watching *Crimson Tide*. "Do you always eat so much junk?" he asked.

"Not always. Just on an occasional weekend."

"How do you stay so thin?"

"I go to work and forget to eat." She shrugged. "Sometimes I even forget to go home at night."

"Oh, yeah. That happens to me all the time." He rolled his eyes and dropped back on the bed, then realized that the water he'd heard running wasn't in the sink.

"What are you doing?" He leaned up on one elbow to see her adjust the knobs on the tub.

"Put on your suit. I thought we could use the Jacuzzi."

"What are you going to wear?"

"Nothing." She smiled slyly.

His heart skipped a beat, or maybe two or three. He stretched to see how she was doing with the water. The bath was nearly full.

"Why the sudden change of heart?"

"Last night I was only willing to play strip poker when I knew there was no real risk that I'd have to disrobe. Which got me thinking."

"About…"

"Those inhibitions you mentioned."

"Right, the inhibitions," he said, playing along.

"My mother actually agrees with you. She says I'm not taking advantage of everything life has to offer."

"And?"

"And I'm going to start opening myself up to new experiences. I figure if I can take off my clothes in front of you, I can take them off in front of just about anyone."

Oh, boy. Somehow he wasn't bothered about her waking him up so early anymore…

"I mean, what could a little skinny-dipping hurt? Most people do it long before they reach my age."

He felt a moment's guilt because he didn't seem

to be a very good influence on her. "Are you sure you've thought this through?"

She wasn't listening. "I'm slowly realizing that there's more to life than work, and if I'm not careful, it's all going to pass me by."

His conscience was bothering him a little, but not enough to stop her. "I'll put on my suit," he said, hoping to hurry things along before she lost her nerve.

The telephone rang.

He planned to ignore it, but he didn't communicate his wishes to April quickly enough. She answered the extension in the bathroom. "I'm fine, Mom," he heard her say. "Nothing to worry about... No, I'm just about to go skinny-dipping with Gunner... Of course I'm serious... So? Maybe I'm ready to take a few risks... I've got to go... Okay, see you this afternoon."

"What did she say?" he asked.

"'It's about time.'"

"Really?"

"I don't think mothers are supposed to agree with something like this. Sort of takes the fun out of it."

"Not for me," he said.

CHAPTER EIGHT

APRIL PRESSED her bare backside to the bedroom wall and tried to peek around the corner into the bathroom. Gunner was waiting for her in the tub, just like she'd asked. His hair was wet and curling around his ears, and the steam rising from the water made his chest gleam. He looked gorgeous, of course, but he was getting a little impatient. Probably because he'd been sitting in that hot water long enough to start sweating.

"April, are you coming?" he said.

She considered backing out, but the memory of her mother laughing skeptically and saying, "I'll believe *that* when I see it," wouldn't let her. She could be bold and daring....

She just wished bold and daring didn't make her feel as if she was about to faint.

Maybe she needed to do this by degrees. That concept was used for conquering all kinds of difficult challenges, right? Today she'd go topless. Tomorrow she'd take it all off.

Maybe.

But a compromise wasn't easy to arrange because she didn't have anything of her own she could wear into the tub. Her sarong wouldn't work, and her panties were the kind that screamed, *I have no love life*. She'd rather go naked than wear those panties in front of Gunner.

So she opted for his boxer briefs. Boxer briefs were sexy. Women were wearing them on billboards all across America, advertising perfume.

"April?" he called again.

"I'm coming," she said as she pulled on the boxers. They rode low on her hips, falling well below her navel, but a glance in the mirror told April that was a good effect. She almost didn't recognize the woman peering back at her—but that could've been because she didn't have her glasses on.

"What did you say?"

Somewhat reassured to be wearing at least one article of clothing, she headed to the bathroom.

"Here goes," she said, and stepped into the open.

Gunner looked up at her, and she felt her stomach plummet to her knees. Her first instinct was to cover up. But she refused to chicken out so completely. She was what she was, she told herself. It didn't matter that he'd seen better. She was breaking out of her humdrum life, tossing away routine, overcoming her fears....

"Say something," she said, her heart thumping wildly when his gaze dropped immediately to her breasts and his mouth fell open.

"You—" He cleared his throat. "You did it."

A sense of empowerment brought a victorious smile. She'd never dreamed she'd see that stunned expression on any man's face—least of all Gunner Stevens's. "I told you I can overcome my inhibitions," she said, and stepped into the hot water.

WITH AN EFFORT, Gunner closed his mouth and lowered his lids so that he was watching her from under his lashes. Just when he felt he was getting the best of his innocent little opponent, she unwittingly pulled out a trump card like this one and changed everything—like his image of the "perfect" female body. He'd thought bigger breasts were sexier. He'd always preferred his women with more curves. But now that he'd seen April, he knew he liked his women slender, with breasts the size of his cupped hand and toffee-colored nipples that puckered to perfection whenever he looked at them.

"You're making some real strides," he said to encourage her.

She took a seat directly across from him, slightly flushed from the heat and the daring of what she'd done. "I know. Isn't it great? The people at my work wouldn't even know me. Last night I played poker. Today I'm skinny-dipping.''

"You're wearing my boxers," he pointed out. "That's hardly skinny-dipping."

"I'm doing this by degrees," she said confidently.

That sounded hopeful. "You planning to go another degree today?" he asked.

She bit her lip thoughtfully, then shook her head. "No."

SHE HADN'T EVEN let him touch her. She got into his Jacuzzi. She got out. That was it.

And now, three hours later, Gunner was still thinking about those few moments and aching for more.

Claire was golfing with the party ahead of them. He returned her wave and placed his ball on the tee of the eighth hole, feeling decidedly morose. He'd never played such a poor game of golf. April was hell on his concentration. Every time he heard her laughing or talking, which she seemed to be doing quite freely with the other two members of their group—her father and Keith Bodine—he pictured her half-naked and out of reach, and hacked his ball into the rough or overshot the put.

This hole he managed a little better. His ball

dropped just inside the green instead of landing in the surrounding desert.

Walt took his turn and managed to get fairly close to the flag. Then Keith made them both look bad by putting himself in position to birdie.

"My turn already?" April said when her father called her to the tee.

Gunner pulled the bill of his hat a little lower as he watched her step up in her sleeveless golf shirt and formfitting white shorts. His mood darkened further when she tossed a grin at Keith Bodine simply because the man had wished her luck. Given Bodine's lovesick expression, Gunner was fairly sure *he* was the plant manager April had wanted to avoid. But she didn't seem too worried about keeping her distance from him now. Bodine had been helping her at every opportunity, choosing her club for her, showing her the right way to hold it, demonstrating a good swing. She was cutting her flirting teeth on him, and the poor bastard didn't even know it.

WHEN THEY RETURNED from golf, April talked Gunner into taking her shopping. But as he followed her through the open-air bazaar in town, he didn't have much to say. "You seem kind of grumpy today," she complained. "Is something wrong?"

He told her there wasn't, but April had noted a distinct change in him since their Jacuzzi experience and was a little mystified that he wasn't more pleased with her progress.

"Are you tired?" she pressed.

"No."

"Then what?"

"Why were you flirting with Keith Bodine if you're not really interested in him?" he asked.

She blinked in surprise. Gunner sounded almost...jealous. But he *couldn't* be jealous. Which meant he really believed she'd been unkind or irresponsible in some way.

April reflected on the afternoon and couldn't come up with a single comment she'd made that might lead Keith to believe she was interested in anything more than being his friend. Gunner had been there, posing as her boyfriend, for Pete's sake. She'd just been thrilled that at last she felt in charge of her love life and her sexuality, that she felt confident enough to offer poor Keith a kind word and a smile.

"I wasn't flirting." She weaved through showcases of silver jewelry and tables bearing T-shirts, tequila shot glasses and Cabo San Lucas bags, mugs and key chains. "I was merely being nice."

"Nice includes letting him put his arms around you?"

She struggled to remember when Keith might have put his arms around her and finally it came to her. "Oh, that." She dismissed his words with a shake of her head. "He was only helping me with my swing."

"He was doing a lot more than that," Gunner muttered.

April didn't really understand why Gunner had a problem with how she'd behaved today, so she shrugged it off. Propping her hands on her hips as they came to the last row of merchandise, which was very similar to what they'd seen in at least a dozen displays so far, she sighed. "They don't have what I need. I guess I'm going to have to ask someone for directions to a store that sells what I want."

"What are you looking for?" he asked.

"Underwear."

"You didn't bring enough?"

"I didn't bring the right kind." She grinned. "This is part of my transformation. I need to buy some underwear that reflects my new liberated self."

She started toward the woman who ran the stall, but Gunner caught her by the shoulder. "What kind of underwear are you talking about?"

"I don't know yet. That's why you're here. You have to help me pick out something that really appeals to a man."

"I can only pick out what appeals to *me*," he said hesitantly.

She nodded. "But there's bound to be some crossover, right?"

The fact that she didn't particularly care whether she pleased him or someone else grated on him.

"I'm thinking a couple of thongs might be fun, if I can get used to wearing them," she confided.

Thongs. That was it. Gunner was tired of letting April Ashton beat him at his own game. Tonight he'd seduce her on the beach, touch and taste her everywhere, make her shudder in his arms while murmuring his name. He'd show her he wasn't interchangeable with any other man.

Except that his breath grew short and his body hard at the very thought of making love to her. And for the first time in his life, Gunner was afraid he'd be the only one enslaved by the experience.

"You can pick out your own underwear," he said. "And you can do it later. Let's go back to the hotel."

She seemed hurt by his gruff tone, and definitely surprised. "I'm not ready to go back."

"I am, but I can't leave you here alone."

"Why not?"

"I'm not sure it's safe."

"Don't be silly. I'm an adult. I shop here by myself almost every year."

"Fine." He started to go, but she stopped him.

"Have I done something to offend you?" she asked, obviously bewildered.

He wasn't sure even *he* understood what was happening to him. He certainly wasn't ready to explain it to her. "No."

"Then what? Are you bored with our friendship?"

Gunner tilted up her chin with one finger and kissed her, battling a sudden longing to pull her against him and whisper things he'd never said to a woman before. "This has nothing to do with boredom or friendship," he said. Then he caught a cab and headed back to the hotel.

WALT SHOVED HIS HANDS in the pockets of his chinos and stared out to sea. He loved Cabo, owned a home on the mountain just north of town. But during the company trip, he'd chosen to stay at the Hacienda Del Mar with everyone else. There wasn't any reason not to. The Hacienda Del Mar was a five-star premier resort and was more than comfortable. And he liked being in the middle of the action instead of twenty minutes away.

The only thing missing from this trip was a companion, he decided. He should've brought Regina for times like this, when he had a couple of hours to kill. If he'd known April was going to be so preoccupied with Gunner, he would have.

Reminded of his daughter and her new boyfriend, Walt shook his head. Who would've thought the race-car driver whose ability he'd long admired would be able to see what so many men had missed—that his daughter was a rare jewel? Walt hadn't expected a relationship to spring up between them, but he was encouraged by the possibilities.

Nodding hello to Nora Phelps, his company controller, who was passing by with her husband, he started down the brick-and-cement steps. He was heading for a seat by the pool when he spotted Claire. Wearing a purple-and-gold swimsuit cut high on the leg and low in back, she was just getting out of the water.

She looked great for fifty-two. He could see why so many men, even younger men, found her attractive. He would've found her attractive, too, if he'd remembered to *look* at her. He'd been so busy building Ashton Automotive, over the past three years especially, that she'd finally faded into the woodwork. No wonder they'd drifted apart. And then he'd gotten involved with Regina.

He veered off to the left, hoping to avoid Claire and the mixed emotions she stirred in him. She was the mother of his daughter. She'd once been the love of his life. Yet he'd broken his marriage vows in a weak stupid moment and caused more damage than he could ever repair. Now he was fifty-five, getting a divorce and having heart surgery.

He glanced up to make sure he'd escaped her notice and caught her staring right at him.

She immediately dropped her gaze and busied herself spreading out a towel on her lounge chair, and he knew she wouldn't bother him. He wasn't sure why he'd been worried about that in the first place. She'd pretty much stopped trying to initiate conversations. Now they handled most everything through their lawyers. But April couldn't be handled through lawyers, and Walt had a few questions he wanted to ask about their daughter.

Changing directions, he rounded the pool. By the time he reached Claire, she was lying on her back with a straw hat covering her eyes. She lifted the hat the moment his shadow fell across her.

"What do you think of Gunner Stevens?" he asked without preamble, because the awkwardness between them made it difficult to begin a conversation any other way.

Her face registered surprise. "I think he's the best thing to happen to April in years," she said.

"You're confident she won't get hurt? A man with that much money and fame typically goes around the block a few times before settling down."

"Gunner seems to have a good head on his shoulders. And April's a bright girl. You know that."

"But she's not very worldly-wise, is she?" He was voicing his worries because he knew that Claire, of all people, would understand how he felt.

"I think she's getting educated," she replied. "She spent last night in his room."

Walt's eyebrows shot up. He wasn't sure he was pleased to hear this information. "If he hurts her—"

"Have some faith in April," Claire interrupted. "It's time she started experiencing life. She's thirty and never been in love. And she's tougher than she looks. She's your daughter, remember?"

Walt couldn't help smiling at that. He *was* a tough old coot. But Claire had always been able to handle him, had always reminded him of the things that were really important. Until he quit listening to her. Until he got sidetracked by something that seemed to have substance but soon turned to smoke.

"I guess you're right," he said.

An awkward silence ensued, but Walt found himself strangely reluctant to leave. There was an open chaise next to Claire. He thought about sinking into it and telling her all about his heart problems and the surgery and his concerns about what might happen to the company if he didn't recover. He wanted to let her know he'd decided to sell so he could cash them all out at the peak, to provide for those he'd leave behind if he didn't make it.

But she'd already lain back and put the hat over her eyes. "See you at dinner," she said.

CLAIRE HEARD WALT'S steps recede and breathed easier when he was gone. She'd had it with the pain, the rejection, the whole emotional devastation of their separation. And she was tired of crying. After last night, she'd decided she'd never cry over Walt again. They'd spent the best part of their lives together. If he wanted to throw that away for someone like Regina, she couldn't stop him.

Adjusting her hat to provide more shade, she slid her sunglasses to the bridge of her nose and gazed down at the legs she'd worked so hard to tone and tan. She'd been knocking herself out for months, trying to become more attractive, hoping to convince her husband that he was making a mistake. But watching April with Gunner had made Claire wonder if pleasing Walt was the real issue. Maybe it was time Claire started thinking about what *she* wanted. Lord knew it wasn't another tattoo. She already regretted getting the first one. She'd chosen a butterfly to symbolize her freedom, but it symbolized her desperation and stupidity instead.

"I'm done scrambling for his affections," she muttered.

"Excuse me? Did you say something?"

Claire lifted her hat to see a man, somewhere in his early thirties, settle in the chair next to her. He was muscular and attractive in a pair of swimming trunks and nothing else, but the toothy smile he flashed simply reminded her that she was twenty years too old for him.

"No, nothing important," she replied.

"It is beautiful here, yes?"

She admired his European accent. "Yes."

"Beautiful like you." His dark eyes twinkled in the sunlight, and she couldn't help smiling back.

"May I buy you a drink, lovely lady?" he asked.

Claire knew that because of her hat and her dark glasses, he probably couldn't judge her age. A few days earlier she would have exploited his ignorance by flirting with him, hoping he'd continue to pursue her just to prove to Walt—and herself—that she was still desirable. But she refused to prop up her self-esteem in such a false way anymore. She'd learned that making a fool of herself didn't help.

Taking off her hat, she lifted her glasses so he could see her clearly. "No, but thank you."

He pressed a hand to his chest despite the fact that he had to realize, by now, that she was too old for him. "Are you married?" he asked.

''No.''

''Then have a drink with me.''

''No.''

''Why not?''

She stood and gathered her wrap and hat. ''Because I have a thirty-year-old daughter, and it's time I start acting my age,'' she said with a sad smile. ''But I'm flattered. Have a wonderful day.''

CHAPTER NINE

UNDERWEAR SHOPPING WASN'T the same without Gunner. April forced herself to buy a few things, because she'd set out to do it and pride dictated she finish. But her afternoon wasn't the good time she'd envisioned. And dinner when she returned was even worse. She wore a wrap-style dress that, with her new push-up bra, definitely made the most of her small bust. Her hair she curled and piled loosely on her head, the way her mother had been trying to get her to style it for months. And she wore her contacts instead of her glasses and even a little bit of mascara and lip gloss. But if she looked nice, Gunner didn't seem to notice. He sat beside her at the table and talked mostly to her parents.

By the time she'd finished dessert, April was feeling disgruntled. She hadn't done anything to upset Gunner. She hadn't done anything to change their relationship at all. So what was his problem? He was supposed to be nice to her for five more days.

''The wind's died down,'' her father said to her

and Gunner as they started to go their separate ways. "Shall we put on our suits and get in the outdoor Jacuzzi by the big pool?"

Gunner shot April an uncertain glance but agreed. April tried to say she was too tired, but her father insisted the experience would be good for her. Then Walt surprised everyone by turning to Claire. "Would you like to join us?" he asked.

Her mother's eyes widened. "No, thank you. I think I'll go read a book."

April couldn't believe Claire had just turned her father down. Recognizing the opportunity to finally get them to socialize, she quickly changed her own mind. "Actually, I'll bet the water will feel good," she said.

"Then have fun, dear," Claire responded. She'd just started to walk away, when April caught her by the arm. "You'll come along, won't you, Mom?"

"April…"

"Please, Mom?"

Claire hesitated but finally nodded when April tightened her grip.

"Great." April smiled at Gunner and her father. "We'll just go put on our suits."

THE JACUZZI TURNED OUT to be no improvement over dinner. Gunner watched April covertly—she could sense his regard even when he was talking to her father or mother. But he didn't speak to her directly, and he certainly didn't apologize for his behavior in town. After a few minutes, he got out, gave her a cursory nod good-night, no more personal than the one he gave her parents, and excused himself.

Then Walt and Claire looked at her as if to say, *What's happened between you two?* and April grew so angry with Gunner that she couldn't stay in the Jacuzzi a moment longer.

Damn him, he wasn't keeping up his end of the bargain!

Getting out, she threw on the sheer cover-up that went with her suit and marched after him. She was leaving her estranged parents in the Jacuzzi by themselves, but she figured they'd just have to deal with it. She had something to say to Gunner Stevens, and it couldn't wait.

When she arrived at Gunner's room, she knocked loudly. He took his sweet time answering, so she banged more insistently and when he finally appeared, he was wearing only a pair of boxer briefs like the ones she'd borrowed this morning. "Can you give me a minute to get changed?" he asked.

She didn't care that he was standing in the doorway in his underwear, looking like a dream. There was the matter of his behavior to address, and she planned to do that here and now.

"Are you backing out on our deal?" she said. "Is that what's going on?"

He peered down the hall, then shoved the door wider. "Come inside."

She stalked into his room.

"Want to sit down?" he asked.

"No. I want to know why you're upset with me."

He scowled and pulled on a pair of pajama bottoms. "I'm not upset with you. Our agreement was founded on something that isn't turning out to be true."

"What's that?" she demanded. "I painted a very realistic picture of what was going to happen here. I never lied to you."

"You said neither one of us would get hurt, April."

"So *that's* it? You think I'm going to get hurt? I'm not stupid, Gunner. I know I'd be crazy to think for a second that—"

"I was talking about me," he said.

It took a moment for his words to sink in. When they did, April felt as though he'd just knocked the wind out of her. *"What?"*

His eyebrows drew together, and he suddenly seemed irritated or impatient or both. "Never mind. It's over, okay? You're handling Keith Bodine just fine, your parents are getting along better than I ever imagined they would, which is really all you can ask, and if your father wants to sell me the company, he'll sell me the company. We don't need to keep up this pretense.''

He opened the door and gestured out with his free hand. ''Good night, April.''

GUNNER COULDN'T HAVE been serious. That was the thought that kept passing through April's mind as she walked numbly down the corridor from his room. Women were a dime a dozen to him, remember? She'd seen the front pages of the tabloids. She knew his reputation with the ladies. Besides, she was so different from the leggy blondes he typically dated. Was he playing some sort of new game with her?

When she reached the lobby, she hesitated. She wasn't ready to face her mother's wrath for abandoning her in the Jacuzzi with Walt. So she headed out a side door to avoid the crowded lobby bar and walked down to the water.

An hour came and went while she sat on the cold sand, watching the black waves roar up onto the beach and thinking about Gunner. He confused her, threw her out of her element. She couldn't make sense of their relationship no matter how many minutes slipped by, so she decided to go back inside, where it, was warm. What did seem clear was the fact that she was capable of caring on a deeper level than he was. Which meant, if she allowed herself to trust him, to trust *in* him, she'd be the one who was disappointed.

She thought of Bill Sossaman and was afraid that this affair would end the same way.

But what about her desire to break out of her staid, safe existence and start living? Someone, somewhere, had said it was better to have loved and lost than never to have loved at all, and she believed it. She just wasn't sure she had the courage to take such a *big* gamble right now. Gunner Stevens, of all men. Surely she'd have a better chance at happiness with someone who wasn't drop-dead gorgeous and devilishly charming. Someone like—

"Hey, April."

She glanced up to see Keith Bodine and some of the other guys from Ashton Automotive standing at the edge of the bar she'd avoided earlier. A television was on in the far corner. It looked as though they were watching sports highlights.

"Hi," she said, trying to pump some cheer into her voice.

"Can I buy you a drink?" he asked.

She started to tell him no, then imagined returning to her room before her mother was quite asleep, and reconsidered. Why not? She never drank because alcohol gave her such a nasty headache. But she felt she could use a margarita tonight.

POUNDING AT HIS DOOR jerked Gunner awake.

"Gunner? It's me. I want to talk to you."

April. Shoving himself out of bed, he opened the door to see that she was still in her swimsuit, which suggested she probably hadn't been back to her room since she'd left him earlier.

"It's nearly two o'clock," he said, growing worried. "Where have you been?"

"Downstairs in the bar."

That he could believe. From the slurring of her voice, she was more than a little tipsy.

"I've been talking to Keith."

Gunner couldn't help the flat tone that entered his voice. "What did he have to say?"

"That sometimes, when your heart's really committed to something, you have to go with it."

"Do I get to hear the rest of that conversation?"

"No," she said, but when she looked up at him, he could see that her eyes were filling with tears.

He leaned against the doorjamb, watching her. "Do you cry every time you get drunk?"

"How should I know?" she asked. "I never drink anymore. It gives me a headache."

"Why is tonight any different?"

"I needed clarity."

He chuckled despite his concern. "Hell of a way to achieve it."

"I've been talking to Keith."

"You mentioned that."

"He's a very nice man, a good friend."

Gunner's jaw tightened. "Glad to hear it."

"He said some things are just meant to be and we have to face them squarely."

"Sounds like words to live by."

"Yeah." A tear slipped past her lashes and ran down her cheek, and he couldn't resist reaching over to wipe it away.

"What's wrong?" he said, softening when she closed her eyes at his touch. God, there was something about this woman that had gotten into his blood. They had absolutely nothing in common. He'd barely heard of quantum physics; she knew zilch about racing. She was serious and intense; he was always trying to rile somebody. She lived a celibate's life; he felt more comfortable raising hell. They'd never be able to make a go of it. Yet she was the first thing, the only thing, to interest him since his mother had died and he'd lost his desire to race.

She sniffed but didn't answer.

"What do you need, April?" he pressed, cupping her cheek.

More tears pooled in her eyes as she looked up at him. "You."

FOR A SPLIT SECOND, April felt as though she'd just dived off the edge of a cliff into total blackness. She'd done it. She'd opened her big mouth and confessed all. Next came the part where Gunner apologized and told her she was mistaken if she thought he wanted her to care about him. Just like Bill Sossaman.

She squeezed her eyes closed, free-falling through space, picking up speed, plummeting faster and faster and faster toward—

She never found out because suddenly Gunner was there, taking her into his arms and pulling her close. She felt him kiss the top of her head, heard him murmur that everything was going to be okay. Then he carried her to his bed, and she fell asleep with her cheek against his chest, listening to the steady beat of his heart.

APRIL WOKE UP in Gunner's bed. Sometime in the middle of the night, he'd taken off her cover-up and the top of her bikini—or she'd done it herself. Her breasts were against his bare back, and she had one arm wrapped possessively around his waist as if she thought he might try to get away during the night.

But he was still wearing his pajama pants, and she was still wearing the bottom of her swimsuit. Which meant she hadn't missed too much.

A good thing, she decided. If she and Gunner ever made love, she'd want to remember it.

Sliding away from him, she started to get up to brush her teeth. It was her first time waking up in a man's bed. She had to vanquish her margarita breath—even if it meant pirating his toothbrush. But the slightest movement made her head threaten to explode, so she shifted gingerly onto her back and tried to figure out how she could get hold of a bottle of Tylenol, and then a toothbrush, without having to move *or* wake Gunner.

He rolled over a moment later and opened his eyes. "Hangover?" he asked, taking one look at her face, which she knew, from the way she felt, had to be ashen.

"Tylenol," she said.

He chuckled at her one-word answer and called the front desk to request a bottle of painkillers and some soda water. Then he called room service and ordered a plate of steak and eggs and a stack of pancakes. "It'll help if you eat something."

"Maybe you could do me a favor and just shoot me now."

"Want a massage?"

"Is that how I lost my top?"

"Don't look at me," he said with a shrug. "You

took it off. You were practically begging me for more intimacy lessons.''

''I was?''

''Would I lie to you?''

''Yes.''

''Well, maybe I would. But you were drunk, and I was a total gentleman.'' He let his fingers slide lightly over her stomach, raising goose bumps. ''If you want, we could start advanced classes as soon as we get rid of your headache. I'd like to repeat yesterday morning's get-naked experience—and have it end with a little less frustration.''

April would have laughed, except the mention of ''advanced lessons'' had triggered a Bill Sossaman flashback. ''Um...I'm afraid I have some bad news,'' she said, finding some of that clarity she'd been searching for.

He sat up, his expression guarded. ''What kind of bad news?''

''The kind you won't like.''

''Does anybody like bad news?''

''This isn't *all* bad,'' she said.

''Then give me the good news first.''

''I care about you and I'm willing to trust you enough to risk my heart.''

He seemed to think that over. ''So what's the bad news?''

''I believe in waiting.''

She could tell from the blankness in his eyes that he didn't have a clue what she was talking about. "Waiting for what?"

"You know…"

Suddenly he straightened, and she knew her meaning had just registered. *"For a ring?"*

She winced at his incredulous tone. "I know it sounds old-fashioned to want to see if a commitment develops before we make love, but…"

"We've only known each other for a few weeks!"

"Exactly. And you're probably not the marrying kind. I'm honestly not pushing for anything you're not ready to give. It's just that, well, there are a few things I need in my own life, Gunner. And I'm simply not cut out for casual relationships. You might have noticed."

He didn't answer. He was still looking shocked. And then the phone rang. Dragging his gaze away from her, he answered—and sagged against the headboard as if his morning had just gone from bad to worse. "Hi, Dad."

CHAPTER TEN

APRIL LISTENED as Gunner talked to his father for a few minutes. The conversation sounded a bit formal for a father and son, but April didn't have time to think about it. Her painkillers had arrived and room service came immediately afterward with breakfast. She ate wearing one of the fluffy robes provided by the hotel. But when she started to feel better, she began worrying about her own father, and his chest pains, and the fact that she'd been so preoccupied with breaking out of her thirty-year cocoon that she hadn't focused much on Walt.

She pulled on her bikini top and waved to get Gunner's attention because he was still on the phone. "We have reservations to go deep-sea fishing with my parents today," she said. "I'm going to visit my dad and check on my mother. I'll see you in the lobby in two hours, okay?"

He covered the mouthpiece as though he wanted to say something to stop her. They certainly hadn't reached any agreement about how they might proceed with their relationship. But now obviously wasn't a good time to discuss it. Instead of interrupting the call, Gunner nodded grudgingly, and she left.

April wondered if she'd be giving too much away if she showed up at her father's door wearing the same thing she'd had on last night. She considered going back to her room to change, but she knew she wouldn't be able to escape again once she saw her mother. Besides, she'd never been much for pretense. Smoothing down her hair, she promised herself she'd have a nice hot shower *soon,* found her father's room and knocked.

"Who is it?" he called.

"April."

April thought she heard voices inside, followed by movement. Then Walt finally called, "Just a minute," and, after a prolonged silence, opened the door wearing a robe.

April glanced beyond him, but didn't see anyone else in the room or anything out of the ordinary.

"Hi, honey," he said. "How'd it go last night?"

"Good." She hugged him and was fairly sure she smelled perfume on his clothes. "Did you have Regina fly down or something?"

His face reddened. "No, no, of course not."

"Then can I come in?"

He stepped more squarely in front of her, as if

he'd actually bar her way, and alarm bells went off in April's head.

"Actually, I was just about to take a shower," he said. "Do you want to meet me for breakfast in an hour or so? You can—" he cleared his throat "—you can ask your mother to join us if you'd like."

Her mother! Of course. That was the scent April had smelled—it was her mother's perfume! She recalled her father's asking Claire to join them in the Jacuzzi, remembered leaving them alone afterward—and felt a moment's terror. *What had she been thinking?* She wanted to get her parents back together. But a one-night stand wasn't what she'd had in mind. If her father returned to Regina after something like this, it would push her mother over the edge.

"Mom?" she called, absolutely positive that Claire was hiding in the bathroom.

Her father winced. "Honey—"

"Don't 'honey' me," she said. "Are you two fooling around? Because I can't take any more of your emotional ups and downs."

Her mother finally came out of hiding—also wearing a robe. "I'm sorry April. The secrecy is my fault. I didn't want you to know we were seeing each other because nothing's been decided."

So now what?

Walt was scowling, his customary expression. But when Claire caught his eye and smiled, April saw her father melt—which completely defused her anger despite what her mother had just said.

"Want to join us for breakfast?" Claire asked.

April looked from her mother to her father. "No, I had breakfast with Gunner. And I think you two could use the time alone. Just don't—" she took a deep breath "—just be patient with each other, okay?"

GUNNER SAT ON HIS BED long after he'd hung up with his father, staring into space. Quincy Senior had talked to him for almost thirty minutes, but he hadn't really said anything. He'd gone on and on about how the Murray town council was considering naming the new park after Gunner, and mentioned that they were thinking of putting up a statue of him—as if Gunner cared about that sort of thing. Then his father had talked about going ice fishing when Gunner came to visit and how he'd found the perfect fishing hole.

Gunner had done his best to act interested, but he wasn't sure how he'd get through the week he'd promised to spend with his father when he returned to New York.

The telephone rang again, and this time Gunner welcomed the interruption. He didn't want to think about his father, didn't want to acknowledge that Quincy Senior had been trying for years now and Gunner was the one holding out…. "Hello?"

"It's me."

April. She wasn't much easier to deal with than his father. Why couldn't she simply fall into his bed and put an end to the desire that licked through his veins every time he saw her? She said she wasn't cut out for casual relationships. Well, he wasn't cut out for any other kind. He was good at fast and fleeting. He'd had lots of practice.

"You all set for deep-sea fishing?" he asked.

"Just about. How did it go with your father?"

"Fine."

"When you were talking to him, you seemed a little tense."

He opened his mouth to dismiss his feelings, as he always did. He was mildly surprised she'd noticed the strain. But he shouldn't have been. April was more sensitive than many other people and he knew he had to respect that by being honest with her, even when it was painful.

"We've had some trouble connecting," he admitted. "Especially since my mother died."

"She passed away just before you retired from racing, didn't she?"

He didn't say anything.

"Is that the reason?"

His throat began to burn, but for the second time he fought the impulse to dodge her. "Yes. At that point, racing didn't hold the same appeal for me." But he hadn't known where to focus his attention after that and it felt like he'd been wandering around lost ever since.

"I'm sorry, Gunner." April's voice was soft and warm, completely sincere. "I can tell you were very close to her."

"She was—" Suddenly he wanted to talk but found it difficult to get the words out. He rarely spoke of his mother, hadn't allowed himself to cry over her death. He didn't feel he had any right to self-pity when his life had been so good. But now the loss felt new and raw, like a giant hole blown through his chest, and he couldn't fight the tears that blurred his vision. "She was a good woman."

"She'll never really be gone, Gunner, you know that, don't you? Not as long as you carry her in your heart."

He closed his eyes, almost certain April had found her way into his heart, too. "I know."

"Maybe we shouldn't go fishing today," she said. "I'll say I'm not feeling well, and we can lie around the beach for hours and make out. I'm pretty sure I need a refresher course."

He chuckled, feeling strange, different…more at

peace somehow. "Don't cancel the fishing. I'm fine."

"Want me to come to your room so we can talk? I can swing by the vending machine first."

"No. I need to call my father back. I'll see you in the lobby in a little while."

WALT GLANCED LONGINGLY at the array of foods at the breakfast buffet. Omelettes, Mexican entrées, waffles with strawberries and whipped cream, sausages, bacon, biscuits and gravy, cheese blintzes and more. It smelled like heaven. But he passed up all those fat- and cholesterol-laden foods and followed Claire to the fruit island, where he loaded up on watermelon, cantaloupe and grapes, adding only a poached egg to the fruit.

She found them a small table in the corner, and he joined her a moment later.

"You're not having any of the Mexican food? Or an omelette?" she said, eyeing his plate as he sat down.

He glanced at the short line in front of the omelette station but refused to weaken. "No."

"Why not? You love omelettes."

He loved sausage, too. But knowing he had open-heart surgery in a couple of weeks had a way of taking the fun out of a poor diet. "I'm trying to lose a few pounds," he said, because he didn't want to broach the subject of the triple bypass just yet. They had several more days in Cabo and plenty of other things to work through first.

"You look good to me." She smiled meaningfully, and he couldn't help grinning in return because he knew she was referring to last night. He hadn't been *that* excited in a long time. But it was more than the sexual high that had made the night unique. Being with Claire was somehow richer and more meaningful for the familiarity, trust and trials of the past thirty-three years.

"I'm glad you came to Cabo," he said, knowing he might never have realized the truth if she hadn't.

She accepted some freshly squeezed orange juice from the waitress, but her smile disappeared as she set her glass on the table. "I'm glad, too, Walt," she said. "Last night was…extraordinary. Something I really wanted. But we should probably talk now, instead of pretending we can simply step back into our old lives. A lot has changed."

Did they have to talk? Walt didn't want to face what might have changed a lot any more than he wanted to face that he could no longer risk clogging up his arteries.

"I owe you an apology, Claire," he said. "I know that."

"We've both been acting like fools."

"But it's mostly my fault. I took you for granted over the years, got too caught up in the business."

"I've always been patient about the business." She took a sip of her orange juice. "I want to hear what you have to say about Regina."

Walt couldn't help wincing. How could he have betrayed Claire, when she'd been faithful to him for so long, when he owed her more than he did anyone else? "I won't see her again, of course."

"That's not enough, Walt." Claire's eyes remained steady. "I need some sort of explanation. What went wrong between us? Not knowing the answer to that question has been the toughest part of the past few months. You came home, told me you were in love with someone else, and moved out. You never even told me what I was doing wrong."

"Because you weren't doing anything wrong." Forced to deal with the issues he'd worked so hard to avoid, he sighed and shoved his plate away, although he hadn't started eating. "Regina was…a diversion. Something different. Something to keep me from realizing—" he hesitated, embarrassed to admit the truth, even to Claire "—that I'm not as handsome as I used to be, that I'm not as strong as I used to be—"

"You're not the only one who's getting old,"

she broke in. "We've been together for thirty-three years. I'm in the same boat."

"I know." He shook his head. "You want this to make sense, Claire, but it doesn't. Even to me. I can't explain *what* was going on in my head. I guess I just didn't appreciate what I already had. And Regina was there, flattering me, building my ego. I suddenly felt as though I needed what she was offering."

She studied her hands, which she'd clasped in her lap. "And after you left?" she said softly, looking up at him again. "Was life any better?"

He admired her clear, direct gaze and the loveliness of her face. Maybe she had a few wrinkles she hadn't had when they were newlyweds, but he still found her beautiful. Still loved her, despite everything he'd said and done. "No. I wouldn't admit it, even to myself. But on some level I knew I'd thrown away everything that really mattered to me."

"You were going through with the divorce, though," she said. "You were actually selling the company."

"After what I did, I didn't see how I could turn back. Trying to save our marriage would mean telling the truth—" he spread out his hands "—about all of this."

"And you had too much pride for that?"

"I couldn't deal with feeling so inadequate."

He saw tears brimming in her eyes and understood just how deeply he'd hurt her. "Can you forgive me, Claire?" he asked, reaching across the table to take her hand.

After last night, after holding his wife in his arms again and feeling as though he'd finally come home, he was ready to ask for another chance—beg if he had to. He'd made a terrible mistake. And now he had to have the guts to make it right.

"I *want* to forgive you," she whispered.

"All I ask is that you try."

Giving him a watery smile, she nodded.

GUNNER SHOWERED before calling Quincy Senior back. He wanted a few minutes to think—about his father, his mother, the lack of direction in his life during the past eighteen months…and April. But the hour at which he was supposed to meet the others in the lobby was fast approaching. If he didn't get on the phone right away, he'd lose the opportunity to make amends for the distant way he'd behaved earlier.

"Hello?"

His father answered right away.

"It's me, Dad."

"Gunner?"

The question in his father's voice caused Gunner

a fresh twinge of guilt. He was beginning to understand that his behavior stemmed from anger, but
looking closer for the cause of that anger, revealed
something he didn't want to see. Basically, he was
angry that the wrong parent had died.

"I..." Now that he had his father on the phone,
everything Gunner wanted to say fled instantly,
leaving him with mixed emotions.

"Is something wrong?" his father said.

"No, I called because..." Why? To admit that
he'd been holding out? He didn't want to put them
both through an uncomfortable apology, so he said
the only other thing on his mind. "To tell you that
I've met someone."

Silence, then, "When?"

Gunner drew in a deep breath. "I've known her
for a few weeks."

"She must be special. You've never called to talk
about a woman before."

"She is. It's just that—"

"What?"

Stabbing a hand through his hair, Gunner sat on
the bed, wishing he could discuss April with his
mother, instead. If Olivia was still there, she'd be
full of good advice. But she wasn't.

Maybe it was time he started accepting the parent
he had left. Quincy Senior wasn't Olivia, but he

was trying to establish a better relationship between them.

"She's the type of girl you marry," Gunner said.

His father chuckled. "Oh, now I get it."

"Get what?"

"This one's serious."

"No…I'm not sure about that."

"Because…"

"We're nothing alike. She's not my type at all."

"Something about her must have caught your eye. And it sounds as though, this time, it wasn't her, uh, legs."

Gunner couldn't help the wry smile that twisted his lips. "Her legs aren't bad, don't get me wrong. But, no, it's not the way she looks that really gets me."

"You see something deeper in her?"

"I think so."

"Then maybe it's time for you to settle down."

Gunner blew out a long sigh. "That's a big step."

"Don't be afraid to take a chance, son."

"I'm not afraid of taking chances."

"I'm not talking about racing."

Gunner remembered the panic that had come over him when April mentioned waiting. Maybe he *was* scared. Maybe he could risk his life but not his heart.

He glanced at his watch. "I've got to go. Everyone's downstairs waiting for me."

"Right. I don't want to make you miss your friends."

"Dad?"

"Yeah?"

"Thanks for the advice."

"I'm glad you called," his father said—and strangely enough, so was Gunner.

CHAPTER ELEVEN

GUNNER NUDGED April as they sat on the back of the thirty-five-foot Bertram Sportfisher they'd chartered. "Did you see that?" he called above the boat's motor.

April pulled her gaze away from the fishing line, which they'd been watching for several hours. There hadn't been so much as a nibble. "What?"

He jerked his head toward the cabin, where her parents were supposed to be getting the lunches they'd brought, and he knew she turned just in time to see what he saw—her father steadied her mother when the boat rocked, then pulled Claire against him and kissed her on the neck.

"They've been doing that all morning," he said.

"I know." April shook her head. "Crazy, isn't it? A week ago they wouldn't even speak to each other."

"I guess your matchmaking efforts are paying off."

"Well—" she crossed her legs "—I don't think I'll box up her stuff just yet. I mean, I'll be thrilled if they can work things out. *More* than thrilled. But I'm afraid—'' she glanced worriedly at her parents again ''—I don't know. A lot has happened.''

Gunner brought his chair closer and draped his arm around April's shoulders. All morning, he'd been trying to tell himself that there wasn't anything special about her. But he didn't believe it. His eyes followed her wherever she went, and he couldn't help brushing against her or touching her at every opportunity. More telling was the fact that he didn't care anymore about buying the business he'd wanted to devote himself to—probably because he wanted to devote himself to *her*.

The wind whipped her hair around April's face as she leaned into him and smiled. ''It's so beautiful out here, isn't it?''

He almost told her that nothing was as beautiful as she was, but quickly bit his tongue. What was wrong with him? He'd scarcely noticed the mild weather or the undulating ocean or anything else. He didn't care if they caught a fish. He was falling in love with the last woman he'd ever dreamed he'd want. And he was doing it in a matter of days. If someone had told him this might happen, he would never have believed it.

But he was actually more worried about April's feelings than his own. She was different from the other women he'd dated. His money and fame meant nothing to her. She'd said she trusted him enough to let herself care about him, but if she didn't think he'd make a good husband, she wouldn't allow their relationship to go very far. And he already knew what she thought of his reputation. How much of a chance did he realistically have with her?

"You're frowning," she said. "What are you thinking?"

"That life is unpredictable."

"Why—"

Suddenly one of the lines tightened, and she cried out in excitement as Gunner jumped up to grab the fishing rod. They had something. He wasn't sure it was a marlin, but he figured it was big.

Taking the rod out of its holder, he motioned for April to put on the harness that would keep her in the special swiveling chair so she could reel in their catch.

"Wow," she said as he handed her the rod.

"Hang on tight," he told her, then called out to the others. "We've got a bite!"

The boat had a crew of two. Both men came out to offer their advice, and Walt and Claire followed closely behind.

"Keep reeling," Gunner told her. "Don't slack off."

The resistance was so great that a few minutes

of reeling left April's arms shaking. Gunner put his hands over hers and helped. The fish was getting closer to the boat, but it was still putting up a fight.

"It's big," April managed to say. "It's...really big."

One of the crew members grinned. "It's a marlin. I can see him out there."

Gunner squinted against the sun but couldn't make out anything except the birds suddenly flocking toward them and the water. "That's it," he told April as she kept the line taut. "There you go."

"That fish has got to weigh forty pounds," Walt said.

Claire touched April's shoulder. "You doing okay, honey?"

April nodded and kept fighting the fish. After another few seconds, Gunner offered to spell her, but she wasn't willing to give up. "I can do it."

He chuckled at her determination and continued to help her, enjoying the feel of her against him even more than the thrill of the catch. Finally the two crew members who'd positioned themselves in the corner of the boat, holding giant hooks, hauled in the flopping blue fish with the long swordlike nose. Then April sagged into the seat.

"I did it," she said, breathing heavily. "I caught a fish in Cabo. A *big* fish. A marlin."

Gunner laughed and . shook his head. She'd

caught more than a marlin in Cabo. Whether he liked it or not, she'd caught *him*. And now he could only hope she didn't throw him back.

APRIL WATCHED television while she waited for her mother to finish showering. She needed to get ready for dinner, too. But she couldn't stop thinking about Gunner and how difficult it would be to go back to her regular life after this trip. He'd shown her what it was like to feel weak with desire, to crave his touch more than anything else, to hear his voice in a crowd no matter how many people were talking. Too bad she and Gunner didn't have the slightest chance of making a life together. He wasn't the type to settle down, and she wasn't the type to prance around on his arm and smile for the cameras. After Cabo, she'd return to her laboratory, and he'd return to...whatever he did. Still, she was glad he'd come, glad he'd shown her that there was more to life than work and pragmatic decisions.

The water went off, and April heard the shower door open and close. "Mom?" she called, flipping off the television after giving Claire a few minutes. She wanted to speak to her mother about Walt, make sure Claire was being realistic and at least a little cautious where her father was concerned. Though Rod wasn't much of an issue, thank God, Regina definitely was. April was terrified that her mother would be hurt all over again, and that she'd be to blame for setting her up.

"What, honey?" Claire replied.

"Can we talk about Dad for a few minutes?"

"What do you have to say about him?"

"You two seem to be getting close pretty quickly. I just want to be sure you're looking at all the angles."

"What angles?"

"Regina, for one. Getting back with Dad would mean forgiving him for Regina. That won't be easy, will it?"

Silence, which was proof enough that her mother was struggling with this.

"It would also mean helping him decide whether or not to go through with selling the business," April continued. "That has a lot of ramifications for both of you, as well as other people we care about."

"We'll keep the business," she stated matter-of-factly.

"Even with Dad's surgery?"

Her mother poked her head out of the bathroom. "What surgery?"

April stared at her. "You mean he hasn't said anything?" Her father had insisted she keep quiet, but she'd assumed he would have told Claire himself by now.

"About what?"

April couldn't imagine why her father was still hiding his condition from her mother, but she hesitated to tell what she knew, just in case he had a good reason. "Never mind." She stood up and reached for her room key. "I think I'll run down and take a swim before—"

"April?"

Hearing the gravity in her mother's voice, April paused at the door.

"Tell me what's going on. What surgery?"

With a sigh, April turned to her mother. "Dad's been having chest pains."

Claire covered her mouth with one hand. "No!"

"He needs surgery."

"*Heart* surgery?"

"The doctor wants to do a triple bypass a couple of weeks after we get back."

The color drained from her mother's face. "Why didn't he tell me himself?"

"I don't think he wants to acknowledge the possibilities. He's acting as though it's nothing serious."

"Nothing serious!"

The telephone rang, and April crossed the room to answer it, hoping the disruption would give her mother a few minutes to cope with the news. "Hello?"

"April?" It was Gunner.

"Hi." She smiled automatically, grateful that they still had four more days in Cabo. She wished it was an eternity.

"You going down to dinner?"

"Um…" She glanced at her mother, who hadn't yet dropped her hand from her mouth. "Not quite. I might be late, actually."

"That's fine. I won't be there, anyway."

Disappointment made April slouch onto the bed. "Why not?"

"I have to take care of something. I just wanted to tell you to bring all your change to my room later."

An invitation. That was hopeful. But one look at Claire told April that her mother was still terribly upset. "Hang on." She set the phone down and walked over to Claire. "Mom, are you okay?"

Her mother nodded stoically. "I'm fine. Go ahead and talk to Gunner," she said, and resumed getting ready.

April watched her for a few seconds, wondering what she was thinking—and feeling. But she didn't want to keep Gunner waiting too long.

Telling herself she'd speak with her mother later, she returned to the phone. "Why do I need to bring change?" she asked. "Are we going to play poker again?"

"Yes."

The prospect of spending more time with Gunner, especially late at night and alone in his room, was enough to make her pulse race. She loved being with him, loved the way he smiled and teased her, loved the appreciation she'd seen in his eyes when she came around that corner and got into his Jacuzzi. She loved...

April's breath stuck in her throat. She loved...*him*. But how could she have let this happen when she knew she was heading for certain disaster?

"I thought you'd lost your nerve about playing with me," she said numbly, trying to keep up her end of the conversation.

"I'm feeling lucky," he said. "And April?"

"What?"

"Tonight, winner takes all."

She wanted to ask what he meant by that—or at least tell him not to buy any more pork rinds—but he hung up.

CLAIRE STARED AT HER HUSBAND across the now-empty dinner table. "Why didn't you tell me?" she asked softly.

Walt's gaze followed the waiters and busboys hurrying around the restaurant, clearing away the dishes. Most of the Ashton Automotive group had already left for the hotel. "Tell you what?"

"About the operation."

Finally meeting her eyes, he sighed. "April mentioned it?"

She nodded.

"I was afraid of that."

"Why should this be a secret from me?" Claire demanded.

"Because I didn't want you to worry. We were having such a good time here."

A good time. Suddenly a good time didn't seem to matter so much. Suddenly a good time seemed terribly fleeting. What if Walt didn't make it through the operation? What if he had a heart attack and died before the doctors even had a chance? Tonight...or tomorrow...or next week?

Fear constricted Claire's heart. She'd been enjoying Walt here in Cabo, but she hadn't truly committed herself to forgiving him. Just when she'd decided to let him go, he'd come back.... No matter how wonderful it felt to be with him again, whenever she thought of Regina, anger and jealousy and the memory of the terrible hurt she'd suffered overwhelmed her, making her want to punish them both.

Only now, all of that seemed so petty. They were talking about life and death. They were talking about the possibility of losing Walt altogether—not to some silly fear of growing old or a floozy massage therapist who took advantage of his confusion. To *death*. And with death there was no winning him back.

"What are you thinking?" he asked when she remained silent.

Claire realized in a new and certain way how selfish it was to continue holding a grudge. Walt might have made some very serious mistakes and hurt her deeply, but he was sincerely sorry, and he wanted her back. That was what mattered, wasn't it? Somehow she'd deal with the rest. "That you're going to get through it," she said, forcing a confident smile for his benefit. "And I'll stand by you every minute."

Tears filled his eyes for the first time since she'd married him, and he reached for her hand. "How can you do it?" he asked. "How can you forgive me so easily?"

She felt his callused fingers close over hers as they had so many times before and a warm sensation flooded through her. "Because I'm not going to let life knock either one of us down just before the finish line."

A single tear escaped and ran down his cheek. "Thank you, Claire."

APRIL KNOCKED hesitantly on Gunner's door. She'd missed him at dinner and knew just how crazy she'd been to fall in love with a famous playboy. She probably shouldn't have come to his room tonight. It would only make her infatuation worse. But she was so head over heels in love that she couldn't stand not taking advantage of what time they had left.

He smiled when he opened the door and saw her standing there with her arms full of vending machine snacks.

"Wow, looks like we're going to be playing for a while."

"I thought I might need to spot you a few snacks before the night was through."

He raised his eyebrows. "Don't start feeling sorry for me just yet."

"So you think you're going to do better tonight?"

"I certainly hope so," he muttered.

She detected an unusual tone, one she couldn't quite identify. But he was already getting out the cards so she didn't question him.

The first hand she won, but before she could feel too confident, Gunner beat her on the next three.

"You're not saying much now," he teased as he raked in the heap of candy bars.

"The game's not over yet."

"No, it's not." He set something small, round

and shiny in the middle of the bed. "But the stakes are changing."

"What's that?" April asked, even though she could see quite clearly that it was a ring.

"Pick it up and see."

Tearing her eyes away from Gunner's face, she lifted the ring and held it to the light. A huge baguette diamond glittered in a white-gold setting with two emerald-cut diamonds on either side.

"It looks like an engagement ring," she said.

"It is an engagement ring," he replied, and it had to be the first time she'd ever heard any insecurity in his voice.

"It's beautiful. I've never seen anything like it. Where did you get it?"

"In town."

"Tonight?"

"That's why I missed dinner." He touched her cheek. "What do you think, April? Do you want it?"

Of course she *wanted* it. But this was crazy. They were so different. "This is what you're betting?"

He nodded and, taking her hands, kissed her fingertips. "That's not all."

"What else?" she breathed.

"My heart."

She must have heard him wrong. He was one of

the most eligible bachelors in America. He couldn't be offering his heart to *her*. "Is this a joke?"

"No."

"But you're not—I mean, we've known each other only a short time. And what about all those other women?" Women who were so much better suited to him!

He scowled. "I haven't been a saint, April. But I haven't been as bad as you seem to believe. I was kidding about the fifteen hundred notches in my bedpost. You know that, right? And I'll always be true to you, I swear."

She swallowed hard at the sincerity in his voice. "But…what's the hurry? Shouldn't we get to know each other better?"

"I already know you well enough." He rose up on his knees, kissed her temple, her forehead, her mouth. "Come on, April. Take a risk," he murmured. "Take a risk on me."

She couldn't find any words.

"Well?"

"I'm thinking. At least, I'm trying to think. My brain isn't really cooperating."

"I don't want you to analyze this. Some decisions have to be based on pure gut instinct. This is one of them."

"You know more about instinct than I do," she

admitted. "Just tell me one thing, Gunner. Because...I have to know."

"What's that?"

"Do you love me?" She held her breath as she waited for his reply.

"I've never proposed to a woman before, April. Does that answer your question?"

April closed her eyes as she felt the most powerful emotion she'd ever experienced. "Okay," she whispered, letting her lips curve in a smile. "I see your ring, and your heart, and will match it with my own."

He grinned. "What kind of wedding do you want?"

"A family-only church affair in California, okay?"

"Perfect. You plan the wedding. I'll plan the honeymoon."

"What about my father's business?"

"I'll leave that up to you. We can buy it if you want. But I should probably warn you that I'm going to be busy for the next few years."

"Doing what?"

"Oh, different things. Buying you a vacation house down here, since you like it so well. Helping out with the kids, giving them racing lessons—"

"Did you say *racing* lessons?" she broke in. "As in *car* racing lessons?"

"Um, I meant I'll be coaching their soccer teams."

She laughed. "And to think I wanted out of my staid existence. Something tells me I just landed in the fast lane."

"Maybe. But it's going to be the ride of your life, sweet April," he said, and slid the ring onto her finger.

Epilogue

CLAIRE ASHTON FELT as nervous as a new bride. There'd been times over the past decade when she'd worried that her bright, serious daughter would never step out of her lab long enough to find a man and get married. Yet here April was, on her wedding day, looking beautiful in her simple but elegant white satin gown and stylish veil. Part of her dark hair was pinned up with tiny pearls for accent and curls cascaded down her back. She was walking up the aisle on Walt's arm, carrying a bouquet of pink roses that matched the healthy blush in her cheeks.

Gunner stood at the altar, wearing a traditional black tux. He couldn't seem to take his eyes off her. Which was perfectly understandable to Claire—April was special.

They make a good couple, Claire thought as Gunner took April's hands and they began to exchange vows.

"I, April Ashton, promise to love, honor and cherish..."

Feeling an overwhelming sense of pride, Claire glanced up at Walt, who'd come to sit next to her after leaving April's side, and found him staring at her. He'd had his surgery nearly a month ago and had lost a good deal of weight. But the color was coming back into his face, and she could tell he was starting to feel better.

When their eyes met, he took her hand and brushed a kiss across her knuckles, and she knew she was back where she belonged, at the side of the man she'd married for better or worse thirty-three years ago. Somehow, despite everything, they'd found new, common ground and deeper commitment.

Turning her attention back to the ceremony, Claire watched Gunner kiss her daughter sweetly once the pastor had pronounced them husband and wife. She sniffed as tears rolled down her cheeks, but she didn't even try to hold them back. Today, happy tears went with the territory.

As April and Gunner broke apart, Claire stood so she could approach them. But Walt stopped her.

April threw her father a conspiratorial smile and guided Gunner to the left, where they sat in the front pew.

"What's happening?" Claire whispered, confused. No wedding she'd ever attended had the bride and groom taking a seat in the audience. The ceremony was over. It was time for the organ music to swell and the young couple to rush out of the church while being pelted with rice. ''Why aren't they leaving?''

''Because there's still one thing left to do,'' he said. Then he stood and led her to the altar.

''Most of you know that Claire and I have had some trouble this past year,'' he announced to their small audience of family and friends. ''We almost divorced, mostly because of my own foolishness. But because of Claire, and her ability to forgive, that's behind us now. To show her how much she means to me, I'd like to exchange vows with her again, if she'll speak them with me.''

As Claire glanced into the audience, more tears slipped down her cheeks. Her widowed mother, who was nearly eight-five, sat in the second row. Her sister and brother-in-law and their large, rambunctious family sat there, too. Gina Roper, April's next-door neighbor, who'd been a friend to Claire throughout her darkest hour, was perched on the pew behind them, beaming at her. Gunner's father and a couple of dozen relatives filled the pews on the other side.

''Will you marry me again, Claire?'' Walt asked, his voice trembling with emotion.

Claire smiled at April and Gunner, then returned her gaze to her husband of thirty-three years. He was watching her with a hopeful expression, his sincerity shining in his eyes. She'd almost lost him. But he was back, and the nightmare was over. "What else can I do?" she said simply. "I love you."

THE ROAD HOME

Jill Shalvis

CHAPTER ONE

IF ASKED, Melissa Anders would say her life was perfect. But when no one was looking, she sometimes took a deep breath, let it all out in a baffled sigh, and wondered how the hell she'd ended up here.

Here being out in the middle of California, in the small, quaint Martis Hills, treating various farm-animal ailments instead of the upscale, spoiled, snobby, pedigreed cats and dogs as she'd planned.

Sure, she loved being a veterinarian. But somehow during those long, exhausting college years, when she'd worked so hard to keep up her grades and scrape together enough cash to live at the same time, she'd never imagined living amongst rolling hills and farmland, where there were more cattle than people, running one of only two vet clinics for miles and miles.

The people in town—and having grown up in Los Angeles she used the word *town* loosely—were all a bit...*too friendly*. They popped in on her uninvited, asked nosy questions and basically talked her ear off. Some even brought cookies, or amazingly delicious casseroles.

She'd waited to see what their angle was, but having been here for a few months now, no angle had materialized. Maybe she'd moved to Mayberry.

It wasn't that she didn't like people, but that she preferred animals. Animals accepted. Animals loved unconditionally. Animals never, ever, gave up their young because they wanted a career in the ballet and couldn't be bothered to raise a baby.

Oops, a self-pity slip, she thought, as she got out of her car, smoothing down her plain black trousers and white blouse. She headed up the path to the large farmhouse that years ago had been converted into an animal clinic by Dr. Myers. He'd just retired to Phoenix to be with his elderly sister, and Melissa had leased it with an option to buy—not that she ever intended to do any such insane thing. But the place was cheap, at least to her LA standard, and with her college loan debt still hanging over her, she needed cheap.

That was what had brought her here, she told herself, curiosity about small-town living. The low cost of the lease. It had nothing, nothing at all, to do with the fact she'd been born here twenty-eight years ago.

And that her mother lived here.

She grimaced and shook her head. No. The truth

was, she'd come here because in some deep recess of her heart she'd wanted to be close to the only family she had. Which really pissed her off when she thought about it too hard, so she tried not to think about it at all.

She unlocked the front door to the clinic, flipped on the lights and took a deep breath, which never failed to make her smile. Nothing like the smell of disinfectant to get her going in the morning.

The converted living room made a nice waiting room. She had chairs lined up beneath the windows, a shelving unit on the opposite wall filled with retail supplies such as bovine toothbrushes and doggy breath mints. The reception desk was tiny, not really a problem since she couldn't afford a receptionist anyway.

She'd just stepped behind the counter and slipped on her white overcoat when the front door opened, the bell above it chiming loud enough to awaken the dead. On her first day, she'd taken it down, only to have everyone tell her that Dr. Myers had brought that bell all the way from Europe forty-five years ago, so she'd put it back up. Tradition in Mayberry—er, *Martis Hills* apparently ran bone deep.

The man coming inside had his back to her while he shut the door. He was tall, lanky, and wore the town's usual uniform of soft, faded Levi's and a white T-shirt. She repressed the sigh for days of old, when on any given day in Los Angeles she could feed her love for fashion by just looking around.

Then he turned and faced her, and oddly enough, every fond thought of the days of old fell right out of her head.

He looked to be thirtyish. His hair was light brown, almost blond. Probably sun-kissed by the hot summer sun, and given the sinewy, rangy look to his body, he probably worked hard farming his land like so many in the county did. He was slightly hunched over a towel-covered bundle that was meowing loudly in protest.

''I've got something for you to fix up, Dr. Anders.'' He let out a startlingly contagious smile.

That he knew her name didn't surprise her. Just another product of living in a small place. Gossip ran wild here, and no one was safe from that. Especially a single city woman running a vet clinic. Often in the dark of the night, she'd lie awake and stress about money or a variety of other things including why she always managed to stick out like a sore thumb no matter where she was. But that was for the dark of the night.

Right now she had a patient, and she loved her patients, every one of them. When he handed the cat over to her, their arms brushed together, hers covered by her long white coat, his bared and tanned and warm, and also sporting four long nasty scratches down one forearm. It'd been a tough morning, she'd guess.

With obvious relief, he slapped his hands together, ridding himself of the feline hair that was sticking to him. His own longish hair, brushing his collar, fell over his forehead as he lifted his head and smiled at her. "So, can you fix him up?"

His eyes were green, and full of an easy warmth and friendliness that she'd never mastered. Not with people, that is. Odd then, how her mouth actually quirked in a smile back. "Let's see. Follow me." She entered the first of three patient rooms and set the poor, shaking cat on the table, keeping firm but gentle hands on his body. "Shh," she murmured, bending close. "I've got you. Name?" she asked.

"Oh." Another quick flashing grin. "Terror."

"What?"

He laughed. "That's what he invokes in me, so I call him Terror. His real name is Bob."

"Bob," she said softly, and rubbed her cheek to the cat's, saying the name again, just as quietly.

The caterwauling stopped at the sound of her crooning voice.

"Ah, blessed silence." The man sighed with relief. He lifted his attention from the cat on the table and smiled at Melissa, another slow, easy one that she was quite certain had set more than a few hearts pounding. "From the bottom of my heart, thank you. Now I'll just wait way over here." He backed to the wall, propped it up with his shoulder. "You go ahead and work your magic."

Mel stroked the cat's chin, and a loud rumble filled the room.

The man straightened. "What in the hell?"

"Haven't you ever heard a cat purr before?"

"Well, sure, but that sounds more like an engine gone bad than a purr." He appeared to be one-hundred-percent rough-and-tumble country guy, and yet he stared at the cat with mistrust, from all the way back at the wall.

Given the nasty scratches on his arm, she supposed she couldn't blame him. In the waiting room, she hadn't been able to see him in a good light, but now, under the harsh fluorescent glare of the bulbs above, she could see that on his extremely hand-some face ran a jagged scar, starting at his forehead, along his temple, and then down his jaw to his chin. It was still red and shiny, indicating it wasn't very old. "Symptoms?" she asked.

He put his hand to where her gaze had remained, his long fingers managing to cover only part of the scar. "What?"

She nodded to the cat, who'd sprawled out on

the table, belly up to be rubbed. "What's the matter with Bob?"

"Oh…" Clearly feeling a little foolish, he dropped his hand from his face and returned to propping up the wall with his shoulder. "He's doubled his food intake, for starters. And also he seems to have to go to the bathroom a lot."

Mel felt the eight swollen nipples and the bulging tummy of the blissfully purring cat. "Well, for starters, he's a she."

He blinked once, then again, before slowly scratching his jaw. "Hmm. That would explain the PMS-y mood then. Bob's been trying to bite a piece out of me ever since I first picked him… I mean, her up."

What was the point of explaining that if a female got cranky around him, maybe it had something to do with his attitude rather than her gender? The man had probably been born and bred here in this place that apparently liked its women barefoot and pregnant.

And speaking of pregnant. "You should also know, she's going to have kittens. In about two more weeks, I'd guess. Is this cat new to you? A stray perhaps?"

"Pregnant?" He stared at her for a moment, then shot her another of those slow, melting grins. In spite of herself, her pulse quickened.

"Isn't that something," he murmured. "Little kittens to play with."

He was afraid of the cat but thrilled to know it was having kittens? Daft, she decided, and continued her examination of the perfectly healthy, perfectly happy cat. "You know, cats can tell when you don't like them."

He'd pushed away from the wall and now stood directly in front of her. So close, in fact, that she could see that his eyes weren't just solid green, but had speckles of gold dancing in them. "If they sense you don't like them, it's all over for you."

"Not so different from females of another species entirely."

She rolled her eyes. "Hold out your arm."

He thrust it out. When she ran cotton-soaked disinfectant along the four deep scratches on his forearm, he hissed out a breath. *"Ouch."*

"Baby," she said, but bent over him to blow on the admittedly nasty scratches.

"Mmm." This rumbled from his chest, and when she looked up at him, he smiled hopefully. "Are you going to kiss it, too?"

She straightened, a hand on her hip. "Are you flirting with me?"

His grin spread. "Well, now, that all depends. Did you like it?"

"I don't flirt with clients," she heard herself say

coolly, and wanted to wince because she sounded just as distant as her friends back in Los Angeles had always accused her of being.

"See, now there's our loophole." He lifted his hands in a surrendering gesture. "I've never been in here before, so I'm not really a client."

The cat butted her head against Mel's hand for more petting. Mel stroked her for another moment, then scooped her up against her chest. The cat rubbed the top of her furry head against Mel's chin and kept purring. "Bob is going to be fine," she said, cuddling for another moment. "But she should be checked again after the birth." She plopped the purring mom-to-be back into his arms.

Because she needed some space, she headed out into the reception area and toward the desk. "I'll just need you to fill out a form for billing. You can leave it when you're finished."

"But…"

She stopped and glanced back at him. He was trying without much success to juggle both the annoyed cat and the clipboard with the form attached to it. "Yes?"

Unhappy at being jostled, Bob dug her claws into his chest. The man yelped.

With a sigh, she bent behind the receptionist's desk and brought out a cardboard kitty transport box. "Here. Use this." She helped him get Bob into it, again within extremely close proximity. She couldn't help but notice how his T-shirt stretched across the muscles of his back when he moved, and how he smelled of citrus soap and wood, and man.

Not interested, she reminded herself. She was absolutely not going to be interested in a man who was nervous around cats and had a sinful smile. So she stepped back, laughing at herself. "Goodbye."

He eyed the box with Bob in it as if it were a bomb ready to detonate. "Do you want to put disinfectant on my new scratch?" he asked, and rubbed his chest.

His T-shirt rose just a bit, revealing a strip of tanned, flat belly. She pictured herself lifting that shirt to treat his scratches and her mouth went dry. "I think you'll live."

He grinned a little knowingly.

"Goodbye." Then, as she always did when someone got too close, Melissa walked away.

CHAPTER TWO

MELISSA SPENT the rest of the day busy at the clinic. Busy being relative, of course. She had only a few appointments, but coupled with her walk-ins for the afternoon, she figured she just might be able to pay the bills for the day.

That night she ate dinner alone in front of her television. She'd wanted Thai take-out, but there wasn't any to be had. Sometimes she really missed Los Angeles, missed all the choices, the culture. Here, culture meant adding blue-cheese dressing onto a burger at the Serendipity Café, and even then, the waitress always gave her an odd look, as if she was massacring a perfectly good meal.

After making herself a quesadilla, she fed her re-ality-TV fix by watching *The Stud*. Watching twenty gorgeous women all competing in various humiliating "trials" for the attention of one man was both repelling and fascinating.

Who wanted a man that badly?

During the commercial breaks, she dug into her mail, most of which were bills, and more bills, ex-

cept for the scented envelope. Staring at it, her heart
kicked into gear.

Rose was trying again. She opened the pink envelope and spread out the flowered stationery covered in her mother's writing. At forty-six, Rose had
decided she wanted to be a part of her daughter's
life, the daughter she'd given up at birth for the
ballet.

To be fair, Rose hadn't *suddenly* decided—she'd
been trying on and off for years. Melissa had deep
misgivings about relationships in general; she had
difficult with intimacy. It didn't take a rocket scientist to figure out that was a product of being abandoned by Rose at age one, into the foster-care system. Moving from one foster-care family to another
made it too painful to keep opening to people who
would soon disappear from her life. So Melissa had
closed up for self-protection, and had done too good
a job of it.

She hadn't seen Rose more than a handful of
times her entire life—again, her own fault because
in the past years Rose had sincerely made an effort—the last time being when Melissa had first
moved here. Rose had shown up on her doorstep
with a basket full of homemade brownies and a nervous offer to go to lunch. Startled, Mel had de-
clined.

She wasn't ready. What if Rose expected something from her that she couldn't give? Mel had gone

too long without a mother to want a doting one now. And yet... Mel had moved here. No one had asked or coerced her; she'd come on her own to Martis Hills.

The why of that would have to be faced sometime, she supposed, but not now. She picked up the letter again.

Dear Melissa,
I want you to know, I'm not giving up. Out of all the towns in the world, you moved here, near me. I'm taking that as a good sign.
Call me when you're ready. I hope that's soon.
         Love, Rose Anders (still your mom)

A good sign? Ha! After all those years of wishing she'd had a mother to braid her hair before school, hold her hand at the dentist, or simply hug her after the end of a long day, it was too late. Way too late.

Wasn't it? Yes, Mel decided, refolding the letter. Long ago she'd outgrown the need for a mom. All the hard work of growing up was over, and she was quite content on her own.

Setting aside the letter, she got into bed. The light from the stars shone through her wide window in a way it could never have in Los Angeles. There the city lights had always blocked them out. She lay there, blinking up at the constellations that were so incredibly beautiful. Unmoved, she figured she'd trade in this view in a heartbeat for a Starbucks run.

"Psst!"

No, he wasn't ready to leave blessed slumber land. Jason Lawrence turned over.

"Psst."

Damn it, he closed his eyes tighter and yanked the covers over his head.

"Jason, please. Please can you try again?"

It wasn't the soft feminine plea that got him, but the squawk of a parrot.

He cracked open an eye. His bedroom was lit with the early-summer morning sun that slanted in through the windows, one of which held the face of…Dr. Melissa Anders?

Now he knew he was still dreaming. Dr. Melissa Anders was petite, with a dark cap of hair that accented her expressive jade eyes and a kissable mouth.

And a serious back-off attitude.

Eyes closed again, he grinned, because she probably had no idea how much he loved a feisty woman, and how her go-to-hell expression had only egged him on.

"Jason!"

He blinked. Nope. It wasn't Melissa Anders standing outside his bedroom window, but *Rose* Anders.

Rose Anders holding a parrot. "Ah, hell," he said.

Smiling sweetly, her short dark hair falling into her green eyes, she knocked on the window again and lifted the arm on which the parrot sat.

"No." He sat up against the headboard. In order to beat back the nightmares, he'd written, pounding out the pages of the thriller he was working on until four in the morning, and it was…he squinted at the clock…just barely seven now.

He couldn't function on so little sleep, he just couldn't. If he wasn't so stubborn, he might have taken one of the sleeping pills his doctor had given him after his accident, but he had a healthy fear of drugs, so he suffered the nightmares and the lack of sleep, and reminded himself that at least he was alive.

"Morning," Rose said cheerfully. "You awake?"

Yes, because of her.

Just as he was alive because of her. And in return, all she wanted was this favor…. "Ah, hell," he said again.

Rose just smiled. "Don't worry. The parrot's easier to handle than Bob. I'll meet you at the front door."

JASON SAT in Dr. Melissa Anders's waiting room, squeezed between an old man holding an even older looking dog, and a teenage girl cradling a hamster. The old man and dog were napping, heads back, mouths open. The teenage girl was chomping a big wad of purple gum and staring at the scar down the side of his face.

In the six months since the accident, he'd gotten used to the stares, sort of. "What's the matter with your hamster?"

"She has an abscess." She stroked the little rodent, who in return, wriggled its nose at her. "Dr. Anders fixed Brownie's sister so I'm hoping she can fix Sprinkles, too. Do you think she can?"

He looked into the earnest face with the hopeful eyes, the sweet freckles conflicting with the myriad of silver hoops up one ear. "I think your hamster is safe with Dr. Anders."

"Yeah. She's new, but she's the best. Rose says so. She's my ballet teacher."

Jason thought about Rose's plea. She was desperate to get to know the daughter she'd given up, and yet afraid, too. He knew that Rose could fully understand, and even justify Melissa's standoffish attitude toward her. That, however, didn't stop Rose from yearning to set things right between them.

Jason had no idea if Melissa was open to giving Rose a second chance. Right now he just wanted to fulfill his favor. "Ouch!" Jason grabbed his ear and turned his head to glare at the parrot. "If I liked the taste of feathers, I'd bite you back."

He'd have sworn the bird smirked.

The old man woke up with a snort. "A bird makes a bad pet, son. You need something that naps a lot."

They both looked at the dog on the floor at his feet who was snoring. Loudly.

"Maybe Dr. Anders can take a look at your face while you're here," the teenager said softly, eyeing his scar again. "Does it hurt?"

He got that question most. "No—"

The door to the middle patient room opened, and Melissa appeared in the doorway. She saw Jason sitting in her waiting room, and then she saw the parrot and lifted a brow. "Problem?"

Yep, I like looking at you. "I have a bird that needs your attention—ouch!"

He slapped a hand to his poor, abused ear in tune to the parrot's happy screech, and also something else. He looked at the teenage girl next to him. "Did you just laugh at me?"

She laughed again. "You scream like a girl."

Melissa put a hand to her mouth, her eyes twinkling, and shook her head. "Don't tell me, another pet problem?"

"Yes. I'm afraid of this parrot."

"Uh-huh." Melissa turned to the man next to him. "Mr. Tyson, I can see you now."

The old man got up and patted Melissa on the

back. The dog, woken by the tug on his leash, licked her.

Melissa appeared to be a little flustered by the pat, but accepted the dog's licking with a genuine smile.

After a few minutes all three reappeared, and then it was the teen's turn. "Rose says to tell you hello."

Melissa's smile faltered, but the girl never noticed as she walked toward the patient room.

And then it was his turn. Melissa led him inside a patient room and stood close to him. Just when he was about to make a flirtatious comment, he realized her proximity had nothing to do with him and everything to do with the carnivorous bird perched on his shoulder. She made a kissing noise.

The parrot made it back.

She nodded her head.

The parrot nodded back.

Smiling now, Melissa reached out.

"I wouldn't," Jason warned. "She likes the taste of flesh."

"No, she likes the taste of *your* flesh." She coaxed the parrot onto her finger. "What seems to be the trouble?"

"Um…" He looked at the parrot and tried to remember what Rose had said to him this morning. *I know it seems obvious using my pets as bait, but*

I'm at a loss here. Nothing else has worked. Get Melissa to trust you. Get her to talk. "Well—"

"Rose," said the parrot from her new perch on Melissa's finger.

Melissa went still and stared at the bird. "What? What did she just say?"

Ah, hell. "She said she wants a rose. She likes to eat them. We're here because she…" He'd forgotten what he was supposed to use as an excuse. Maybe it was Melissa's fathomless green eyes, or maybe it was the heartbreakingly endearing way she'd tried to keep her patient's owners at arm's length…or maybe because he'd been half-asleep when Rose had dropped off the damn parrot.

"I think she ate a twig," he said brilliantly. "And I'm not sure that's good for her. I just wanted to have her checked out before I start work for the day."

"Ten o'clock in the morning is pretty late to be starting the chores a farm requires."

Farm. He lived in an old farmhouse, yes, but he was a writer, not a farmer. Then he remembered the form he'd filled out yesterday. She'd seen his address and assumed he farmed for a living.

Wouldn't she be surprised to know that for years he'd been a misplaced city rat, not so unlike herself. "I set my own hours."

Melissa gave him a long look, then silently

checked out the parrot. "She appears to be fine. And if you stop antagonizing her, she'll relax."

"*Me* antagonize *her?*" He laughed. "Oh, baby, have you got that wrong. Check out my poor ear." Before he could think about what he was doing, he'd shrugged his hair away from his face and turned toward her, exposing his ear. And his scar. He remembered almost instantly, and stiffened, but before he could move back, Melissa put her free hand on his shoulder, holding him still. Her soft, warm breath fluttered over his skin and he was torn between mortification and an age-old stirring of his body.

"I have good and bad news," she said.

Lifting his head, he managed to look her in the eyes.

"The bad news is that she did indeed get a good chunk out of you. The good news is that you have another ear."

He stared at her, waiting for the inevitable, for her to mention his scar, to ask questions....

Instead, she lifted her eyebrows in a royal gesture. "Is that all? Because I probably have more patients waiting. And you probably have to get to work."

"Maybe I'll find another animal that needs you."

Her pretty, glossy lips quirked. "I'm going to charge you every time you do. Is it really worth it?"

She thought he was coming here to flirt with her. Did she think he wanted a date? Wanted to kiss her?

Unexpectedly it hit him. He really did.

But his being here wasn't about him. It was about Rose, and suddenly that put a sharp twist of guilt in his gut. He'd been concentrating on just being alive, living day to day, enjoying every single second. But not only had he begun a deception he didn't know how to get out of, he did actually want what Melissa thought he wanted.

A date.

A kiss.

"Goodbye, Jason," Melissa said quietly, with a finality to her voice that made him blink.

Goodbye. Damn. He'd had a lot of goodbyes in his life. His parents had died five years ago. His brothers, both in the army, had been overseas for the past six years.

He hated goodbyes. "See ya," he said lightly, and felt a grim smile cross his face.

Because like it or not, he *would* be seeing her.

Knowing Rose, he'd be seeing a lot of Melissa.

CHAPTER THREE

THE NEXT DAY, Melissa carefully locked up the clinic at exactly six o'clock in the evening, just as she always did. She took a moment on the steps of the clinic to breathe in the clear air and to look around. The sparse landscape was punctuated by gentle, rolling hills dotted with the occasional tree or cow. So much…land. It definitely took getting used to.

Her usual routine was to head down the street to get her mail from the post office, and then to grab dinner. More often than not, this meant something to microwave from the freezer section of the grocery store. Once in a while, she'd grab something to go from the café. Either way, dinner usually came from a box.

She just didn't have the time, nor the inclination, to cook. Maybe if there'd been a family waiting for her…

Nope. She couldn't imagine herself a success in the kitchen even if a family was waiting for her.

But every so often, she wondered what it'd be

like to have dinner with people who loved her, who depended on her, who craved her company.

Then she remembered she wasn't a people person. She was an animal person.

She went into the post office and unlocked her mailbox. Another pink envelope fell out.

With a sigh, she opened it right there on the spot. This way she could read it and toss it into the trash can at the end of the aisle, avoiding all tendencies to dwell, which she'd definitely do if she brought the letter home.

Dear Melissa,

I'm not going to give up. Please let me come see you. I just want to get to know you, and hopefully, have you get to know me.

There are two sides to every story, and I'd love to have you hear mine. It won't take away your pain, but maybe we can come to a place where it's the *now* that matters.

Love,
Rose (still your mother)

Mel read it again, and then again, evaluating her emotions. Maybe Rose could concentrate on the here and now, it certainly suited her to do that, but Mel wasn't ready. She held the letter over the trash can, taken aback at the wave of regret that hit her.

"A bill, huh?"

With a little jerk, she turned and faced...Jason Lawrence. He stood there in his faded Levi's, a dark T-shirt with an opened plaid shirt over the top of it, and a wide smile. He had his sunglasses shoved on top of his head, which left his hair sticking straight up. In his hand was a stack of mail.

She glanced at the letter in her hand again, and felt her heart tighten. "A bill would be preferable to this."

"Really?" He reached for the pink envelope, but she yanked it behind her back.

"It's none of your business."

"No," he agreed quietly, watching her face. "It sure isn't. I just thought I might help you get rid of it, since it's upsetting you."

"I'm not upset."

"If you say so." He cocked his head and studied her. "You work hard today?"

"I suppose."

He laughed. "I imagine you work hard every day, don't you?"

"I like my work."

"Listen, why don't you let me buy you a drink? You can relax a muscle or two, maybe even breathe all the way in and out—"

"I'm fine."

"You don't seem fine."

"You don't know me."

He scratched his jaw, the sound of his stubble making her fingers itch inexplicably. "I think I have a pretty good idea of who you are."

She crossed her arms over her chest. "Do you?"

"You're the woman who works from sunup till sundown because work defines you. You love your job and don't understand others who don't work as hard as you do. You go home most nights and look around at your quiet life and think, it's okay that I'm alone, I have my work. You eat, also alone, you watch a little TV, and then you fall into bed, exhausted, staring at the ceiling wondering what it would be like to have someone hold you. Then you wake up in the morning and laugh at yourself, because you don't need anyone to hold you, you're fine, and then you start all over again."

She could only stare at him. How did he know? How could he possibly know?

"How am I doing?" he asked softly.

"I don't watch TV," she said. "Much."

He laughed. "Come with me tonight, Mel. Come enjoy yourself, away from the vet clinic."

"Are you saying I never enjoy myself outside of work?"

"Are you saying you do?"

"All the time," she lied.

"Really." He leaned back against the row of

mailboxes, crossed his feet and took a lazy, easy-going stance as he called her on that lie. "Tell me the last thing you did just for fun."

"That's easy. I..." Honestly, this couldn't be that hard. "Well, I—"

"Don't hurt yourself now."

The man was insufferable. "Just last night I took a bubble bath," she said defiantly.

"Woo-hoo, party time." Moving away from the mailboxes, he dumped his junk mail into the trash, then smiled at her, a slow, drawn-out smile that somehow made her pulse accelerate. "I've got a radical idea, so don't pass out. How about trying something else that's fun within twenty-four hours of your bubble bath?"

She eyed him. "What do you have in mind?"

"So suspicious. Dinner is what I have in mind."

"Dinner," she repeated. That didn't sound so difficult. "I don't know...."

"Too much fun for you?"

She had to laugh. "Okay, but just food, right?"

"Are you saying wild animal sex is out?"

She opened her mouth, saw the teasing glint in his eyes and let out a breath.

Stepping closer, he tugged lightly on a lock of her hair. "Relax, Doc. I'm not going to make you do anything you don't want to do." Serious now, he looked deep into her eyes. *"Ever."*

She looked down at the pink envelope in her fingers. Her mind wanted her to trash it, but apparently her heart had a bigger say in things, because she tucked it into her purse, which for some reason, made Jason smile at her.

Then he led her out of the post office and into the bright, warm sun, where the rest of the evening loomed large and terrifying in front of her.

THERE WEREN'T MANY CHOICES for dinner in town. They could eat at the Serendipity Café, the Taco Bell Express, or at the bar at the Bulls Inn.

Deciding that none of those would do, Jason pulled up to the only grocery store in Martis Hills. He turned off the engine of his truck and looked over at Melissa. "You don't by any chance trust me yet, do you?"

She lifted a brow.

"Thought not." He eyed her carefully. She was nervous, he decided, and probably already sorry she'd agreed to this. He'd have to change that. "Okay, you can come inside with me, but you can't change your mind about dinner until the next stop."

He grabbed some fancy cheese and crackers, then ordered fried chicken and macaroni salad from the deli counter. Because he'd never been an organized shopper, they wandered through the store looking for wine and ended up in the pet aisle.

"Are you a dog person?" Melissa asked curiously.

He looked at the cans of dog food and tried to decide how to answer. He wasn't much of an animal person, plus in his previous life—which hadn't been that long ago—he'd traveled extensively, researching for his books, which ruled out having a pet. He'd loved that globe-trotting lifestyle but it had lost much of its appeal, so he didn't do it anymore. Yet he still hadn't amassed any animals.

But his neighbor, the woman who'd pulled him out of his car only seconds before the wreck had blown sky-high, now *she* was most definitely an animal person.

He'd told her he owed her, that he owed her big. He'd told her that he'd do anything, anything at all to help her when she needed it.

And damn if Rose hadn't cashed in on that rash promise. Damn if she didn't want him to help her get close to her daughter. Rose had told him how she'd put Melissa into the foster-care system because she was intent on finding a better life for the both of them. Rose had to get away from her abusive boyfriend and strict parents—parents that would in no way let their unmarried daughter bring a child out of wedlock into their house. She'd always planned on going back for Melissa, but it turned out to be harder than she had thought to go back. Rose knew that asking for forgiveness of Melissa, and properly explaining herself while she was at it, would probably be the best route. But it was difficult, because Melissa harbored deep feelings on the matter.

As a result, Rose believed her only way into Mel's heart was through the animals her daughter loved with all her heart.

Which meant Jason was most likely going to have to go through an entire menagerie before this was over in order to plead Rose's case for her.

It was a long shot, both Rose and he knew that. But as he watched Melissa smiling at the posters of puppies advertising dog food, he had to admit, Rose might have been on to something. Only suddenly he didn't want to be on to something at all, but out on a simple dinner date with no ulterior motive except for maybe getting a good-night kiss. Sorrier than hell that he'd ever agreed to Rose's crazy plan, he hitched his head toward the next aisle. "Come on, we're not quite finished."

She followed him to the cookie section. "Dessert," he said. "Pick one."

A little laugh escaped her. "If I'd have known I was going to watch you go food shopping, I'd have grabbed a cart for myself."

"Just tell me what kind of cookies float your boat."

"I don't eat cookies. They're bad for you."

"Sure, that's what makes them so yummy." He dumped some fudge cookies into the cart, then looked over their bounty and decided they were good to go. "Ready?"

"For what exactly?"

"You'll see." When he reached for her hand, she pulled it back.

"I'm not big on surprises," she said.

And she wasn't big on touching, either. He wondered if he could change both.

He paid for the groceries, loaded them and Melissa back into his truck and drove through town. He went past the second and then the last stoplight, and then went past the turn to get onto the main highway.

And he kept going, heading directly toward the still green and beautiful rolling hills.

"Where are we going?"

"I promised you dinner."

She gazed at the wide-open scenery, but said nothing. As far as the eye could see there was nothing around but gentle hills lined with occasional fencing, holding in horses and cattle. They turned onto a dirt road that rose and twisted like the gnarled oak trees they'd passed.

And then they finally came to a small lake. Jason had been born and bred in this area, and though he'd spent the past twelve years away, he still had fond memories here. Once upon a time while still in high school, he'd come here to make out. Not that he had any hopes for that tonight.

Melissa watched him guardedly. "What's here?"

"A picnic." He came around to help her down from the truck, then grabbed a blanket and the bag of food.

She looked at the blanket, and then at him. "You're not going to need that."

He laughed. "We're going to eat on it."

"That's all we're doing on it."

"Right. No wild animal sex. I remember."

They sat on the blanket at the water's edge. Melissa just as far from him as she could get. In her neat black trousers and crisp white blouse, surrounded by the brilliant blue of the calm water and the wild green of the hills lining the lake, she looked beautiful. Her face was shaded by the three oak trees they sat beneath, and her dark short hair, cut in neat little layers that flipped up so adorably they made his fingers itch to touch them, lifted lightly in the breeze.

He poured the wine and took out the food, which they ate while she asked him about his work. "I should tell you, I'm a novelist," he said, smiling at her surprise. "At the moment I'm trying my hand at a psychological thriller."

She set down her piece of chicken and licked her fingers, the little sucking sound her mouth made being the most erotic he'd ever heard. "What does a laid-back, easygoing guy like you know about terror?"

The memory of his car accident flickered through him: fierce rain, a wild storm, slippery roads, a damn deer in the way, brakes not responding... The moment of stark horror as his car careened out of control toward the huge tree at the end of his driveway. Then being dragged from the wreckage by a wet, trembling Rose...and waking up days later in the hospital.

What did he know of terror? Plenty. But he gave her an easy smile. "It's fiction, Mel."

She laughed at herself, and he loved the sound of her amusement, getting the feeling that she didn't do it very often.

"What does your family think of what you do?" she asked.

"My mom and dad are gone, and my brothers are in the army. They're a little mystified by the fact I'd rather use a pencil than a gun, but they're proud." He brought out the cookies. "What about you? Where's your family?" He hated himself for asking when he already knew.

She busied herself cleaning up her trash. "I grew

up in foster homes. It was okay,'' she said quickly, probably used to being defensive about that.

''And your real parents?''

''I don't know my father.'' She shrugged. ''And my mother…she's around. That's why I was never put up for adoption. The social workers kept hoping my mother would eventually take me back. Just so happens she didn't get around to wanting to do it until I was already grown.''

He handed her a cookie. ''In the name of being bad.'' Their fingers brushed, and she pulled away.

''Why do you do that?'' he asked quietly. ''Shy away from my touch?''

''I don't know you very well.''

''And if you did…would that change? You not liking to be touched?''

She looked away. ''I'm not much of a people person. I'd have figured if you'd learned anything about me in the past few days, it'd have been that.''

''Mel…''

He waited until she looked at him and gave her a slow smile meant to charm. He handed her another cookie. ''Why did you think I came back with that damn parrot?''

She sighed. ''I knew there was nothing wrong with that parrot. I thought you came back with it simply to—'' She let out a little laugh and sipped her wine.

"To…?"

"To see me."

"I did." And that was the truth. He didn't want this to be just for Rose anymore. He wanted to do it for himself. He wanted to get to know her because she was the real deal. A real woman, who was into her job, who really cared about what she was doing with her life.

And then there was something else. Unlike everyone else he'd come across in the past six months, she hadn't mentioned the scar rolling down the right side of his face. There'd been so many questions, from both strangers and friends, all of which drove him nuts.

But not from Melissa.

Bottom line, she threw him off-kilter. More than his looming deadline, more than his promise to Rose, more than anything.

And he had no idea what to do with that.

CHAPTER FOUR

THE NEXT DAY at the clinic was hectic for Melissa. Her waiting room was constantly full, and though she did the best she could, and everyone was extremely polite about the wait, she felt she could have done more. Should have done more.

She really did need help in the front office. She needed someone other than herself to sign people in and organize all the paperwork. Soon, she promised herself.

Finally she saw her remaining patients—a chicken with a limp, a cat who'd swallowed a dime and a pet rat with a broken tail. She was attempting to figure out how to print the next day's schedule when the door opened again.

The biggest Saint Bernard she'd ever seen bounded into the room, tongue hanging out, ears flopping, big body exuberant as he tugged in his master by the leash.

Melissa followed the leash up—and burst out laughing.

"Now hold on, Bear—" Jason was jerked to the

middle of the room, where he shot her a rather sheepish glance, just before he was hauled over to her by the dog. "Hi," he managed, just as he was jerked again, to the far corner this time.

"Let me guess... Bear has a problem." She knew she should question him about this, his third and most obvious visit, but quite honestly, she felt herself enjoying the game. Coming around the desk, she bent down and whistled softly. The huge dog gave one bark of joy and then galloped over to her, dragging Jason in its tow.

"Watch out," he warned as she let the dog sniff her hand before petting him. "He's a monster of a dog with no idea of his own strength. He'd just as soon drown you by drooling than anything else, and his entire mission in life has been screwing up mine today."

"Sit," Mel commanded Bear quietly. The dog sat.

She'd already noticed his limp. "Shake."

The dog lifted his sore paw, and when she took it in her hands and studied it, he let out a soft cry. "Oh, you poor thing."

"I know," Jason said with a long-suffering sigh as he hunkered down next to her. "I'm exhausted."

"I'm talking about the dog."

"Oh. Right." Jason watched her let Bear lick her face. "You going to let me kiss you like that?"

She ignored the flutter in her tummy and looked into Jason's laughing eyes. "Are you as good at it as he is?"

"Better," he promised silkily. "Much better."

She had no doubt of that, but given the way her pulse had kicked into gear, it would be nothing short of dangerous to find out. "You promised no kissing."

"No, I promised no wild animal sex."

She let out a nervous laugh. "Promise no kissing."

"Mel—"

"Promise."

He sighed. "No kissing."

"Thank you." She drew a steadying breath. "Bear has a nasty splinter." She got to her feet, and so did the dog, quietly now, right at her side. She'd always had this effect on animals, and they on her. They calmed her soul, soothed her in a way no person had ever managed. And yet she never took it for granted, and when it happened, like right now, she felt...needed. She had a purpose. "Come," she said, and moved to a patient room.

Bear obediently followed.

Jason stared at her. "How in the hell do you do that?"

"I have the touch."

His eyes darkened. "Do you?" he murmured in

a voice that had the opposite of the calming, soothing effect dealing with Bear did.

Her smile slowly faded, replaced by a shakiness in the knees, damp palms and heart palpitations, not to mention a clenching in parts that hadn't clenched in a good long time. "Jason—"

Bear sat down in the room and lifted his paw with a soft whine.

Melissa, who couldn't stand to see anything in pain, looked at the examining table. No way was she going to be able to get the dog up there—

Just as she thought it, Jason squatted down, wrapped his arms around Bear and lifted him to the table. Melissa found her gaze drawn to the muscles straining in his arms as he did, and when she lifted her eyes to his face, she found him smiling. "I might be a writer now," he said in that slow, lazy drawl. "But I still have the strength of a farm boy."

He sure did. She busied herself removing the splinter from Bear, who licked her face every few seconds or so, bathing her in doggie breath and doggie love, which she could never get enough of. Finally she tossed the tweezers into the sink and tried not to watch as Jason lifted Bear down.

The dog promptly let out a bark that assured everyone within earshot he was on the trail of something good, and ran out the door, and because

Jason had left the front door ajar, Bear ran right out that, as well, on his way to freedom.

"Damn it," Jason said, taking off after him.

Melissa went, too, knowing she had no more patients, and that the small-town atmosphere meant she didn't have to worry about leaving the place unattended for a few minutes. Directly behind the converted house lay a wooded area, beyond which was a river and more wide-open space.

Naturally this was where Bear was headed, hot on the trail of a squirrel or whatever had caught his fancy. As they ran after him, Melissa was grateful for her daily torturous run she took in the mornings before heading into work, and couldn't help but notice that Jason ran with ease, as well, that long, leanly muscled body working like a well-honed machine.

She forced her eyes straight ahead, and on Bear, whom they caught up with when he treed his squirrel and sat at the base of the trunk barking his head off.

Jason bent for his leash, and gave the dog a long-suffering look. "Buddy, the less energy expelled on any given day, the better." When Melissa laughed at that, he cocked a brow. "You don't agree?"

There was a path that she knew wound its way along the narrow river, and by silent agreement, they started walking. "You act like you're so lazy, but I just ran alongside you flat out for a quarter of a mile and your breathing hardly changed at all.''

He lifted a shoulder. ''Maybe I'm just in decent shape.'' He turned to face her, halting their walk. Shaded by an oak tree, listening to the river run, watching him watch her, it occurred to her she was smiling. For no special reason other than he made her want to smile. His hand settled at the crook of her elbow and she didn't shrug him off.

''Just because I talk slow,'' he said, with a grin, ''doesn't mean I move slow.''

She realized his other hand had come up and made itself at home on her hip. A lock of his hair had fallen over his forehead, and before she even realized what she meant to do, she stroked it out of his face. Her fingers came in contact with his warm, tanned skin, then the pale ridge of his long, jagged scar. She lightly ran one finger down—

''Don't.'' Lifting a hand, he pulled hers away.

''I'm sorry.'' She might not know much about relating to another human being, other than for the most basic of needs, but here, finally, was something she could understand. She was good at healing, good at dealing with pain and suffering, though it wasn't pain in his eyes but embarrassment.

''I'm sorry,'' she whispered again, and lifted her free hand to touch him once more, wanting him to be soothed at her touch as an animal would. ''I hate to think of how much agony this must have cost you, and not too long ago, given the texture of the skin and the degree to which it still has to heal. Are you using anything to reduce the scarring?''

He let out a shaky laugh, and dropped his forehead to hers. ''Melissa.'' Another low, rather mirthless laugh. ''I don't know what to do with you.''

''How about talk to me?''

He lifted his head and searched her gaze, she had no idea for what, but he must have found what he was looking for, because he nodded. ''Yeah, I'm using something the doctor gave me for the scarring.'' He was quiet a moment, then told her the rest. ''I was coming home late one night about six months ago. I'd taken a trip for some research, and the flight home had been long and exhausting, the drive up from LAX even more so. I think I was half-asleep when Bambi darted out in front of me.

''I didn't want to kill it so I swerved. My first mistake. I wrapped both myself and the car around an oak tree, and because I'd removed my seat belt about a moment before to reach into the back for a soda—my second mistake—I took my second flight that day. Right out of the car and into the air, and smack into another oak tree.''

''My God.''

''Well, I didn't exactly meet God, but I did see a bright light. When I woke up three days later, I was told I would have died before I'd even gotten to the hospital if it hadn't been for one very curious woman who'd come out in the middle of the night to see why a horn was going off."

"Oh, Jason." Her heart stuttered for him. "How terrifying."

"Without her and her cell phone, I'd have been goners—Hey," he said softly, seeing that her eyes had filled. "Hey, I'm good now." He covered her fingers, which were still touching his scar. "Or as good as I get."

"Which is pretty damn good," she whispered fiercely, and blinked back her tears. He wouldn't want them.

"Mel..." He cupped her face, leaned in a little, and unbelievably, she leaned in, too. And then suddenly he was ripped away from her when Bear found a new squirrel to chase.

Melissa took a step back and watched Jason try to wrestle the one-hundred-and-fifty-pound dog to a stop. He managed it, but not until he was knee-deep in the river. By the time he splashed his way out, Melissa was laughing so hard she could hardly stand.

"Oh, you think that's funny." He came toward her. "Me getting all wet."

"Well, yes—" She broke off with a startled squeak when he dove for her. Whirling, she went running, laughing when both man and dog tackled her down to a patch of wild grass. Turning, she found herself in Jason's arms, staring up into his eyes.

She looked at his mouth, and he let out a low groan. "I promised," he said, his hands coming up to cup her face, his thumb skimming over her lower lip in a way that made her ache. "I promised no kissing."

The restraint was costing him. She could see a little tic in his jaw, feel the tension in his body as it covered hers, and it made her melt as nothing else would have. "That was earlier." Slipping her arms around his neck, she brought his head down. Their lips connected for one glorious heartbeat before Bear thrust his large face between them, eyeing them with bloodshot eyes. Then he tossed his head back and let out an earsplitting howl.

Jason groaned, then rose to his feet, pulling Melissa to hers. "Damn dog, you're supposed to help my cause, not ruin it."

With the moment passed, Mel had a hard time looking him in the eye. She felt the need to run, far and fast. "I've...got to go, I left the clinic door unlocked."

"Mel—"

She took a step back. "Goodbye, Jason."

She ran back to the front steps of the clinic, then

watched as Jason loaded Bear up into his truck. He waved to her as he drove off, but all she could do was stand there.

She wished she could still taste him.

As she was thinking this, it occurred to her she could hear something inside the clinic, and thinking someone had let themselves in to wait for her, she entered the front door and scanned the waiting room. Someone had taken over the arduous job of sweeping up the animal hair that had been shed there during the day. The chairs were all neatly lining the walls again, the retail shelving unit nicely organized.

The front desk had been taken care of, as well, with the paperwork that she'd so hastily tossed around all day piled in the proper stacks. Sitting behind the desk, fingers tapping away on the keyboard of her computer sat a lean, willowy, attractive woman in her mid-forties. She had short, dark hair layered around her face, and bright green eyes. She smiled nervously. "Hello, Melissa."

"Hello, Mother."

CHAPTER FIVE

"MELISSA." Rose stood up and smoothed her sundress, showing off her still-fit dancer's body. "I hope you don't mind, I just wanted to help."

"Actually, I—" *Do mind.* Melissa moved closer to the desk, but she could see just how organized Rose had gotten her. The schedule for tomorrow was in the printer tray. The box of office supplies on the floor had been put away. Suddenly the area looked like a functioning receptionist area. She hadn't been gone more than half an hour, but apparently her mother had some serious office talents. "How did you do all this?"

"It's easier if you clean up as you go, that's all. Maybe you could put each patient sheet away as they leave, open the mail as it comes—"

"I don't have time for that." She glanced at Rose. "I don't have time for you."

Rose lifted her chin, only her eyes reflecting her hurt. "Because I never had time for you."

"Sure you did. After you retired from teaching ballet in London." Melissa crossed her arms and looked away, knowing she looked defensive, but damn it, she felt defensive. "Look, thank you for all this, the cleaning and straightening up. But just because you got a bug to start acting like a mother to me doesn't mean I have the same bug to act like your daughter."

"But you are my daughter," Rose said softly, coming out from behind the desk. She put her hands on Melissa's arms, even though Mel stood there stiff as a board. "I'm sorry," she whispered. "I'm sorry I was a selfish, horrible person when you were young, but for years now I've regretted that and you haven't let me in."

"I wasn't ready."

"I know. I know you're still not, but baby, I've decided to stop letting you waste what time we have left."

Melissa's tummy dropped. "Are you...sick?"

"No," Rose said quickly, with a little squeeze of her hands, her eyes shining. "But I want to hug you for that spurt of panic you just felt."

Melissa took a step back. "That wasn't panic. That was...me just being a healer."

Rose smiled. "Know what I think?"

"I'd rather not."

Rose held up the pink envelopes, every one of them, which Mel had rubber-banded and kept in her desk. "I think you're going to like me."

"Don't push your luck." Feeling hounded, Mel went to the front door and held it open.

Rose nodded and came close. "I can come back and sit at your front desk tomorrow, if you'd like."

"Don't you have something more important to do? Fly around the world? Dance? Something?"

"No. I only teach ballet on Saturdays." Rose's smile was as stubborn as…Mel's.

Gee, guess she knew where she'd gotten it from.

"I have nothing more important than you," Rose said softly. "Nothing."

"Now."

Rose's smile faltered. "I was only eighteen when you were born. I—"

"No. Please. I don't want to do this." Her chest had tightened, along with her throat, and behind her eyes was a horrifying sting of tears. "I can't."

Rose stared at her for a long moment, then slowly nodded.

"I'm fine without you," Mel said thickly. "I am."

"Of course you are. It's just that sometimes it's easier to be fine if you're not alone."

"I like alone."

Rose sighed, looked like she might say something else, but Mel opened the door wider in a not-too-subtle hint. "Good night," Mel said.

"Good night." Rose's voice reflected her sadness.

Melissa turned away, no idea why she felt guilty. No idea at all.

A FEW DAYS LATER, Jason had just ordered himself a nice big cholesterol-filled breakfast at the Serendipity Café when Dr. Melissa Anders walked in, looking like her usual put-together, uptight self.

Just the sight of her made him smile.

She didn't see him, mostly because she kept her eyes straight forward as she headed toward the counter, her sensible low heels clicking on the worn black-and-white checkered linoleum. He wondered if she saw the charm in the place that hadn't been redecorated since sometime during John F. Kennedy's era. This place with the jukebox and the red vinyl booths faded to a dark rose, the movie posters on the walls…it wasn't some wannabe retro café, but the real deal.

But she didn't take the time to look around, instead set her hands on the counter and ordered coffee.

The breakfast of champions.

Or the breakfast of a vet always in a hurry.

The waitress behind the counter smiled warmly at her, and thanked her again for fixing up her dog last week. Then the cook came out to ask her a question about his cat's bowel movements. An older couple sitting at the counter told her a story about a kitten she'd delivered for them.

All the while Melissa seemed to squirm.

Jason's smile widened just a bit. Poor baby. Give her a dying animal, or even one who just needed its shots, and she was in her element.

Give her humans to deal with and she wiggled like a five-year-old who'd downed too much apple juice. He decided to rescue her. "Melissa."

Her short dark hair spun when she looked over at him. She remained cool, he'd give her that, but her eyes gave her away, going from quick surprise to a flash of awareness and excitement, to a wariness he wanted to kiss away.

He'd concentrate on that awareness and excitement. "Come sit down and eat with me."

"I'm just having coffee."

"You can't work on just coffee. Marge, add another special to my order."

Marge smiled. "Coming up."

Melissa sighed but walked over to him. Standing, he reached for her hand, urged her to sit. Before she could protest, he'd slid into the same side of the booth with her.

When she shot him a look, he simply smiled. "I was thinking about you, and then in you walked. Fancy that."

"Fancy that." She glanced at his arm and the healing scratches. She made a show of craning her neck to look at his ear and the bites there from the parrot. "You're healing nicely."

"Is that your way of saying 'how are you?'"

"I guess it is."

"Well, then, I'm good," he said, and stroked her cheek when she smiled.

Marge showed up with two full plates of food, set them down, popping her gum. "Gotta say, Doc," she said to Melissa. "I'm enjoying seeing you actually sit and enjoy. Don't take this wrong now, but you're usually so…stoic. This morning, you seem real. It's a good look on you." She winked at Jason. "Keep it up."

Melissa stared at him as she walked away. "What does that mean? I'm a real person all the time."

"Sure you are. It's just that sometimes you forget to show it, that's all. You're doing a great job lately though." Picking up his fork, he dug into his scrambled eggs. "This is far better than staring at a blank page."

"You're having trouble with a book?"

"Plot trouble. Character trouble. Hell, I've even got font trouble."

"What's your story?"

He never talked about a book before he turned it

in to his editor. But she was looking at him, sweet and curious, so what the hell. "My hero has a recurring nightmare about not being able to get home. It's hell all night long, then every morning he wakes up covered in sweat, terrified. Only, as it turns out, it's not a nightmare at all. It's real. He's not home and he can't get there. I just can't figure out why."

They ate for a while in silence, and then Melissa said, "Maybe he doesn't know *how* to get there."

"Yes, but—" He stared at her. Thought about it, and suddenly laughed. "Yes. He doesn't know how to get there—not physically, of course. But getting home is complicated by his past, his issues, his...everything." He scratched his jaw. "Yeah." He smiled. "Thank you."

"Anytime." She pushed her food around. "It's always easier to solve someone else's problems, you ever notice that?"

"Oh, I've noticed. Tell me yours. Maybe I can solve one for you."

"I'm fine." She took a few quick bites, avoiding his gaze, breaking his heart.

"Melissa." He put a hand over hers. "Come on, share."

She pulled her hand free.

"I thought we were past the no-touching-allowed thing."

"This is going to take some getting used to."

She pointed at him. "*You're* going to take some getting used to."

"Yeah." He smiled. "I've been told."

She sighed, then looked at him, that spark of awareness and a whole host of other things in her eyes now. "I'm trying to get used to you. I...I want to get used to you."

His heart swelled in his chest so that it hurt, it physically hurt, to look at her. "From you, that's quite the declaration."

That made her laugh. "How is it I feel like you know me so well after, what...a week?"

"Some things just are," he said, shocked to find it so.

"Yeah." She eyed him then rolled her eyes. "Do you really want to hear my problem?"

"Please."

Her mouth curved into a reluctant smile. "I guess maybe I'm a little stressed. My office needs help I can't give it. My mother showed up out of the blue and thinks she can help, that I ought to just let the past be the past and start anew. For some reason that I don't really like to admit, I don't feel like letting go of the past and giving in." She released a breath. "So. How am I doing?"

Guilt was like a knife. "Good," he said quietly, knowing he needed to tell her that he knew Rose, that he knew what Rose wanted from her, and in fact, knew the extremes she was willing to go to.

Instead, he leaned in and kissed her once, softly. He'd always been better at kissing instead of talking, and given her response, the quick intake of breath, the way her lips clung to his, the sleepy, sexy look in her eyes as he pulled back and looked into her face, she clearly felt the same way.

"Maybe you're afraid of getting hurt," he said very quietly, and held her hand when she would have pulled away. "I think it would be natural for you to be afraid of being hurt."

"But it seems so…childish of me. I mean, I'm the one who moved here, to where she lives. I just can't seem to stop myself from remembering how much I needed her years ago, back when she couldn't be bothered."

Here was his chance. He could explain how Rose had been forced by circumstance to walk away from Mel, how difficult it'd been for her, and how she regretted that decision made by a scared eighteen-year-old.

But he didn't want to pressure or guilt Melissa into anything. He wanted these two women he cared very much about to find happiness together, not because one had been manipulated into it, but because they both wanted it to work. "Maybe…" He lifted their joined hands and kissed her fingers. "Maybe you'll find a middle ground, where it can work for both of you.''

''Maybe,'' she said, not seeming too hopeful on that score. ''But I've gone this long without her, it seems silly to need her help now.''

''It's never too late.''

She looked unhappy about that, and it occurred to him maybe she wasn't used to asking for help. He thought of how she'd grown up, how she'd probably not had anyone just for her, to love her, and that made him ache for her. ''Sometimes, Mel, you only have to ask.''

She was silent for a long time. ''I'm not good at asking,'' she finally said.

Oh, baby, he thought, no kidding you're not good at it. ''Maybe you could practice.''

''I like my life the way it is.''

He started to open his mouth.

''*Just* as it is,'' she said firmly.

He cocked his head and sent her an easy grin. ''You sure about that? Because things can always get better.'' Tugging her close, he kissed her.

She went still for a beat, then kissed him back.

Afterward her eyes were doing that sexy sleepy thing again. ''Okay, point taken.'' She was just breathless enough to make him feel really good. ''But for right now, I've got to get to the clinic.''

He walked her there, and as he watched her walk inside to face her day, he found himself wondering, hoping, that Rose had another animal for him. But nothing that slobbered, bit or scratched.

CHAPTER SIX

THE NEXT DAY went well for Melissa, if she discounted her out-of-control front desk and the fact that she was beginning to doubt she could do it all.

The amount of business she did every day meant that soon, very soon, she could run in the black and maybe actually make a living for herself.

It also meant she'd need help. The thought of hiring another person and learning to trust that person was enough to make her keep putting it off.

So by the end of the day, with her desk looking like a cyclone had hit and the front room looking like…well, like animals had lived in it all day, she stood there pleasantly exhausted and wondered how long it would take to straighten up before she could go home.

She hadn't yet locked up when the front door opened. She turned with her welcoming doctor face on, and promptly burst out laughing.

Jason stood there, tall and lean and heart-stoppingly gorgeous, holding a leash attached to a potbellied pig. "Hi," he said with a mischievous smile. "Got time for one more patient?"

"You are kidding me."

"Nope." He scratched his jaw. "Miss Piggy here needs her shots."

"*You* have a pig?"

"Well…" Suddenly his smile was gone. "I'm doing a friend a favor."

"Uh-huh." She bent and scratched between the pig's ears, who grunted in pleasure. "Hello, Miss Piggy," she said softly. "Let's get you all fixed up." She straightened to her full height, which was to Jason's shoulder, and he reached out, stroking her cheek, tucking a strand of hair behind her ear with such tenderness, she froze.

She liked his touch. She even…craved it. Not sure how that had happened, or why she'd let it, she smiled at him a little shakily and turned to move them into a patient room.

"Wait." He held her there. "Hold up a second, I just want to look at you." Slowly he shook his head, his gaze filled with heat, affection and a tenderness that made her throat burn. "Mel—"

"No, wait." His closeness suddenly scared her, not physically, never physically, but she instinctively knew this wasn't just a passing fancy, for either of them. "Are we doing this? Because I've got to—"

"Yes." He pulled her a little closer, bringing his mouth down. "We're doing this—"

She slapped a hand to his chest to hold him off. "I meant inoculating Miss Piggy. We have to do it now because I've got things to do—"

"Right. You're a busy woman on the go." He followed her to the patient room and left when she was done, just a few minutes later, without any more touches or teasing.

Feeling a little empty, and as if maybe she'd just been really stupid, she locked the front door after him, then set her forehead to it.

For the first time in her life, she had no idea what to do.

So she did what she did best—she buried herself in work.

THE NEXT DAY she got to the clinic her usual half hour early so she could try to wrestle the receptionist desk into order. She dreaded the task but had to face it.

She'd received another pink envelope, and a phone call in the same tone, in which Rose had said she wasn't going to give up, not until Melissa gave in.

Melissa had honestly figured her mother would have lost interest by now. Or at the very least, have gotten frustrated and annoyed.

As she turned on the lights and music, and then inhaled her first whiff of Lysol, the phones started. Before she could blink, she had two dogs, a cat and a family of rabbits waiting to be seen, and the paperwork was overflowing on her desk again.

Feeling unaccustomedly harried, she took in the front room, wincing a little at the mess.

From behind her came a set of heels clicking on the floor. Rose stood there wearing a sunshine-yellow sundress with matching accessories—purse, earrings, and sandals. Her hands were clasped together in what might have been a show of nerves. ''I'm hoping you need my help this morning.'' Rose's eyes took in the mess of the office but didn't say a word.

It's never too late to need help.

Jason had told her that, something Mel had thought about all night long.

All you have to do is ask.

Why did that have to be so hard? Because she was out of practice. No, that wasn't it. Truth was, she'd never been *in* practice. When she'd been two, if she'd wanted something high on a shelf, she'd crawled to get it herself. When she'd been four and needed her shoes tied, she'd carefully slipped in and out of the already knotted shoes. When she'd been eight and walking home alone, dodging the occasional taunt or harassment of an older kid, she'd walked faster. And when she'd needed help with her homework, she'd simply studied harder.

Asking for help wasn't in her realm of experience, and the thought of doing it now stuck in her throat.

Behind her, the phone started ringing. A puppy whined. The sound softened her. She was here for the animals.

Rose was still standing there, eyes hopeful.

Okay, fine. "Obviously, I haven't hired a receptionist."

Rose nodded. "So are you...asking?"

"I'm not ready to make a permanent decision."

"I see."

The phone kept ringing, joined now by Mel's second line. Perspiration broke out on her brow. "But...I do need a temp, at least for today."

Rose kept her face carefully neutral. "Could you spell it out for me? I don't want to assume anything here."

"I'm asking you, for—" she drew in a deep breath "—help. I need your help."

The smile Rose sent her was shimmery with emotion. Before Melissa could draw another breath, she found herself engulfed in Rose's arms, squeezed close and hard.

"Thank you," Rose whispered fiercely.

Mel pried free from her tight grip. "Sure."

"Sorry," Rose said, looking anything but. "I like to hug."

"I don't. The phone is ringing. That falls in your category. Can you really do this?"

"Yep. Get the phones, handle the paperwork, and no hugging." Rose moved toward the desk. "That last one is going to be the hardest, though."

Melissa ignored that and surveyed her patients. She couldn't handle her mother right now, didn't know *how* to handle her mother right now, so she wouldn't.

But she had a feeling Rose wouldn't let that go for long.

THAT NIGHT Mel left the clinic earlier than usual. This, she had to admit, was because Rose had been worth her weight in gold.

Standing on the steps looking toward her car, she blinked like an owl. The sun was still up. The day still had hours in it.

And suddenly she didn't want to go home alone.

Jason hadn't come today with an animal for her to fix up, and she knew that was her own doing. She thought she'd feel relief, but instead she'd been on edge all day, constantly checking the waiting room, wishing he'd show up.

Either he'd finally run out of animals, or she'd chased him off for good.

She'd chased him off for good. Damn it.

She drove to the grocery store and picked the items carefully. She even bought a basket to put them all in, and because she was nervous, she spent a few moments arranging everything in it before she drove to Jason's house.

She'd gotten his address off all the forms he'd filled out over the past week and a half, and even her anxious wondering what he'd think of her showing up out of the blue didn't stop her.

His large property was lined by oak trees. She turned into the driveway and eyed the largest oak tree at the end of it, knowing that was the one that Jason had hit. She shivered thinking about it and all he'd been through.

She passed half a mile of wild grass over unused fields before she saw the old, restored farmhouse, surrounded and shaded by more gnarly old oak trees swaying in the evening wind.

Getting out of her car with the basket over her arm was easy. Walking up his steps with the intention of making the first move on a man for the first time in her life was not.

Fortunately—or unfortunately, depending on how she looked at it—she didn't have far to go. He sat on the wooden swing on his porch, with his laptop resting in his lap.

"Hey," she said softly.

Clearly lost in concentration, he looked up distractedly, but then he blinked, as if waking from a dream.

She felt silly standing there holding the basket, and stupid for interrupting him when he was obviously deep in work mode. "I'm sorry, I'll just—"

"No, don't go." He closed his computer and set it aside. "I was just thinking of you."

"With such a serious expression on your face?" Her pulse doubled when he stood up. Tripled when he came toward her.

"Was I looking serious?" he asked. "I don't usually do serious."

But he had, and she wondered why. Then all the wondering flew out of her brain when he put his hands on the small of her back, then glided them over her spine, up and down, down and up, in a hypnotizing motion that had her wanting to stretch and purr like a kitten.

Now the only thing on her mind was his kiss, his easy ways, and she felt the urge to toss her arms around his neck and let him take her.

And why not let him? It was why she'd come. "Jason..."

He looked down at her mouth, his eyes heating. "Yeah?"

"I came here to..." She bit her lip, laughed a

little at herself. "To tell you how much I've enjoyed your company."

He let out a long breath, looking suddenly serious again. "Mel, wait. There's something you should know—"

"I can't wait. I want you, Jason," she blurted out. "There." She offered him a shaky smile. "There."

He put his fingers over her mouth, his jaw bunching tight. "Don't. God, Mel, don't."

Confusion, also some humiliation, burned in her gut. "I thought you'd be glad."

He groaned, a low, raw sound, then with an oath that blistered her ears, he kissed her, long and wet and deep. Then he gently pushed her away. "You've got to go."

His voice was rough, his breathing ragged and confused. She stared at him. "I don't understand."

"I know. Go. Please, just go. Don't waste your time on me."

CHAPTER SEVEN

JASON STOOD THERE on his porch with his back to Mel. He squeezed his eyes tight and barely resisted the urge to throw something. Hell, yes, he'd wanted her to want him, but having not told her about Rose made him feel like the biggest jerk on earth.

He'd met her under false pretenses. He'd kept talking to her under false pretenses. Bringing those damn animals. Maybe if he'd only done that the first time with Bob, maybe if he'd opened up and told her the truth…but he hadn't.

Not once.

How the hell had this happened to him, when all he'd wanted to do was help out Rose with her daughter, he hadn't a clue. But he'd underestimated the amount of baggage and pain that had come with Mel's past, and he shouldn't have. She'd be pissed when she found out, and rightfully so.

He felt a hand on his back, urging him around to face her. She was smiling at him with the sweetest, sexiest smile he'd ever been on the receiving end of, and suddenly he knew she'd started to fall for him every bit as much as he'd fallen for her. The victory was bittersweet. "Mel—"

Leaning in, she gave him a soft, melting kiss. "I'm scaring you. I don't mean to."

Now *she* was worried about *him*. He was so undeserving of her—

"I brought you a picnic. But I don't want to eat yet. Actually, I had something else in mind—food was just sort of a bribe."

Oh God. "What—" He had to clear his throat. "What did you have in mind?"

Her eyes heated. "Take me to your bedroom and I'll show you." Before he could say a word, she'd taken his hand and opened his front door.

Then she shot him a smile over her shoulder, a smile that promised an evening he'd never forget, a smile that promised oblivion from his torturing thoughts, a smile that promised everything he'd ever wanted.

But after he had followed her down the hall to his bedroom, the sheets tumbled all over because he hadn't bothered making his bed that morning, he got a good, long look at her from the low-burning lamp on his nightstand.

Beneath that sensual expression danced an anxiety that told him she wasn't comfortable making the first move, that she was half-braced for his rejection.

As if he'd ever reject her. And yet, how could he do this before he admitted—

She kicked off her heels, and her hands went to the buttons on her white blouse.

He swallowed hard as she slowly revealed a strip of creamy skin and the curve of her breasts. His entire body reacted, but he forced himself to stand there with his hands at his side because how in good faith could he make love to her with his little secret between them. "Melissa—"

"This is really out of character for me," she admitted with a shaky laugh. "But I wanted to be bold tonight. Shameless."

She was doing a damn fine job, and it was his job to stop her. Stop her from feeling free and open and—

Ah, hell, he couldn't. He couldn't take this away from her.

Or him.

The material fell open and her fingers moved to the fastener of her black trousers.

His mouth went dry. "You—we…"

"I want you," she whispered, suddenly the sure, calm one in the room. "I'm tired of ignoring all my emotions. I want you, and I am going to show you how much."

Her pants fell from her hips. She shrugged off

her shirt, leaving her standing before him in a white lacy bra and matching panties and nothing else.

Which made him Dead Man Walking.

MEL WATCHED HIM as he moved close to her. She saw need, hunger, even fear, everything she felt as well, and her heart lightened. She wasn't just acting on her lust, though there was plenty of that.

This was more, so much, much more. And she wanted him to feel it, too.

"Melissa…"

She put her fingers against his mouth. "Please, Jason. Just for tonight."

For a long beat he simply looked at her. "Please," she whispered.

In response, he yanked his shirt off over his head. Beneath, he was solid, tanned, and rippled with a lean strength that made her mouth water.

His mouth skimmed her jaw softly. She turned her face toward him so that their lips connected, and her entire body relaxed as the tension she hadn't realized she'd been holding slowly started to drain.

"Melissa…" His arms banded tightly around her while his lips nibbled so softly, so sweetly against hers. "You are so beautiful, you take my breath. And there's no way this is just for tonight. Know that right now."

And then he changed the angle of the kiss, deepening it, tasting just as good as he smelled, which was one-hundred-percent male, and she thought she might die of the pleasure of it. This was what she'd needed tonight, and she'd been right to come and get it, to do something for herself, with a man she both yearned for and was beginning to trust.

This, with him, was right, and she felt her loneliness ease. But it wasn't all about her loneliness. She'd been alone a good long time and she'd never sought to ease it before.

It was Jason. He was different, and he enthralled her. She knew it was crazy, and far too soon, but so much about him made her forget to hold back. He was physical yet tender. Smart, confident. His own man.

And in her, he saw something unique, something special, and when he looked at her with that knowledge in his eyes, she felt a little unique, a little special.

A little…his.

His pants joined hers on the floor, and then he pressed her back, until her legs bumped into his mattress. He followed her down, surrounding her body with his, gliding his hands up her back to hold her close, sliding a muscled leg between hers.

Between the sounds of the night coming in his opened window, the beautiful stars lighting their way, and the feel of his body rocking to hers, she started to come undone.

He was a stranger, really. Nothing about his body was familiar to her, and yet she felt as if she'd known him all her life. Her body certainly seemed to know him, arching, writhing beneath his skillful hands and even more talented mouth as he skimmed both over her body until she was panting, whimpering, poised on the very edge and shaking with it.

A stranger.

And yet not a stranger. Not at all. "Jason—"

"I know." He groaned when she touched him back, murmuring his encouragement, showing her with his hands over hers how to bring him pleasure.

His mouth came down, more hungrily this time, and that hunger was contagious. "Jason…now. Please now."

He'd buried his face in her neck, his breathing ragged, but he reared up, grabbing a condom from his nightstand, pressing her into the bed, gliding his hands down her thighs to hold them open while he slid into her.

Before him, she'd been lost. This entire night, with his hands and his mouth on her, she'd held that feeling at bay, and now, with him buried inside her to the hilt, she suddenly realized she wasn't lost at all, not in his arms. As he began to thrust into her, driving her higher and higher, taking her into a shattering climax and beyond, she discovered the truth.

In his arms, she was where she was meant to be—she was home.

It was as simple and terrifying as that.

SHE MUST HAVE DOZED because when her eyes fluttered open, full darkness had descended.

She was still in Jason's bed.

He had her snugged in tight to his body. Her face was pressed up against his bare chest, their legs entangled. His hands were roaming free, severely hampering her ability to remain sleepy.

"Again?" she whispered thickly, tilting her face to look into his.

"Oh, yeah," he breathed, and then they were rolling over his great big bed, until he had her back beneath him. Smiles fading, they stared into each other's eyes. He brushed her hair out of her face, stroked a finger down her throat, over her breasts.

She wrapped her arms around his neck and tried to press closer. He held back only to take her face in his hands and study her for a long moment before dipping his head to kiss her long and deep.

It was slower this time, and even hotter for it. He touched her with his eyes, his hands, his mouth, and when he finally entered her again, he took her to the point of release and beyond, and then before she could even begin to catch her breath, started again.

Everything they did to each other in that bed—the kisses, the touches, the entwining of bodies, everything—lifted her up and away from the woman she thought she was. If he hadn't been right alongside her, just as out of control, she wouldn't have been able to face him afterward, wouldn't have been able to smile and nod when he'd softly asked her to stay, wouldn't have been able to fall asleep in his arms with a sated, dreamy smile of hope on her face.

JASON WOKE UP as he always did. Slowly. He'd dreamed last night, dreamed about his book. Love was the answer for his hero, and the way to find his way home was to follow his heart. Too bad he didn't know how to write a romance.

Maybe he could try to figure it out in real life instead.

Follow his heart.

He reached out for the woman who'd made him feel that way, but he was the only one in the bed. He sat straight up. "Mel?"

No answer, and he craned his neck to the left to eye the floor where they'd dropped their clothes the night before. Only his. Not a good sign.

He craned his neck the other way to look into his bathroom. The door was open, the little room empty.

Leaping out of bed, he skidded to a halt in the doorway to the kitchen, but no hauntingly beautiful Melissa there, either. She'd ditched him.

Naked, out of sorts, he padded back to his bedroom and saw the note on his nightstand.

Jason,
I had to run, the clinic opens at eight. You were sleeping like…well, like a man who had a long night.

Here she'd drawn a picture of a smiley face, making him grin like an idiot.

See you later.
I hope.

Melissa

He read the note again, then plopped back onto his bed and studied the ceiling. She hadn't ditched him. She'd just gone to work.

She'd drawn a smiley face.

Slowly his smile faded.

He hadn't told her the truth. He'd made love to her without telling her the truth. Why had he done that?

Because she'd taken off her clothes. Because she'd kissed him, because...because nothing. No excuse was going to work here, and he knew it.

He pulled a pair of loose sweats over his hips and opened his laptop. At least his hero now had a clue.

He just wished he did, as well.

CHAPTER EIGHT

MELISSA PRACTICALLY SKIPPED into the clinic. She couldn't believe how good she felt, or the silly smile she knew was all over her face.

Leftover from last night, and what a night it'd been.

In Jason's arms, she'd glowed, she'd laughed, she'd cried. She'd felt alive. For so long she'd been on her own, and for so long, she had thought that's how it had to be. Without a lot of experience letting people in, without a lot of trusting, she'd convinced herself that was just the way.

Now she'd let this town in. She'd let Rose in, at least for a job.

And she'd let Jason in.

It felt good.

Curiously enough, the lights were already on in the clinic, as was the music. Rose sat behind the front desk in a bright green sundress today, with a matching visor and sparkly lipstick. She was click-ing away at the computer, the desk neat as a pin around her. Melissa had the sudden urge to both laugh and cry.

On Rose's shoulder sat a parrot that looked an awful lot like the parrot Jason had brought in, which come to think of it, she hadn't seen at his house.

It couldn't be the same one.

"Rose," the parrot squawked.

Rose laughed. "Rose, *hush.*"

It *was* the bird from Jason's visit. Melissa moved closer, noting in some distant recess of her mind, which was still reeling, that the floor had been cleaned, the countertop reorganized. Even the windows sparkled. "You and the bird are both named Rose?"

"Well, I had the name first, but she just kept calling herself Rose, from the moment I first got her a couple of years back. Hard to argue with a parrot. Honey, I have a stack of billings ready to go out. Do you want to look them over?"

"The parrot belongs to you?"

"Since the moment I walked into the shop where she was for sale, singing her little heart out to the elevator music playing there." Rose laughed in memory, and without looking up, pointed to the printer, which was spitting out paperwork. "Now I know you don't think you need my help, but I intend to make myself so useful you can't turn me away. I want to do this, Melissa, please let me do this—''

''I thought the bird was Jason's. He said it was his.''

Rose went still, her finger in the air pointing toward the printer, which fell silent suddenly.

The entire world went silent.

''Rose,'' squawked the parrot, and bobbed her head to some beat only she could hear.

Or maybe she was rocking to Melissa's heartbeat, which was roaring in her ears. ''You live on his street,'' she said to Rose. ''I noticed that last night when I went to his house. You live only a few houses away.''

''Melissa—''

''Do you by any chance own a cat named Bob and a dog named Bear?''

''Well, I—''

''Or a potbellied pig named Miss Piggy?''

''Uh—''

''Do you?''

Rose dropped her hand to her side. Looked away. ''I knew it would come to this, I just couldn't help myself.''

Melissa sat in one of the patient waiting chairs, mostly because her legs had gone weak, but also because she'd just realized something else.

Her natural high on life was gone. Crash and burn.

Back to normal.

"Honey." Rose came around the front desk, crossing the floor in her fancy little sandals with a natural grace and elegance Mel had never achieved. "I was going crazy. You wouldn't let me in, I had to find a way in."

"So you bribed a guy to make me—" She couldn't even say it out loud. Her mother had bribed a guy to make her fall for him, sneaking past her defenses, opening her heart, ripping it in two.

And it had worked.

"I can see what you're thinking, and stop it. Stop it right now. It's not true, any of it." Rose kneeled before Melissa and took her hands in her own two frozen ones. Pale, eyes suspiciously damp, she squeezed until Melissa looked at her. "I didn't mean to hurt you, not now, not twenty-eight years ago, and not in any of the time in between."

"Let's stick with the now."

"Okay." Rose pinched the bridge of her nose. "No, wait. Not okay." She took a deep breath. "I was eighteen when you were born. Old enough, yes, but—"

"Rose—"

"You're going to hear this, Melissa. I'm sorry, but you have to."

"No, I don't. I—"

"I was in an abusive relationship."

Mel let out a breath and stared at Rose as conflicting emotions swamped her. Fear for Rose, empathy…compassion. "My…father?"

"Yes. I was afraid for you," her mother said quietly. "So afraid. My parents…they didn't approve of me, of you, they didn't understand. When they found out I was pregnant, all they wanted me to do was…fix it." Her eyes went fierce, and as if thrown back to that time, she put a hand over her belly in a protective gesture that tore at Melissa. "I refused, and I kept you as long as I could, but…"

But by the time Melissa had been one year old, it'd been too much. Mel closed her eyes. "I didn't know." She opened her eyes now and let out a helpless sound. "I'm sorry for what you went through."

"I don't want your pity, I want you to let me into your life."

Melissa rubbed her temples. "I need to think."

"You can do that, but just understand something for the here and now. I wanted to find out about you. I wanted to know if you were happy, if you were lonely. I wanted to know if you could find it in your heart to ever want me in your life. But you wouldn't open up, and yes, I thought maybe Jason could help me somehow. I admit it was a pathetic attempt, a desperate attempt, and quite stupid in hindsight.''

''I feel really stupid.''

''Oh, honey, no.'' Rose stood up and wrapped her arms around Melissa. ''I was so frantic that poor Jason didn't have a choice but to help me.''

''He helped you.'' Calmly as she could, she untangled herself from Rose. It was all sinking in. Jason had been helping Rose the whole time, including when she—

Seduced him.

That one hurt the most. He'd just been warming her up for Rose, and she'd slept with him.

''Melissa, please,'' Rose said urgently. ''Listen to me. Whatever's going on in that head of yours, don't blame Jason.''

But she did. It was easier than admitting she'd been fooled, lulled into a trust that had never existed. ''I blame all of us.''

Rose nodded, misery pouring out of her. ''I'd like to say I wouldn't do it again, but I'm still so desperate I probably would. Oh Melissa, I just wanted a small, little piece of your world, just a small piece. Hell, I'd even take a crumb.''

The door to the clinic opened and a baby goat ambled in, followed by Mrs. Dot, who was at least eighty years old and the town librarian. ''Dr. Anders, I have a goat emergency," she said. "Sweetie Pie is eating all my flowers."

How this was a medical emergency, Melissa didn't have a clue. "Mrs. Dot," she said, managing to sound completely normal by sheer will. "I need a few minutes before I open."

"No problem." The elderly woman sat in a chair a few feet away, folded her hands in her lap and smiled. "I have a few minutes."

Sweetie Pie meandered over to the retail shelves across the room and started to eat the display poster for feline vitamins.

The door opened again, in came Walter McKnight, the owner of the Serendipity Café and also the mayor of Martis Hills. In his arms was his cat Jezebel, who happened to be the fattest cat Melissa had ever seen. "I think she blew her diet, Doc," he said with a sigh, and sat next to Mrs. Dot. "You know I can repair just about anything, but…" With a helpless shrug, he settled in for the long haul.

Mel turned back to Rose. "I think you should leave. We can't fix this, not right now."

"You're going to have a very full house. I really think I should stay and help—" Rose's voice fell away at the look on Melissa's face.

"Ah, now, Doc," Walter said. "I'm sure whatever's broken can be taken care of. What happened, did she jam your printer? Because I can fix it."

Melissa rubbed her temples. "That's not quite it, but thanks."

"Did she get here late?" Mrs. Dot frowned. "The traffic out there is a son of a bitch this morning, isn't it. There's two cows on the highway, causing all sorts of havoc. Cut a gal some slack, Dr. Anders."

Melissa glanced at Rose. Her eyes were still just a little wet but damn if that wasn't a smile tugging at the corner of her mouth. When she saw Melissa looking at her, she lifted her hands and shook her head. "I'm sorry. It's this place—it's so beautiful, isn't it?"

"Rose—"

"Please let me stay."

"If you fire her," Walter said. "You'll up the unemployment rate in town back to five percent. I'm trying to get reelected, you know."

Mrs. Dot patted him on the hand. "You have my vote, Walter. Oh, let her stay, Dr. Anders. A gal's got to have work."

"Yes," Rose whispered. "Let me stay. I promise to never, ever, mess up again."

But that wasn't a promise she could keep, Melissa thought miserably. She just wanted to crawl back into bed and wallow in this, if only for a little while. She wanted to be alone.

She was used to being alone.

She was good at being alone.

At least she had been, until she'd come here.

Then the clinic door opened again, and everything within her went still as stone when Jason walked in the door. He took one glance at her and Rose, at the looks on their faces, and closed his eyes for a long moment. When he opened them, Melissa saw regret in his eyes.

If she'd held out any hope at all that this was somehow one big mistake, it faded away right then.

"Hey, Jas." Walter pumped his hand.

"Jason Lawrence," said Mrs. Dot very sternly.

"I don't have any overdue books," Jason said, lifting his hands. "I swear."

Mrs. Dot smiled. "Of course you don't, you're such a nice young man. I just wanted to say stand in line—the good doctor is booked."

Jason let out a little breath and nodded. "I'd like to, Mrs. Dot, but I really have to speak to Melissa now."

"But I got here first." She smiled sweetly.

"Yes, I know." Jason looked at Melissa, and she tried to turn away, honest to God, she did. She wanted to be furious but somehow the hurt kept getting in the way.

"You see, Mrs. Dot, if I don't talk to Melissa right now," he said quietly, still holding her gaze,

242

THE ROAD HOME

"things are going to go very badly for me. So I'm going to ask you to let me go first."

Mrs. Dot took a stubborn stance. "Let's hear a really good reason for this, boy."

"Yes, let's," Walter said.

Both looked at Jason expectantly.

Jason turned to Melissa, and she couldn't help it, she gave him a brow raise and nothing else. He was on his own.

So on his damn own.

"You don't even have an animal with you," Walter noted.

"Nope," Mrs. Dot agreed. "Not an animal in sight."

Rose bit her lip. "Well—"

"Don't you dare help him," Melissa broke her silence to say.

Rose closed her mouth.

"I think we should talk in private," Jason said to her in a low voice.

No. Talking in private would allow him to sweet-talk her, maybe even touch her, and she couldn't let that happen because clearly she had no judgment when he did.

What she needed was simple. Him to go.

Rose to go.

Scratch that. She needed to go. The timing was perfect. She'd seen a vet clinic for sale in the trade papers, located in Los Angeles. She'd have to double her current debt, but she'd do whatever it took to get out of Martis Hills. She could lose herself in the crowds of snooty cats and pedigreed dogs and never treat another animal of Rose's again. She could convince herself that she was happy there.

Probably.

"Still waiting for your reason to cut in line," Walter said to Jason.

Jason never took his eyes off Mel. "Dr. Anders is under the mistaken impression I've lied to her."

Walter shook his head. "Women hate that. So did you? Lie?"

"Only by omission."

Mrs. Dot tsked.

Rose bit her lip again.

And Jason, clearly realizing he was on the losing end of a jury, let out a disparaging sound and walked close. Too close. Mel couldn't see anything or anyone but him.

Rose quickly rose to her feet, too, and Melissa knew a foreboding.

Her mother and Jason were going to gang up on her together, and God help her, she couldn't take it. She'd underestimated the blood tie she had with Rose and what Rose's story would do to her anger, which was dissolve it.

And she'd underestimated the deeper soul mate tie she'd started to develop with Jason.

Because just them looking at her with their hearts in their eyes made her burn. Before she could make her escape, Rose gently took her hand in a grip of steel, and then Jason's, and led them to patient room one. "This is all my fault," she said. "And somehow I'm going to fix it."

"Hey," Mrs. Dot called out. "I didn't hear a good reason from Jason to cut in line—"

Rose shut the door on Mrs. Dot. And in fact, on Rose as well.

Leaving Mel alone with Jason.

CHAPTER NINE

JASON DREW in a deep breath, scrubbed his hands over his face and then looked at Melissa. How the hell to fix this?

"Rose said she used you to get me in her life," Mel said, cold and distant, arms crossed. She stood right in front of him, and yet she might well have been a thousand miles away.

His fault, his own damn fault.

"She wanted me to be sure not to blame you."

"But you do."

"I'm pretty sure I do, yes."

She looked relatively calm, for a woman who should be furious. Calm, and scarily removed. "You've already decided we're not worth the trouble, is that it?" he asked.

"Oh, you were definitely worth the trouble." Turning her back on him, she walked around the patient table, putting the long piece of steel between them. "Look, I'm going to be blunt. I'm too busy today for this."

"So you'd rather talk tomorrow?"

"Well—"

"Don't do this, Melissa." He wanted to go around the table and get her, but she already had one hand on the handle of the second door, the one that led to the back of her clinic. She would have no problem locking him out, just as she'd clearly already done with her heart. "I wanted to tell you."

"You wanted to help Rose."

"Yes, that, too. Rose screwed up, she made some bad choices, and she's paid the price of that by not having her daughter in her life. She wants to fix that."

"Maybe I didn't want it fixed."

"Why? Because being alone is easier? Come on, Melissa, you don't want to be alone, either, or you wouldn't have come here. I just wanted to help."

"Oh, you helped," she said with only a dab of sarcasm.

He studied her bowed face, her crossed arms, her stiff shoulders. Oh yeah, she was good and hurt. He hated that, because all he'd wanted to do was make it right for her and Rose. The last thing he'd ever wanted was to hurt her. "To be honest, I hadn't really thought of you with your own reasons and emotions for not wanting Rose in, not until after we started to get to know each other."

"And yet you came again to the clinic with another animal. And then again. We ate together, we walked together, we—" She closed her mouth tight and shook her head. "I hate being your...your *cause*."

He caught her just as she opened the door. Hands on her arms, he pulled her in close, where he could feel her body heat, could feel her shaking. Or maybe that was him. "My...*cause?* Is that what you think you were?"

"Yes. For Rose."

His voice was hoarse. "No. Mel—"

"Last night—who was that for, Jason?"

"My God, are you kidding? Melissa, from the moment I first laid eyes on you, it was all for me. Your smile, your voice, your eyes, everything...you turn me completely upside down."

Her eyes filled, and he cupped her face. "Yes, maybe it started out about Rose, but I promise you, it became something else very quickly." He caught one of her tears on his thumb, his chest tightening. "Melissa, I love you."

She put her hand over his mouth. "Please." She swallowed hard. "If you care about me at all, I want to be alone right now. I want to think."

What could he say? He had to give her time— he knew her enough to understand that. So when she left the patient room, shutting the door, leaving him alone in the very room they'd first spoken, he let her go.

He had to, and he had no one to blame but himself.

STARTING BEFORE DAWN the next morning, Melissa drove the four hours south until palm trees ruled and the heat suffocated. Until traffic was the norm. She got out of her car and looked at the For Sale sign. The vet clinic was on a very busy street in Burbank, just outside of Los Angeles, and the price was astronomical.

But she'd spoken to the current owner, who was willing to work with her on terms. He just wanted to retire to Florida. She'd figured she could speak to a few of her fellow veterinarian friends about a possible partnership so she wouldn't have to do this alone, because suddenly, or maybe not so suddenly, alone didn't seem nearly as freeing as it once had.

At least here she'd be far away from her past, far from Rose and...and her extremely welcome help in the office, not to mention her kindness, and the way she had of making Melissa feel...loved.

Even when she thought she didn't want it.

Her throat burned but she blinked quickly. She hadn't cried in years and years, and yet in recent days she'd turned into such a wimp. Well, she was over that, over letting it all get to her.

Here, she wouldn't have to deal with Jason and the way he had of making her feel as if she was the only woman on the planet. He made her feel special, smart…sexy; he made her brain happy and made her body hum in anticipation.

Yep, boy was she glad that was over.

Damn it. A shaky sigh escape her, while all around her trucks and cars zoomed by, honking and jockeying for superior position on the road. Pedestrians walked past her, jostling her a little in their hurry to get to wherever they were going.

No one in Martis Hills was ever in a hurry.

She got back into her car. Twice she tried to talk herself out of it, but it all just made sense. She pulled out her cell phone and called Dr. Myers in Phoenix, who was thrilled to hear from her.

"I hear you're doing wonderfully in Martis Hills," he said.

"Better now, thank you. Dr. Myers, I no longer want to lease the clinic. I want to buy it."

"Ah." He sounded pleased. "You're ready for roots."

"Yes," she whispered, liking the sound of that. Roots.

THE WAY HOME TOOK six hours instead of four, thanks to a jackknifed big rig just outside of Bakersfield. And a stop for a Big Mac.

She loved comfort food.

By the time she pulled back into Martis Hills, the sun had set. There was no traffic in town, no rude pedestrians ruling the streets. Her clinic looked dark and locked, just as she'd left it.

Heading past it, for the outskirts of town where Jason lived, she pulled into his driveway and walked up the porch where she'd only a few nights ago seduced him into taking her to his bed.

The power of that moment had been incredible, and her heart ached. She wanted more of that.

But he wasn't home. His truck was gone, his house dark.

Deflated, she drove by Rose's. Stopped. Got out of her car.

Melissa watched Rose open her front door and stand on the porch, to see who'd driven up. She then let out a gasp of surprise, and ran down the steps to meet her.

She came to a stop just before Melissa, clearly fighting the urge to toss her arms around her.

Melissa had done that to the two of them. She'd pushed Rose away. She'd pushed everyone away, just pushed and pushed until they didn't know what to do with her or how to treat her.

No more. She wanted this, she wanted these people in her life. So she smiled, and the knot in her chest loosened. "I went to Los Angeles to see a vet clinic that's up for sale. I figured I belonged there."

Rose clasped her fingers together, her smile fading. "I see. And did you? Belong there?"

"Once upon a time, I did, very much."

"And now?"

"Now I belong where my heart leads me. And...and it's led me here. I was drawn here, drawn by being born here...by the fact I knew you'd come back here. I didn't understand the need then, but I think I do now. Being here, allowing people in, you for example... I think that's what I was looking for without even knowing it."

Rose's eyes filled. "So...you've forgiven then?"

At the hitch in Rose's breath, her own throat went even tighter. She reached out for her mother's hands. "My past made me, it molded me. My past is a part of who I am. But I've forgiven, if you'll forgive me for taking so long to listen to your story."

"Oh, honey." She threw her arms around Melissa's neck. "There's nothing to forgive." Her eyes wet, she cupped her daughter's face. "From right this very minute we're starting over."

They hugged for a long moment before Rose pulled free. "What about Jason? I know you feel he betrayed you, but—"

"He's not home."

Rose tried to look indifferent, but it was clear this was not news to her.

Mel eyed her. "What are you up to now?"

"Well...in the name of a new start and all, I'll confess. Mr. Myers called me. Told me you were looking into buying his place."

"You're kidding. He *called* you?"

"Right, he shouldn't have done that, but honey, this is Martis Hills. People talk. Besides, he wasn't trying to gossip, he wanted me to give you money to help. He's worried you'll strap yourself, and he really cares about you and that clinic."

"If he's so worried, tell him to lower his price."

Rose smiled. "I got him to do just that, so you're welcome."

Melissa's head was spinning. "And what does all this have to do with Jason not being home?"

"Well..." Rose had guilt all over her. "I might have told him the good news, that you were coming back. I might have told him to make the most of my little tip because I wasn't going to ever interfere again.''

''After this time, you mean?'' Melissa had to laugh, but hugged her mother again when Rose stood there looking miserable. ''It's okay. I think I just might get used to a mother who cares so much she meddles in my life.'' With one last hug, Melissa headed toward her car again.

''Honey? Where are you off to?''

Mel smiled. ''The rest of my life.''

CHAPTER TEN

MEL FOUND JASON waiting on her porch, sitting on the top step, with a chocolate-brown Lab puppy asleep in his lap. "Hey," she said, feeling all soft and mushy at just the sight of him.

"Hey, yourself." Despite the clear tension in his long, rangy, beautiful body, his smile was slow and lazy and just for her.

"What are you doing here?"

"Waiting for you." Picking up the puppy and tucking it against his chest, he rose. "I've been waiting for you all my life, Mel."

"Jason—"

"No, let me say this. I have to say this. Ever since my accident I've taken a what-the-hell attitude about life. Casual. Cavalier, even. Mostly because I knew exactly how short life could be, but also because nothing was worth stressing over if I could die any second."

"Oh, Jason. I understand. I—"

"I was wrong, Melissa. I took it all wrong, and everything in my life, including my writing, suffered. Hell, I couldn't even figure out that my hero's problem was *my* problem. *I* couldn't find my way home, and that didn't make any sense because I was living in a house I'd known all my life. But it wasn't about the damn house, it was about *me,* and what I did with my heart. Yeah, life's short, but I need to live it, I need to live it every single day, even if it means getting hurt. Are you following me?"

"Yes. I agree with you. I…I went to Los Angeles to get the most out of my life."

He looked grim. And, if she wasn't mistaken, just a little vulnerable. "Did you find what you were looking for?"

She nodded, and his body tensed even further, but he let out a long breath and a smile that didn't quite meet his eyes. "I'm glad," he said, then shook his head. "No, scratch that, I'm not glad, I'm—"

She put her fingers over his mouth, and stepped closer so that their bodies brushed together. The puppy mewled a little but stayed asleep. "I found that I don't belong there anymore," she said. "I belong here. With Rose trying to boss me around, with crazy patients coming in and out of my clinic, and…"

He tugged her hand loose from his mouth but kept her fingers tight in his. "And…?"

"And you." She cupped his lean jaw and kissed him. Kissed both sides of his mouth before pulling back. "I belong here with the man who wanted me so badly he kept coming in with animals just to see me."

He winced. "I'm so sorry—"

She kissed him. "I know," she whispered against his mouth. "I get it now. You care. You all care. And God help me, but I care back. I missed you when I was gone, even though it was only one day. I missed you so much. And I came to understand something, Jason. I came to understand what I've been missing all these years."

"Yeah? What's that?"

"Love."

With his one available hand, he squeezed her so close the puppy mewled again and lifted its sleepy head.

"She's adorable," Melissa whispered. "Another of Rose's?"

"No." He tipped her chin up to see into her eyes. "Back to that love thing. Are you—"

"Yes." She swallowed hard. "I'm saying that I've fallen in love with you. I know it's silly, it's such a short time, but I'm figuring we have lots more time to figure it all out."

"Yeah." He looked down. "I came here with a shameless bribe thinking I'd have to talk you into letting me see you. I said it before, and I meant it. I love you, Mel.''

Her eyes filled. ''Oh, Jason.'' They kissed, sweet at first, but quickly heat and need jockeyed for position, until the puppy let out a surprisingly loud bark for such a little thing, right in their faces.

Jason grinned. ''Melissa, meet your bribe. Sissy.''

''*Sissy?*''

The little puppy blinked and yawned wide, her eyes a dark, dark brown and filled with adoration.

''She's a big sissy. She cried all last night. Please say you'll take her.'' He kissed her again. ''I think a vet should have her very own pet, don't you?''

She'd never had a pet before, never. She'd never had time, she'd never had space, she'd never—

She'd never wanted to open her heart. She took Sissy into her arms and melted when the puppy set her head on her chest and sighed as if she'd found home.

They'd all found home.

UPSTAIRS, DOWNSTAIRS
Alison Kent

To my daughters, Megan and Holly.
For living their own lives and allowing me to live mine.
I love you both.
Smoochies.

CHAPTER ONE

AVERY RICE TURNED onto the street where she lived, just in time to see her mother's white Toyota Camry back out of their shared driveway and head away from the three-story Victorian.

So much for their weekly ritual of coffee and croissants. And for the second weekend in a row, no less. Her mother was taking this business of moving on with her life too far. Especially as her plans obviously included leaving her daughter behind.

They'd shared Saturday-morning coffee and croissants—the croissants fresh from Avery's bakery—since the death of Avery's father five years before. For the past month, though, Suzannah Rice had been busy doing her own thing to the exclusion of the shared things that had been a big part of both of their lives for so long.

Avery wasn't complaining, though a little voice whispering in her ear argued otherwise before going on to tell her to get over it already. She readily admitted her quasi-isolation and homebody tendencies were no one's fault but her own. But she'd found a great comfort in safety—especially after the near disaster she'd barely escaped when she had taken a risk years ago.

Another three houses and she bumped her pickup into the driveway. The driver's-side door was hit twice with a blast from the sprinkler dousing the front lawn—and spraying the front of the house, she realized. She'd have to use the back door into her mother's kitchen rather than the main entrance that directly accessed the staircase to her second-story apartment in the converted triplex.

Of course, doing that meant making her way down the long narrow driveway and around the overgrown SUV that belonged to her mother's third-floor tenant and the longtime bane of Avery's existence, David Marks. David, the know-it-all who was constantly riding her about still living at home with her mother when she didn't live at home with her mother at all. She only lived in the same house. Yes, it was the house she'd grown up in, but it was now very clearly a multitenant dwelling, which he should know since he lived here, too.

Wicker bread basket hooked over her elbow, Avery shut off the engine, climbed down from the truck and pocketed her keys. Slamming the door apparently drew David's attention—though what he was doing in her mother's kitchen, she didn't have a clue—because he was standing in the open doorway before she'd even climbed the first of the six back steps.

"Hey," he said, wiping his hands on a workman's knobby red rag and getting on her nerves by just standing there, wiping, silent now, his jeans slung way too low and his chambray shirt hanging open as if he'd just slipped it on. "What's up?"

"Just me and the breakfast trying to stay dry." She walked up one step, two, three.

"You just missed your mother."

"So I saw." Four steps. Five. She stopped there, leaving the sixth step between them because he hadn't moved except to tuck the red rag into his front pocket. He'd been so much easier to take when she'd led cheers and he'd run around the Tatem, Texas, football-field sidelines wearing their high school mascot's tornado costume.

A tornado she'd always thought looked more like an upside-down soft-serve cone than a threatening storm—even if later, she admitted, the threat had been real. For all she knew, it still was. He made her nervous—another admission she couldn't afford not to make, just as she couldn't afford not to keep her wits about her. Their history left her less than certain where she stood with him today.

He'd been just as maddening fifteen years ago as he was now, but from age eight to eighteen he'd been nothing but a muddle of arms and legs and freckles who'd bugged the crap out of her and the rest of her friends with his stupid jokes and lame attempts to get her attention.

Now he was all broad chest and six-pack abs, with a disheveled head of thick, sandy-brown hair, fans of crow's-feet at the corners of his eyes, a short sexy goatee, and a really fine backside that...

"What are you doing?" she asked, pulling the basket of croissants away from his greedy, groping fingers.

"Looking for breakfast. I'm wasting away to nothing in here." He wiggled both brows in a suggestive way that drove her nuts. "And you know how I feel about your buns."

Oh, good grief. "You have way too much meat on your bones to be starving," she said, blushing as his eyes grew all sleepy looking when she knew he wasn't the least bit tired. She pushed past him into the kitchen that would've been classified as sixties retro if it hadn't been the original decor. With all the changes her mother was making these days, Avery wouldn't be surprised to find a kitchen makeover next on the list.

Why in the world Suzannah had ever rented the top-floor apartment to David was a bone of contention Avery hadn't quit gnawing. Her mother claimed that David, now Suzannah's colleague on the faculty at Tatem High, deserved to feel at home, returning as he had to West Texas, to the town he'd left on the heels of scandal, to teach the high school's one and only computer science class.

Avery agreed in theory. She couldn't imagine a better mentor for the high school's whiz kids than Tatem's team mascot-cum-resident geek. But in practice…no. David did not deserve to feel at home when she was at the root of that old scandal and when the home in question was hers. Or at least above hers.

And when getting to his home meant sharing the same staircase and having to pass each other between the first and second floors. A staircase that really was much too narrow for a man as broad as David Marks.

He shut the kitchen door behind her, and a shiver of intuitive apprehension told her that walking through her mother's living room of roses and mahogany and chintz and up the stairs to her own apartment before either of them said another word would be the smartest thing she could do. He made her uneasy in ways she hadn't taken time to define since he'd moved in ten months ago, and she feared that lapse would prove to be her undoing.

Then he flipped the dead bolt, locking the back door. She lifted one brow in question and tried to breezily add, "That's really not necessary, you know."

He shrugged, obviously not sharing her opinion. She further pled her case. "There hasn't been an incident of breaking and entering in Tatem since Buck Ester climbed the trellis to propose and crashed through Yvette Lapp's bedroom window."

Long lashes sweeping slowly down then back up, David shrugged and headed toward her. "Better safe than sorry, I always say."

See? This was why she didn't like having him here. He said things like that to make her crazy. Now she wanted to ask about his years away but couldn't. Or wouldn't. She'd promised her mother that she wouldn't bring up the past that had driven David away from Tatem in the first place and now, fifteen years later, had brought him back.

She set the bread basket on the white-and-gold-flecked Formica top of her mother's old aluminum-legged kitchen table. David dropped to his back on the floor and wormed the upper half of his body up into the cabinet beneath the kitchen sink.

"What are you doing here anyway?" she asked, though the answer was fairly obvious, and her question was actually more a case of wondering why.

"I ran into your mother this morning when I went out for the paper." David's voice was muffled and punctuated with the sound of metal tools on metal pipes. "She was watering the flower beds and asked if I could take a look at her clog."

"Weird."

"What?"

"She hasn't said a word about a plumbing problem."

The banging and grunting stopped, and David blew out a long sigh. "Maybe she thought she could handle it."

"It's just that usually Buck Ester takes care of her home repairs. I would've called and scheduled him for this morning if I'd known she needed him to stop by."

"Your mom's a smart cookie, Avery." David shifted on his hip, and drew up one knee. His jeans stretched tight in all the right places, hung loose in all the right others. "Give her some credit here for taking care of her own business. Shouldn't be that hard for you to do. You know as well as I do that she's more than capable."

"True." Avery hardly needed this man's reminder of her mother's growing independent streak. "Not that you know her *that* well."

"She taught me English for most of four years. And now we're on the same faculty." Another grunt and David went back to his banging.

"She taught four years of English to everyone at Tatem High."

"And I've lived and worked with her now for ten months."

"You haven't lived *with* her. You've rented living space *from* her." She wasn't sure why the distinction mattered, but it did. Especially with the way David seemed to be making himself at home.

"Believe what you want, Avery."

The aluminum legs of her chair scraped the linoleum like nails on a chalkboard as she pulled it out to sit. "What's that supposed to mean?"

David grumbled beneath his breath. "Whatever you want it to mean. Obviously you're the expert here on your mother." He paused, grew still, as if making sure he had her full attention before he added, "Bringing breakfast when she's not even here and all that."

And why wasn't she here? Surely Suzannah had done no more than make a run to the grocery for sugar, butter or cream. Avery noted the gurgle and steam from the coffeemaker and the white ceramic mug sitting on the countertop. Oh, but she needed coffee. "So…she asked you to look at her sink, then just left you here?"

Again with the grumbling and grunting and banging—each one louder than the last. "Yeah. But she locked up her jewelry and extra cash first."

"That's not what I meant." And it wasn't, she thought, cringing. It was just that she'd had trouble saying anything around David and making her meaning clear for ten months now.

No, that wasn't true.

Since football season of their senior year at Tatem High and that night beneath the bleachers neither of them had spoken of since, she'd been unable to say anything to him without wondering what he expected of her...if he expected anything at all.

Not knowing bothered her. It bothered her a lot. "I just thought she might've mentioned where she was going. Or maybe when she'd be back?"

"Nope. Not a word."

Avery sighed. She really felt out of sorts here. Over the past five years, she'd become quite used to her routine. A routine filled with work, church and time spent with her mother. A routine she told herself was part of a very good and comfortable life, one that made her happy. She sighed again.

"Coffee's done. Would you like me to pour you a cup?" she asked, out of her chair now and on her way for one of her own. Years of observing her mother at work in Suzannah's circle of friends had taught Avery that food and drink were the great equalizers when it came to discomfiting situations.

And no one had ever unbalanced Avery Rice more than David Marks. She had no explanation except chemistry, and being a baker, not a chemist, limited her knowledge of chemical reactions to that of yeast.

He squirreled around and backed out from under the sink, staring up at her with lazy, sleepy eyes that sent her stomach tumbling. He gave her a wink and a grin and nodded. "I'd kill to have you pour me a cup," he said, and she turned away before her stomach fell completely to her feet.

Behind her, he got up. She sensed rather than saw his movements as he washed his hands and rebuttoned his shirt, and she had to admit relief. It was impossible to think of him as the soft-serve tornado mascot when his body brought to mind all things...hard.

Chair legs squeaked as David sat, and she found creamer, sweetener and sugar to add to the tray bearing the two full mugs. She turned in time to see him lift the corner of the white linen napkin covering the bread basket and decided they might as well eat while the croissants were hot.

She turned to the refrigerator for the ever-present bowl of butter balls and a jar of her mother's homemade peach jam, desperately thankful for the distraction and knowing she would only be able to get through this shared breakfast by avoiding his eyes.

David was pouring cream in his coffee when she returned to her chair. "You're a good woman, Avery Rice. No matter how many times in the past I may have said otherwise.''

''The croissants won't be good when they're cold,'' she said, refusing to rise to his bait. ''That's all.''

''Right,'' he said, splitting a roll with his hands then stabbing a butter ball with the end of his knife. ''Tell yourself that if it makes it easier.''

''Makes what easier?'' she asked, slipping a knife through the layers of her croissant.

He lifted a brow as if the answer and not steam from her coffee rose to heat her face. ''The truth.''

''And what truth might that be?'' she asked, because she wasn't going to allow him to win too easily.

He sat back, sighed, his hands at his sides holding to the chair's aluminum tubing. ''Why don't you trust me alone in your mother's house?''

Avery returned her croissant to her plate and twisted her hands into the napkin in her lap. She didn't like her mother leaving him alone, but for none of the reasons he was probably thinking.

The simple explanation was that he'd surprised her, and she hadn't had time to think, to process the scope of the situation. She realized that her mother would never have gone out had trust been an issue.

The more complicated version was that what she

was feeling was a long-dormant uncertainty about her history with David finally rising to the surface.

She glanced around the kitchen that had changed so little from her childhood and not at all since her father's passing. It was the idea of David in this space that had always been her refuge causing her now to act out.

"I do trust you. I apologize for leading you to believe otherwise." She breathed deeply. "It was just strange…and a bit…difficult to understand you being here."

David leaned forward again, his forearms on the edge of the table, his hands held in loose fists. He'd buttoned his shirt wrong, she noticed, as her gaze slid away from his to the relative safety of his now-covered chest. "Avery?"

She looked back up, her heart wedged tightly at the base of her throat. It was a wonder she was able to speak. "Yes?"

"We're going to have to talk about it."

Speaking was nothing; swallowing was the problem now. She reached for her coffee mug anyway. "Talk about what?"

David's eyes twinkled and flashed. The corners of his mouth wrapped like parentheses around his wide grin. "About the fact that I saved your life. And that you ruined mine."

CHAPTER TWO

AVERY'S COFFEE SLOSHED from her mug to the table when she slammed it down. "You did not save my life."

Yeah, she was probably right, David admitted, though he did take note that she hadn't refuted his comment that she'd ruined his. She hadn't, of course, which caused him to wonder why she didn't stomp his claim to the ground. Or if this was another demonstration of her unhealthy tendency to hold too tightly to the past.

Still, they'd been circling this itchy thing between them now for ten months—if not for the fifteen years since the incident beneath the bleachers—and it was time to put it to bed.

"Maybe, maybe not." He spread the melted butter on his croissant and spooned up a serving of peach jam. "I seem to remember a few months later at the Dairy Queen you telling me that I had."

Avery pinched off first one end of her croissant then the other, no doubt imagining the bread to be his neck. "I was frightened the night it happened, yes. Especially knowing what Johnny was capable of. But he wouldn't have hurt me. I overreacted.''

David begged to differ; he'd seen the look in Johnny's eyes when he'd pulled him off Avery and thrown him to the ground. "Another matter of opinion,'' David offered with a shrug.

She paused, swallowed; her eyes darted to his, then away when he dared to hold her gaze. "You weren't there for the whole thing.''

David huffed with more bitterness than he'd intended. He'd been there for way too much. "Yeah. I just saw the part where good ol' Johnny Boyd ripped open the top of your cheerleading uniform.''

Avery sat back. Slowly she drew her hand along her collarbone, her fingers slipping beneath the V neckline of her dusky-blue sleeveless tunic. Her voice barely reached a whisper when she said, "He didn't mean to hurt me.''

God, but she was wrong. So very wrong. Johnny Boyd had been all about getting into her pants whether she consented or not. Shoving half his croissant into his mouth kept David from demanding Avery admit her mistake.

Not that he thought she'd defend her position if he did. He was surprised she was talking at all, because even then, that night, all those years ago, she'd turned and run without saying a word.

Not even a halfhearted thanks.

He hadn't wanted her thanks. He'd wanted her to see, to really *see*, who he was, how he felt about her. How he'd always felt about her. But like everyone around her, all she'd seen was what he looked like, the clothes he wore, the way his mouth wouldn't shut the hell up.

Stupid. He'd been such a stupid freak to think she would pay him any attention when he'd been the school geek and she'd been queen of the prom. She sure as hell hadn't wanted anything to do with him or the attention he'd received *after* the fight with Johnny Boyd beneath the bleachers.

He'd returned to school at the end of his suspension as the bad boy, the only kid in any of the four classes who'd taken on Johnny and won. It was the peer respect he'd always wanted, had foolishly wished his 4.0 grade average would earn.

But no. That sort of awe only came with pounding another kid's head to a near pulp.

Hell, he was still a stupid freak even now for thinking back to a time that was over and done with and had no bearing on who the both of them were today. Except he wasn't so sure of that truth. Which meant he had no business bad-mouthing Avery for not letting that night go.

It was that night beneath the bleachers and the look in Avery's eyes, in fact, that had brought him back into her life. He'd moved on since high school, had graduated university with honors. He was more than content with his circumstances, pleased by the enthusiasm of his students, fortunate to be part of a dedicated teaching staff.

No, he'd never planned to end up in Tatem. But neither had he ever been able to get Avery's wounded-animal expression out of his mind. He'd wondered for years what that night had done to her, knowing exactly how it had changed him, turned him from freak to punk.

So when she reached a tentative hand across the table and wrapped her fingers over his, he didn't even question why his pulse decided to race. He looked up from her hand, from her fingers so pale and delicate and, yeah, so really, really strong, and into her big baby blues.

"Thank you, David. I don't think I ever said that." One side of her mouth turned up. "I thought it." She gave a quiet laugh. "I've thought it now for fifteen years." Finally her expression grew solemn. "You suffered for my sins, and I never even expressed my gratitude."

Gratitude. Right. That was exactly what he wanted. He pulled his hand free and reached for his mug, scraping his chair around and squaring an ankle over a knee so he no longer faced her. And then he got back to eating his breakfast. Food he could deal with. Fixing clogged drains, simple stuff.

Not having Avery try to make nice when he wasn't in the mood for forgiveness.

And then she huffed.

Avery huffed and snorted. "Oh, now you don't want to talk about it, is that it? You want to rub my face in the fact that you rescued me, but the minute I offer you the thanks I should have given you years ago, you're done talking."

Here we go. "It's not about thanking me, Avery." He tried not to glare, and wasn't sure he'd succeeded. "It's about you always being so blind to people."

"Blind? Me? What are you talking about?"

As much as this was about how she'd never seen him for who he really was, it was more. About how she was unaware of her own fixation on the past. About how her own mother had moved on. "Johnny Boyd, for one."

"I've already admitted I made a mistake following him under the bleachers, all right? I kicked myself a thousand times over after that night." She threaded her fingers through the handle on her mug and held it tight. "What else do you want me to say?"

He looked at her then, unsure if her naiveté was real or if she was still deceiving herself all these years later. He thought for a moment. "Did you tell your parents what had happened?"

She had the grace to drop her gaze, her face coloring slightly as she shook her head. "They heard what everyone else heard."

"That we were suspended for fighting," he offered before she reminded him of all the other rumors that had taken off and raged like a rampant wildfire upon his and Johnny's return to school.

She nodded, used the tip of her knife to push around the torn ends of her croissant. "I thought if I stayed quiet, if I didn't tell anyone what Johnny had been trying to do, then he wouldn't—" she shrugged "—you know, make things bad for you when y'all came back to school."

He didn't want to talk about his return to school. He wanted to talk about her. The weariness, the sadness, hell, the guilt he saw in her expression now hit him harder than Johnny Boyd's fists had. Why couldn't she let it go?

He pictured her getting to her feet that night in what had felt like a movie set when he'd first walked up, a dark city underbelly ripe for breeding crime. The bright yellow top of her uniform gaped where it hung torn from the neckline to just above her waist, the flap of material exposing one breast covered in a plain-Jane bra.

He'd pictured her like that for years, dusting gravel from her bottom and the backs of her thighs, digging stubborn grit from the palms of her hands.

She wore little makeup then, but her mascara had run in dotted lines down her cheeks as she silently cried.

The fact that Johnny Boyd had six inches and sixty pounds on David hadn't deterred him a bit. He'd done his damnedest to keep the inevitable from happening.

And he had, surprising Johnny and suffering in the process, but gaining a world of brutal experience to replace his innocence lost. An innocence that had kept him believing he had a chance to win Avery's heart. Pathetic.

One heartbeat, two, three and David pushed out of his chair. He headed for the coffeemaker, realizing too late Avery had left the pot on the table. Hell, he didn't want another cup anyway. He only wanted the distraction and the distance.

"Avery, look. I need to finish up your mom's sink," he said, turning to find her standing there beside him, the coffeepot in her hand.

He didn't know what else to do so he held out his mug and she poured, setting the carafe on the coffeemaker while he made his way back to the table for sugar and cream and, hell, why not, another croissant.

Avery, however, stayed where she was, leaning against the countertop, crossing her arms over her chest. "It's not the end, David, and you know it as well as I do," she said softly. "We're stuck with this connection neither of us seems to want."

He poured cream into his coffee, added sugar, stalling as he weighed his response. Truth-or-dare time. Put up or shut up. She'd given him the perfect opening. And he'd be a damned fool not to take it.

He'd been a damned fool for this woman too long already.

"Answer me this, then. How come it's taken us ten months to have this conversation? We could've gotten this out of the way last summer, and you wouldn't have spent all this time avoiding me."

"Avoiding you?" Her eyes went wide. "You think I've been avoiding you?"

"I know you have." He shrugged, glad to see he'd struck a nerve. "I've seen you turn around on the staircase when I've been on my way up."

A pink flush dotted her cheeks. "That's because the staircase isn't designed for two people."

"Sure it is. We fit just fine," he said, thinking that the way they fit together would be a whole lot of fun to explore further.

"Maybe your idea of fine," she muttered, but not so low that he couldn't hear.

"It bothers you, then. When we're that close." She didn't say a word. She unscrewed the top to check the level of coffee in the carafe instead. "Avery?"

"No, David. It doesn't bother me." She hesitated; he waited. "It's just a personal-space issue."

"Uh-huh," was all he said, getting back to his breakfast and waiting for her to come around.

"Fine. Don't believe me." She huffed again.

"I don't." She may have hung around the Dairy Queen when he'd been working, but even then she'd kept her distance.

She'd been keeping her distance since she'd backed away and left the scrawny beanpole he was to face down the one kid in Tatem High's student body of seventy-five no one was ballsy enough to call down for being a thug.

She stewed for a long moment, finally coming back with, "Why?"

"Why don't I believe you?"

She nodded. "You have no reason not to."

"I don't?"

"No." She shook her head. Too vigorously. "It's a space issue, like I said. It's nothing personal at all."

And, at that, he laughed. He had to. His frustration was off the charts, and he was digging himself an early grave chasing this circle of a conversation into the ground.

So he laughed. Then he got up, pushing away from the table and to his feet. A button of his chambray shirt caught on the table's loose aluminum flashing and rolled across the floor to Avery's feet. To the toe of one sandal. To her nails painted a soft frosty blue. Blue. Her toenails were blue.

He bent. She bent. She picked up the button. He hesitated, then ran his thumb over the tips of her blue-painted toes. She caught her breath but didn't pull her foot away. He smiled to himself, straightened and stepped as close as he could, waiting for her to bolt as he invaded the very space she claimed to value so highly.

She didn't bolt. She remained exactly where she was. He could see the flutter of her straight blond hair where air from the vent above the kitchen sink blew down. He could see the half-moon shadows of her lashes above her cheeks. He could see the girl who'd been frightened all those years ago in the face of the woman frightened now.

The last thing he wanted to do was scare her, to make her nervous or uncomfortable. He only wanted some sort of peace so that passing on the staircase would be a normal course of daily affairs. One they both could live with.

Yeah. That was all he wanted. He lifted a hand and tucked loose strands of hair behind her ear, his hand lingering as he asked, "What are you afraid of, Avery?"

Her chin came up; her blue-eyed gaze met his undauntedly. He saw the things she wanted to say, watched them flash brightly then fade, the retreat into the safe harbor that he instinctively knew she'd been making for years.

"I'm not afraid," she said. "I'm…worried. About my mother. I assumed she made a quick trip to the market and would be home by now."

"I'm sure she's fine." And he was. Suzannah had looked like a million bucks, like she hadn't a care in the world but for her clogged sink. He knew the truth about what was going on with her, but he wasn't going to share it with her daughter per Suzannah's request. Her private life was hers to keep secret or to share in her own time.

"I know," Avery was saying. "It's just that she's always home on Saturday mornings. And anytime she plans to be out, she lets me know." And, as she said it, she continued to stare into his eyes.

David swore the room's heat descended from the ceiling and entered his pores. He drew his hand down the strand of hair he still held and moved his palm to her shoulder. He squeezed, his fingertips slipping beneath the edge of the shirt's armhole so that he grazed the strap of her bra.

Her tongue darted out to wet her lips, as if she knew his intent was to kiss her when even he hadn't yet made that decision. It was what he wanted. God, but it was what he wanted. Yet he hadn't quite figured how to slide into the crack between what she said with her eyes and what she told him with her mouth.

Right now, he was listening to her mouth. Not spoken words, but the dampness of her lower lip that appeared to quiver as he lowered his head. He moved his other hand to cup her neck, his thumb beneath her chin to lift her head. Her breath was warm where it brushed his cheek. Her mouth was even warmer when he settled his lips over hers.

He kissed her softly, sweetly, nothing but a light brush of contact when he could easily have taken more. For a moment she remained still, simply letting him have his way. Then he felt her hands move, and she settled them at his hips, beneath the loose tails of his shirt, hooking her fingers through his belt loops as if to keep him near.

Temptation slid the length of his body, fired by the tenderness of her shy movements, the hesitation of her response. He wanted to press, to push, to show her how much he wanted her, but he knew this wasn't the time or the place. He'd known her too many years to risk making a wrong move now, now that he had her this close.

In the seconds that followed, however, she turned him inside out, stepping fully into his body as her hands left his hips, her palms sliding up his bare rib cage and on around his back where she kneaded the strap of muscle running along his spine. He groaned; he couldn't help it, his body reacting to the sensuousness of her touch.

He deepened the kiss, moving his hand to her nape and holding her still as he urged her lips apart. She opened with no hint of indecision or uncertainty, allowing him the intimacy he sought and returning the same. The beat of his heart grew painfully hard.

The taste of her tongue, the show of her willingness, the sense that she shared his desire quickly became his undoing—or would have had their tryst not been interrupted suddenly by a sharp clearing of a throat and teasing "Ahem."

Avery jumped back, her mouth red, her eyes wide as she met her mother's humorously curious expression. David simply accepted the inevitable scrutiny as Suzannah's gaze moved from one to the other, her brows arched, the corners of her mouth lifting despite her obvious battle not to smile.

CHAPTER THREE

SUZANNAH RICE WAS fifty-eight years old, yet appeared young enough to be her daughter's contemporary.

Sitting next to her mother on the living room's rich burgundy-and-floral chintz sofa, Avery felt as if she were looking at one of her girlfriends rather than at a woman twenty-five years her senior.

Suzannah brought her cup of coffee to her mouth to blow across the steaming surface, her lips smooth with a light mauve gloss, her expressive eyes emphasized with no more than a dusting of taupe shadow.

Her brown hair was colored and highlighted in her one and only display of vanity. She'd told Avery repeatedly that until her body gave out, she refused to give up her contact lenses or to let her hair go gray.

She'd also refused for years to butt into Avery's life. Or so that had been the case until recently. The past few weeks Suzannah had been relentlessly insisting that Avery was stagnating, that the hours she kept at work were unhealthy, as was her lack of a personal life beyond the bakery.

But Avery didn't want to think about her mother's new penchant for meddling or her self-improvement issues needing to be addressed. All she wanted was an answer to her question about her mother's whereabouts this morning instead of this grilling over the kiss with David, who was back to banging away beneath the kitchen sink.

"If you were going out, why didn't you just let me know? It's not like my showing up here was unexpected."

"I know, sweetie. I'm sorry. I hardly had time to get dressed and meet Leslie, much less let you know I was going out." Suzannah gave a quick pat to Avery's denim-clad knee.

"I bought you a cell phone for a reason, you know." Avery kicked off her sandals and pulled her knees to her chest. "It doesn't do a bit of good when you leave it in the charging cradle."

"I love the phone, Avery. I just forgot to take it. This morning was so hectic. Leslie was only in town for a few hours, and deciding to have break-fast together was a very last-minute plan."

"Do I know Leslie?" Avery thought back to the photos and keepsakes in her mother's albums from her pep club and sorority days.

"I'm sure you don't. We lost touch after school

and only recently became reacquainted. Suzannah smiled as if that was a sufficient explanation to get her off the hook for skipping out without a word on their longtime, mother-and-daughter routine.

And if Avery were to be honest with herself, it was. Her mother didn't owe her any explanations. Avery certainly wasn't ready for a role reversal in their relationship. Yet here she was, sounding like she was the old fogy who couldn't deal with change.

Ugh. How unattractive was that?

Suzannah lifted her coffee again and smiled at her daughter over the cup. "Tell me, sweetie. Did you have a nice time here with David?"

"You mean did your lawn-watering, sink-clogging matchmaking work?"

"Well, yes. Though none of the morning's plans were premeditated. Except, perhaps, using the sprinkler to send you to the kitchen door." Another sip of coffee. Another smile. "So, when did you and David get so cozy?"

"About ten seconds before you walked in." Avery had welcomed her mother's interruption even as she'd hated it. She'd longed to go on kissing David forever. The feel of his hands, his lips, his tongue, even his body pressed to hers had resonated with an unexpected sense of rightness.

But as he'd said, she thought she had ruined his

life. Even if he'd been exaggerating, what right did she have to feel anything but guilt and regret? If she hadn't taken that disastrous risk with Johnny Boyd, David's future could've turned out so differently.

Yet she shivered, remembering. She'd kissed David Marks. After ten months of circling, avoiding, retreating and hiding, it was all she could do to sit still knowing he lay on his back in the next room.

"It was nothing," she finally said to her mother. "It didn't mean a thing."

"Oh, Avery, of course it did," her mother argued. "A man doesn't kiss a woman the way David kissed you without a measure of intent."

Intent? What was that supposed to mean? How long had her mother been standing and watching, anyhow? "Mom, it was just a kiss. Besides, I've known David for years." She waved a hand dismissively.

Suzannah sighed. "Don't discount what might develop, sweetie."

Avery looked at her mother quizzically. "Is this more of your matchmaking?"

"Of course not," Suzannah denied, the very picture of innocence. Avery didn't believe her mother for a minute. "Not that I don't think you and David wouldn't make a perfect couple, mind you. But I would never push the two of you into a relationship.''

''Thanks for that,'' Avery said, really not liking this conversation. ''I enjoy my life as it is. I doubt I even have time for a relationship. The bakery keeps me plenty busy and the hours are insane. You know that,'' she finished, pleading her case.

''Yes, I know. But I like to see you happy.'' Suzannah arched a brow. ''And kissing David definitely made you happy.''

''Mother, please!'' Avery felt a flush rise up her neck. She was not going to sit here and have a birds-and-bees conversation with her mother. ''Kissing David has nothing to do with happiness.'' In fact, she had no idea *what* it had to do with. ''I don't need a man to be happy.''

''No. Of course you don't. I would never maintain that any woman does.'' Suzannah's expression grew wistful. ''But it's certainly nice to have a man with whom to share one's happiness.''

An unexpected pang of sadness settled like a cloak on Avery's shoulders. It was so hard to believe her father had been gone for five years—especially when she was in this room, on this floor of the house where they'd lived as a family for all of her life.

It was one of the reasons she loved the time she

spent here so much. "I know, Mom. I miss him, too."

Suzannah frowned. "Miss who, sweetie?"

Miss who? *Miss who?* "Uh, Daddy? Isn't that who you're talking about?"

With a slight, melancholy laugh, Suzannah shook her head. "Oh, Avery. I'll always miss your father. But I was talking about you, dear. I want you to be happy, to know what I knew for so long, the joy of sharing that feeling with a man who loves you."

Avery squirmed where she sat, thinking of loving David, of David loving her, wondering if he'd thought of her over the years as often as she'd thought of him.

And then Suzannah's smile deepened, brightening her face. "Who knows? That man could be David."

Rolling her eyes, Avery ignored the thumping of her heart that reminded her of David's kiss. "You just told me you weren't matchmaking."

"And I'm not," Suzannah insisted. "It's just as I said. I want you to be happy."

"And just as I said. I am happy." Avery smiled reassuringly, telling herself that she was only listening for David because visiting with her mother was difficult when a third party hovered. Not that David hovered. "Besides, David and I will never be anything but casual friends."

"Kissing friends."

When Avery glared, her mother capitulated.

"Okay, okay. No more matchmaking."

"Thank you." Avery breathed a short-lived sigh of relief, because her mother's next words hit her like a blow to the chest.

"I suppose it would be difficult anyway for you to have a relationship with David considering your history."

Avery stared at her mother while Suzannah sipped at her coffee. It was as if now that she'd dropped her bomb, nothing mattered but the caffeine.

Ooh, it was unfair how sneaky mothers could be.

"I'm not falling for your tricks, Mother. You can't possibly know anything about what history I might or might not have with him."

"Of course I do. I visited David when he was in the hospital, you know. Before he returned to school from his suspension."

"What did he tell you?" Avery demanded after swallowing the lump of dread in her throat.

"Nothing, really." Suzannah shifted on the sofa, leaning back against the overstuffed arm opposite Avery who said, "Okay, then," right before her mother added, "But Johnny Boyd told me everything."

God. What was happening here, and could it please stop? "When did you talk to Johnny?"

"I tutored him at the alternative center before he was allowed back to regular classes. He talked about the girl who had been with him and how David had been jealous and tried to take her away."

Avery let her head fall back into the cushions, closing her eyes and bouncing her head as if beating it against a brick wall. "He was such a liar."

"I know, Avery," her mother said softly. "Anyone who knew David knew he would never go after Johnny Boyd out of jealousy. Which meant he went after him for another reason. Knowing a girl was involved made the rest of the puzzle fall into place. There was only one girl over whom David would have been so protective and reckless."

"Me," Avery said softly. She hadn't breathed a word about what had happened that night to anyone. Not even directly to David until this morning.

She'd been wrong not to tell all then, thinking her silence would prevent Johnny from going after David. Young and selfish and deathly afraid of rumor. Fearful of anyone knowing how close she'd come to being truly hurt because curiosity had driven her to find out how much of Johnny's bad-boy reputation was rumor, how much was truth.

Stupid and selfish and very, very ashamed.

Yet all the time she'd thought her secret safe her

parents had known. And never said a word. Who else? she wondered. How many others were aware of what had happened beneath the bleachers that night?

"I need to say something, Avery." At the wounded sound of her mother's voice, Avery opened her eyes. "I should have asked you about it, but I didn't. I wanted you to come to me. I knew that was wrong, but mothers are not always sensible when their own children are hurting."

"It wasn't that I was hurting…" Another half-truth because, of course, she had been—as much for David as for herself.

"Yes. You were. But I think you were more confused than anything." Suzannah paused, her caring eyes meeting Avery's, which had become watery and blurred. "I watched you for signs of depression, for signs of drug use—"

"Mom!"

"I know, I know." Suzannah waved a hand. "It sounds so dramatic now when I speak of it. At the time, however, I was worried that you might need help to cope, and had I hovered or been too insistent I feared that you wouldn't have come to me if you did."

Avery's coping had been dealing with the unbearable guilt over what had happened to David as much as anything. Or perhaps knowing what he'd gone through had kept her from thinking of her own near miss.

At this point in time, she wasn't sure her past mental state mattered. She wanted her mother to know the truth so they could both put away all that had happened.

She reached up, unbuttoned the top two buttons of her tunic and pointed to the old scar along her collarbone. "Do you remember asking me how this happened?"

Suzannah frowned, studying the narrow strip of light skin. "Of course I do, sweetie. You caught the top of a chain-link fence while papering a house. I remember telling you that you could pay to replace your own uniform top."

Avery smiled ironically at the lie she'd told. She'd known the story would never raise an eyebrow with her parents and would work as a perfect cover-up. "It wasn't a fence. Johnny cut me when he sliced off my top."

Suzannah's eyes widened; she smothered a gasp. Avery watched the pulse jump in her mother's throat. "I'm sorry I never told you," she whispered. "I should have told you. If I'd told the truth about everything then, told all of the truth, I would've saved so many people so much hurt."

"Oh, Avery—"

"Sink's done, Suzannah."

David's voice from the doorway drew Avery's attention away from her mother's forgiving expression. He stood there in his wrongly buttoned shirt, drying his hands, his hair disheveled, a short smear of grease on one cheek.

He was gorgeous, beautiful, a man made to turn heads. He sent her heart racing by doing no more than standing still. And her stupidity could have gotten him killed. *She could have gotten him killed!* And she'd lived with that truth now for fifteen years.

Shame came in waves, a tide of emotion causing her to feel very small. She was surprised he had any desire to speak to her, much less the sort of desire he'd shown her minutes before in the kitchen. How blind she truly had been.

"What was wrong?" her mother asked, following Avery's cue and turning her attention to David.

He shrugged, blinked, moved his frowning gaze from Avery to Suzannah. "Looked like celery strings. And eggshells."

The celery strings and eggshells could wait. Avery was done holding it in. "David, were you aware my mother has known the truth all this time about what happened with me and you and Johnny Boyd?"

David's hands stilled on the rag. His focus

moved from Avery to her mother and back. "All about it?"

Avery narrowed her eyes. "So, you did know."

He shook his head. "I only knew what Johnny had told her. About me trying to steal away his girl. Not that she knew you were the one involved."

"Actually, David, my daughter was just telling me, or rather, showing me the extent of her involvement," Suzannah said, giving up Avery's last secret. "It seems neither you nor I knew the full extent of the truth."

At David's fiercely questioning expression, Avery leaned forward over her knees and buried her face in her hands. She heard his footsteps on the plush mauve carpet as he came farther into the room and knew she wouldn't be getting out of there without revealing all.

"Avery?" He said her name softly, as if she would bolt should he raise his voice. It didn't matter what tone he used; his determination was clear.

Opening her eyes, she saw his work boots and realized he was standing too near, and she was going to have to face him with more of the truth, and why oh why hadn't she moved to Tibet years ago and lived out her life as a monk?

Hands on her knees, she pushed to her feet to stand toe-to-toe with David, watching the pulse beat in the hollow of his throat even though she spoke in response to her mother when she said, ''I never told anyone about the knife.''

''What knife?'' he asked with a growl, his eyes flashing.

''The one Johnny used on my uniform top. I knocked it out of his hand before you arrived. I don't think he knew where it landed.'' She pulled aside her unbuttoned tunic and showed him her scar.

And then, as if her mother wasn't sitting on the sofa three feet away, he reached up and touched her.

He ran his thumb over the faded welt along her collarbone, once and then repeated the caress again until he'd raised her temperature there, as if he could rub away the evidence of the long-ago crime. ''I should've killed the bastard.''

''Which is why I never told anyone. It's been hard enough living with the hurt I caused by being so stupid. Living with anything else...'' And that was it. She'd had enough.

Stepping back and buttoning her top, she glanced toward her mother. ''I've got to go to work to cover the afternoon for Yvette. You and David are welcome to the croissants that are left. I'll pick up the basket later.''

Suzannah got to her feet, held out a hand. ''Avery, sweetie, if you're still speaking to me, I'd like to ask a favor of you.''

"Of course I'm speaking to you." She was surprised anyone was still speaking to her! "What is it?"

"Well, Leslie will be back in town next weekend," Suzannah was saying, as if already having put the last few minutes behind her. "And I was wondering if we could come up on Saturday evening for dinner at your place?"

"Dinner?" After a morning of witnessed kisses and confessions, her mother was making weekend plans for dinner?

Suzannah's expression was hopeful and also a bit mischievous. Even challenging. "We were talking about our children this morning, and I would like very much for the two of you to meet. David, you come, too. We'll play cards and have a relaxing evening."

Avery looked from one to the other, thinking it would be a miracle if she ever had a nice, relaxing evening again.

CHAPTER FOUR

LEANING CLOSE to the oval mirror hanging over her bathroom's pedestal sink, Avery applied a light pink gloss to her lips, the shade a match to the summery frost with which she'd painted her nails earlier.

Painting her nails, of course, had brought to mind David's touch. Shivering, she curled her toes in her purple leather slides. Two days later, Monday morning now, and the feel of the thumb he'd rubbed over her blue polish was as real as that of his mouth pressed to hers, as that of the imprint his fingertips left on her shoulder.

She needed to shake this obsession that had intensified a thousandfold in the past forty-eight hours. It had to be unhealthy the way he seemed to be so much on her mind. She'd spent too many stolen moments over the past fifteen years allowing her thoughts to drift in his direction.

It had to stop here and stop now.

No, she hadn't put her life on hold waiting to hear from him or wondering about what might have been and what had happened to him. That would have been even more absurd than thinking of him in the first place as often as she had.

In fact, until he'd walked back into her life, she still pictured him as the freckled and gangly teen he'd once been.

That image had been erased in one long breathtaking moment the day he'd followed her mother up the staircase to where Avery had been standing on the second-floor landing, trying to fit her key into her front-door lock.

She'd known, of course, that her mother was showing the empty third-floor space to a new tenant, but when she'd looked down to see broad male shoulders taking up most of the narrow staircase's width, she'd reacted the way single women did to gorgeous men—she'd checked for a wedding band and then she'd moved her gaze to his.

It was a strange thing, the familiarity she'd felt, looking into eyes that searched out hers with the same curiosity—though a curiosity more intense. After all, David had been well aware of who she was. She'd been the one at a disadvantage.

And then he'd smiled.

That moment, that smile, had defined the past ten months of unrest she'd been living—just as that moment beneath the bleachers had impacted her life. She'd wondered so often what sort of boy David Marks had really been that he would take on Johnny Boyd for her? Why had she never taken the time to know him? She'd been so self-involved, so shallow, that's why.

She slipped the pot of lip gloss down into her bag and chose a small compact of smoky-mauve eye shadow, her stomach tightly knotted with old guilt but also with a new anticipation brought by Saturday's kiss. And, oh, what a kiss.

She couldn't remember any man's mouth ever sweeping her away as David's had. Sure, she'd dated, had relationships, come close once to an engagement until realizing that something didn't click quite right.

Not the way she and David had clicked there in her mother's kitchen.

The fact that she was putting on more than her usual mascara and blush, that she was wearing lacy rather than practical panties, that she was timing her departure for work to coincide with his, tempting fate and that very narrow staircase…those were the most obvious pieces of evidence that she was skating on thin ice here by focusing on that kiss. She had no way of knowing if taking this risk—*God, but she hated risk*—would result in another disaster.

The fantasies she'd had of taking their kiss further, of unbuttoning David's shirt and slipping it from his shoulders, of moving her fingers to his belt buckle, the button fly of his jeans, of what might have happened had her mother not interrupted....

She hadn't yet shaken the feel of his bare skin, the resilience of flesh and muscle on his back, the strength he so easily checked as he touched her gently, reverently, as if he was the one who'd been nervous. David Marks, nervous. She couldn't even imagine.

Shivering, she fluffed at her blown-dry and bouncy blond layers that she usually wore pulled back in a scrunchie. See? She was primping and preening when she had no guarantee of seeing him and no business making herself up for a man in the first place. She was setting the women's movement back decades, dressing for a man instead of for comfort and practicality.

She glanced at her watch. *Ack!* She was out of time and probably too late as it was. He left for school at seven, and it was already three minutes after. She quickly finished her eye shadow, having decided to add it at the last minute after applying her mascara. It would serve her right for her vanity to ruin her seduction.

Seduction? Funny! She stopped, frowned, then shook off the ridiculous thought and returned the rest of her makeup to her bag. If anything, she was engaged in a harmless flirtation. A simple testing of the waters that had been swirling around her ankles now for months. Or that's what she would have been doing had she been more on the ball here this morning.

As it was, when she finally pulled open her door, it was to the sound of the triplex's shared entrance closing downstairs. Well, crap. She was obviously more out of practice flirting than she'd realized. So much for the best-laid, last-minute plans, she thought with a sigh, turning her lock and closing the door behind her.

She'd only just headed toward the staircase when she heard the door at the foot of the stairs open. She paused on the edge of the landing, looking down as David walked inside and glanced up. Her stomach's resident butterflies fluttered their wings wildly at the smile spreading over his face.

One hand on the staircase railing, she took her first step down. "Forget something?"

He nodded, climbed two steps toward her. "I heard your door."

The butterflies were joined by dozens of hummingbirds.

"You came back because you heard my door?"

Another step up, another nod. "I wanted to test my new staircase theory."

She forced her feet to move, managing to descend two whole steps. Her chest tightened. Her throat ached with her effort to speak. "What theory would that be?"

"It's pretty simple, really." One step, two steps, three steps, four. His eyes glittered and he stopped. He stood almost at eye level now. Only one lonely step remained untaken. "Now that there's not so much baggage in the way, I thought we might want to test out how narrow this staircase really is."

She pulled in a deep breath. "That baggage has weighed me down for a very long time, you know."

He nodded. "I know."

"I just wanted to be sure that you did. That you didn't think I'd forgotten anything that happened." A shiver coiled sharply at the base of her spine; her fingers trembled and she tightened her grip on the railing. "That I'd blown it off as if it were nothing."

His expression softened as he studied her, his hands shoved into his navy Dockers front pockets. She watched him flex his hands, wondering if he wanted to reach for her because she so wished he would. "I never thought you blew off anything, Avery. You're not that type."

Curious that he thought he knew her, she mused, tilting her head to one side. "What type am I?"

He inhaled deeply, exhaled slowly. His knee shook as if he wanted more than anything to move up that one last remaining step. But he stayed where he was. "Do you remember when we played that football game in Alpine? Our senior year?"

She smiled. "And it was, like, ten degrees?"

"More like twenty," he said with a laugh. "But, yeah. It was cold. And afterward everyone was on the bus ready to go and yelling at me to hurry up?"

"But your zipper was stuck and you could only get halfway out of your costume." She hadn't thought of that night for years.

"Pretty damn humiliating, I gotta say." The corner of his mouth quirked enough for his dimples to appear. "But you got off the bus and came around behind me to—"

She interrupted him with a laugh. "I almost smacked you because you wouldn't stand still. It was like trying to help a dog who wouldn't stop chasing its tail."

"You were so close," he said, his face coloring slightly. "I wanted to see you. To see what you were doing. I wasn't used to having cute girls feeling up my backside," he added with a grin.

He was so cute, so vulnerable in his admission. Her heart beat harder, faster, against the walls of her chest. "It was your shirttail. You wouldn't have been able to get it loose on your own. You'd probably caught it when you zipped the tornado top to the bottom."

Chuckling, he shook his head. "You never told me that."

She shrugged. "I'm telling you now."

"Dumping more of that baggage?" he asked, one brow lifting.

"David?"

"Avery?"

She relaxed her tight grip on the railing, knowing she was going to have to touch him and touch him soon or totally go out of her mind. "I don't think of all of our shared history as baggage. Only what I caused to happen to you."

His face darkened. "It was my choice to go after Johnny."

"You should've run for help," she said, because she'd wished so often that he had.

"You're kidding me, right?" His voice echoed gruffly, painfully, as if the choice to intervene had been one he'd never consciously made but one that had been preordained. "You think I could've run off and left you there?"

"Johnny was almost twice your size," she said, sensing the argument wasn't going to get her anywhere. Not judging by the fierceness of his expression.

"Yeah, but I was crazy in love with you."

The tone of his voice caressed her, a soft breeze stirring the exposed tips of her feelings, a gentle tug on her heartstrings playing their song. She'd known of his crush, had recognized the puppylike affection behind his flirtatious bids for attention and ignored him, discouraged him.

But love? Crazy in love?

"Oh, David," she said, closing the distance between them, taking one last step, the final step, a literal movement that meant more than putting them face-to-face as she stood on the stair above.

And then she swallowed hard because his eyes flared with a heat she longed to feel on her body, a heat she knew would burn her from the inside out.

Her arms went around his neck, his came around her waist and he pulled her close, nuzzling the skin beneath her ear and whispering soft words she couldn't make out. She didn't care what he was saying. His meaning couldn't have been more clear when his big broad hands settled one above the other in the small of her back.

He felt wonderfully right in her arms. She wanted his kiss, and he readily complied, his lips settling over hers with an intent that was nowhere as hesitant as that of Saturday morning.

This time he was sure of what he wanted and increased the pressure accordingly. Avery willingly parted her lips and took his tongue into her mouth, responding in kind and teasing him with quick flicks in and out and around until he growled and moved one determined hand to the back of her head.

He was no longer gentle but sweetly demanding with a pressure she was loath to resist. When he turned her body and backed her into the wall, her bottom contacting the staircase railing, she simply closed her eyes and accepted the weight of his body as if she'd been waiting all of her life to feel him like this.

Like this, with one of his hands threaded into her hair and the other cupping her backside and pulling her firmly to him. Like this, with his chest pressed solidly to her breasts, his breathing hard and heavy. Like this, with a knee wedged between her legs and pushing upward.

She wanted him now; she wanted him naked and moving above her and forever. She was out of her mind with the way she wanted him, with the way he knew to make her body sing. Her heart thundered madly. Her breasts grew heavy, the taut tips aching to feel the brush of his smooth, bare skin.

A whimper escaped her mouth, and David swallowed the sound, growling in answer, grinding his hips to hers. The hard ridge of his erection settled firmly against her belly. She lifted her arms from around his neck, slipping her hands behind him and tugging his white oxford shirttails free.

She skated her hands up and down his back, loving the feel of skin on skin, wanting more than was allowed by their position and by the narrow width of the staircase. David took her cue, finding the elastic waistband of her lavender capris beneath her white polo shirt and slipping his fingers beneath.

This time the sound she made was one of hunger and need. She tore her mouth away from his and begged. "David, please. Let's go inside. My mother could come out any minute. Please, I don't want—"

He silenced her with a finger to her lips. And then he shook his head. "I'm late for class. I've got to go." He took a deep, shuddering breath and rested his forehead on hers. "Besides, going inside means going to bed. And I'm not sure we're ready."

She shut her eyes tightly, not wanting to hear what he was saying because she knew that he was right. Just because they fit together on the staircase—

"Avery, look at me."

She did, and her heart went wild.

"I didn't say that I didn't want you." He pressed her lower body flush to his and made his meaning known. "I want you more than I want to breathe right now. But I've got to go."

She nodded because it seemed like an obvious

response and he'd robbed her of the ability to speak. Wanting her more than he wanted to breathe. She swallowed and found enough of her voice to say, "I know."

But he wasn't through. "What do you know?"

"That you have to get to class."

"And?" he asked, one brow lifted.

She felt the heat sure to be splotching her cheeks bright pink. "That you want me."

He exhaled as if she'd freed him from a fifteen-year-old burden. "Good. Now. Dinner. Tonight, yes? We'll pick this up again where we left off."

"Okay," she agreed, nodding. "I can meet you wherever you'd like."

"Your choice," he said, his eyes sparkling with an intensity that was nothing if not deliciously, wickedly, all about sex. "Your place or mine."

CHAPTER FIVE

"OH, THANK GOODNESS," Avery said, opening her front door to her mother later that evening. She took the fresh tomato Suzannah offered from the palm of her hand. "I picked up two tomatoes this afternoon and both are as mealy as wet bran."

"Bran? And here all this time I've been thinking of you as the Cheerios type," Suzannah said teasingly.

Heading back to the kitchen, Avery glanced over her shoulder and grinned at her mother trailing behind. "That's because you still look at me as your little girl."

"Well, of course I do. The younger you are, the younger I am," Suzannah said with a laugh that Avery didn't find convincing.

She washed the tomato and pulled a chef's knife from the block on her navy-tiled countertop. "And here all this time *I've* been thinking that you considered age to be nothing but a state of mind."

"True. But there are times I can't help but wish I was your age again with so much time still ahead of me.'' Leaning a shoulder on the archway separating the kitchen and dining areas, Suzannah crossed her arms.

Frowning, Avery cubed the tomato and told herself not to worry. But her mother remained silent, and by the time she scooped up the handful of tiny chunks and tossed them into the bowl of shredded lettuce, Suzannah's scrutiny had intensified fourscore and seven.

Enough was enough. Avery rinsed her hands and reached for a dish towel, drying as she asked, ''Mom? What's going on here?''

Suzannah considered her daughter from head to toe, then shrugged and pushed away from the archway. ''I've decided you're not the Cheerios type after all.''

Mothers! Argh! ''What is that supposed to mean?''

''Seeing you preparing dinner for David certainly doesn't have me thinking of you as a little girl.''

Avery shook her head and turned back to setting the table with her aqua stoneware, relieved her mother's moodiness was about something so simple. ''You act like I've never cooked dinner for a man before.''

''You've never cooked dinner for David.''

Placing flatware on napkins beside the plates, Avery couldn't deny the flicker of anticipation brought on by her mother's comment and the memory of the stolen moments she and David had shared earlier that day. For a moment she simply stared at the muted colors of her reflection in the brushed silver of the knives, forks and spoons atop the ivory linen napkins.

She turned her gaze to Suzannah. "It's funny that after so many years it would be David making me nervous. I'm worried about getting this right. I guess it's because this is the first real date I've had in a year."

"Then you're guessing wrong. What you're feeling is all about David."

Her mother was far too intuitive. The tightness in Avery's chest intensified. "I owe him so much."

"No, sweetie, you don't. You absolutely do not. Nothing beyond honesty." Suzannah came farther into the room and wrapped her daughter in a one-armed hug, rubbing a hand up and down Avery's upper bicep. "And I think the two of you already have a good start in that direction."

"It's just…" Avery paused, not even sure she knew how to phrase what she wanted to say. It was that precipice thing. One wrong step and…*splat!*

"Just what?" Suzannah encouraged, reaching up to tuck a fall of hair behind Avery's ear.

Avery moved to sit in one of the dining room's shaker pine chairs; her mother followed suit. "I think about what you had with Daddy, and it makes me sad that you lost that. I know I can't fill his shoes—"

Suzannah gasped. "Avery Marie! Do not tell me that you have been putting your own life on hold for five years now because of me."

Avery glanced up sharply, unsure whether she'd ever seen such a stern expression cross her mother's face. Not even when Suzannah had called down disruptive students in class. Or when she'd been presented with Avery's ruined—and pricey—cheerleading uniform top.

"Of course, I haven't," Avery hedged, recalling for the first time how much of her comfort level had to do with familiarity. And how she'd been loath to taking chances since that night fifteen years ago. "It's just that lately the boom in the bakery's business has been eating into what little social life I did have."

Suzannah wasn't buying it. "And breaking your engagement to Tom? Not even a month after your father's passing?"

"Tom and I wanted different things out of life. It shouldn't have taken us as long as it did to figure that out."

At least, that was the truth, though her mother's emotional state *had* played a part in her decision to end the engagement. She'd been with Tom two years, yet she had been unable to picture herself ever mourning him the way her mother had mourned the loss of her father.

It had taken that enormous heartbreak for her to recognize the crux of all her relationship issues before and since. She wanted the life her mother had lived with her father. That perfect pairing. That ideal match. That rare coupling of souls that happened but once in a lifetime. She'd been afraid for so long that she would never know such bliss.

For the past forty-eight hours, however, she'd been more afraid that she was going to find she couldn't have what she wanted with a man when their history, and David's "ruined life" comment—even if made in jest—factored in.

Sighing, Suzannah turned her chair so that Avery's and her knees met. "Avery, listen to me. I've wanted to say this to you for a very long time, but I hate the idea of butting into your life. Your father and I raised you to be independent and we always respected your decisions, even when we didn't necessarily agree with them."

"But?" Avery asked, because she sensed a really big *but* on the way.

"But you must stop living in the past." When Avery opened her mouth to interrupt, her mother shushed her and went on. "I've suspected as much for some time now. I love our Saturday mornings together, but I know for a fact that Cicely Linden has invited you more than once to go shopping at Canton.''

Avery didn't know what to say. She'd put off her good friend repeatedly even though a trip to the North Texas antiques bazaar was so incredibly tempting. She'd thought of asking her mother to come along....

''Avery?''

She glanced up at her mother. ''It's not that big of a deal.''

''It's that big of a deal to me.'' Suzannah took hold of her daughter's hands, rubbing her thumbs over the backs of Avery's fingers. ''I feel horribly responsible that somehow I'm holding you back. That you're living in the past out of a misplaced loyalty to me.''

''You're my mother. How could any loyalty I have to you be misplaced?'' Avery asked, feeling torn between her own feelings and the truth her mother spoke.

Suzannah's expression grew solemn. ''If it's keeping you from living your life fully, then that's exactly what it is. Let me ask you this. Would you want me to remain static the rest of my life out of my loyalty to you?''

''Of course not,'' Avery answered, squeezing her mother's hands. ''I want you to be happy.''

"Which I am. Very." Suzannah smiled brightly.

Avery's smile was dim in comparison. "Besides, you're hardly remaining static, not with all the coming and going you've been up to lately."

Suzannah sighed. "Avery, listen to me. I'm not a doddering old fool who has to have every moment of her day managed for her. I'm perfectly capable of entertaining myself, living on my own, making my own decisions—"

"I know that," Avery interrupted, facing the fact that she *had* been hiding in the safe harbor of parental concern. After all, who could fault her for her devotion? "I just knew that losing Daddy would leave a void in your life."

"Yes. It has. Of course, it has. But it's a void I have managed to fill by refusing to live in the past." Suzannah got to her feet and returned her chair to its place. "Now, I want you to promise me you'll do the same. And start tonight by having a good time with David."

DAVID SAT ON THE TOP STEP outside his front door, elbows digging into his knees, fingers laced, head down and thumbs rubbing the pressure from his temples as he waited for Suzannah to leave Avery's place.

Minutes ago, he'd been on his way down, but hearing the knock on her door followed by the voices of both women, he'd stopped above on his third-floor landing. He'd decided to hang out upstairs until the coast was clear, not wanting to interrupt whatever mother-daughter thing they had going on.

More than that, however, he wanted to get his hands on Avery, and with her mother around that wasn't going to be happening.

He knew he had Suzannah's blessing should he wish to pursue her daughter. She'd made her approval of him perfectly clear, hinting on occasion how she wished Avery would get out and have more of a social life.

None of the hints had been blatant matchmaking attempts; Suzannah was more subtle than that. Well, except for the obvious lawn-watering ploy. But catching her drift didn't require a rocket scientist— even if that was exactly what he could have been. Instead, he taught computer science, his higher education plans diverted by one of life's big fat detours.

In a truly twisted irony, he owed his career to Johnny Boyd and that fight beneath the bleachers. Returning to school with a reputation as a badass had been his first step into the hell that had been his senior year at Tatem High. He only made it two months in before his father yanked him out of school and moved their small family of two to El Paso.

An oil-exploration geologist, his father had been comfortable leaving his overachieving son home alone in the small town during his short trips around the state. That comfort had turned to an unease that blossomed in proportion to David's dropping grades and rising incidents of trouble. Once enrolled in school in El Paso, he'd been reduced to the same status he'd had in Tatem. The one with the nearly perfect 4.0 GPA.

In the end, the experience had taught him a lot about himself, and he'd married his geek's love of computer science with the newfound fulfillment he found in teaching when working in after-school programs with kids from El Paso's barrio. Life was strange, but he couldn't complain about the twists and turns since he was sitting here waiting to complete a circle that had begun so many years ago. He loved what he did and wouldn't trade the small-town classroom for the moon.

At the sound of Avery's door opening and that of her mother's descending footsteps on the staircase, he got to his feet. He dusted off the seat of his khaki Dockers with one hand as he walked down. When he looked toward Avery's door he saw her watching his approach.

Her expression was both hesitant and one of anticipation, and he couldn't help but wonder whether she was responding to her mother's visit or the thought of the evening ahead.

He slowed his steps as the beat of his heart picked up speed. "Am I too early?"

Avery shook her head. "You're just in time to save me from talking myself to death while the casserole bakes. King Ranch Chicken. I hope that's okay."

"Are you kidding?" She could've baked dog biscuits and he would've been fine with it. He offered her the bottle of Pinot Grigio he'd brought.

"Mmm." She smiled as she read the label. "I'm so pedestrian when it comes to alcohol. I was going to offer you Dos Equis or Corona. This will be so much nicer."

"I'm good with the beer," he replied, closing her front door and following her through the apartment. The two-bedroom layout of all three floors was identical, and he wasted no time looking around Avery's place.

Not when she was the reason he was here. And when he had the choice between looking at her furnishings and watching the set of her shoulders, the sway of her hips, the way she shook back her hair as she walked.

He caught the groan rolling up from his gut and stepped into her kitchen. She snagged a corkscrew from a drawer, turned and handed it to him. He took it and placed it on the countertop next to the bottle of wine. And then he hooked an elbow around Avery's neck and tugged her body flush to his.

"I'm starving," he said, his forehead resting on hers as his lips brushed the corner of hers and tickled her cheek.

"Dinner's almost ready," she answered, her hands moving to his waist, settling there at his belt instead of unbuckling it as she wanted to. She nuzzled her nose to his. "We can start with the wine and the salad."

"Sounds good." It sounded awful compared to starting with her mouth. And so he did, opening his lips over hers, which parted willingly.

He swallowed her whimper, devoured her desire, swept his tongue through her mouth and backed her into the countertop. She pulled him with her, urging him closer than the distance he'd forced himself to keep.

He settled his weight fully against her slight frame, wanting more than anything to explore their fit without bright overhead lights glaring down and too many layers of clothing between.

When the tension in the room grew too razor sharp to bear, he eased away slowly, first his body, then his arm from her neck and finally his mouth from hers. He wasn't going anywhere; they had a long night ahead. The possibilities held by the next few hours were worth a trip taken minute by minute.

And so he let Avery go, and opened the wine.

CHAPTER SIX

DAVID POURED the wine while Avery set bowls of salad and a spouted serving boat of dressing on the table. He'd told her he was a fan of buttermilk ranch and would've been fine pouring straight from the bottle.

Avery, however, had insisted on completing her well-set table. He didn't know if the effort was meant to impress him or to keep their evening structured within whatever boundaries she'd set—a strange thought considering the way she'd so easily welcomed his tongue and his body, but there it was.

And now here he was, sitting directly across from her at the rectangular table designed for six, a linen napkin in his lap, his salad bowl centered on his plate. He felt as if he were taking an Emily Post test. One wrong use of a fork, and bam! He was history.

He lifted his wineglass as Avery reached for the salad dressing. "Are you practicing for Saturday night's dinner party?" he asked.

She frowned, offering him the serving boat before she picked up her drink. "I hadn't thought of it that way, no. Why do you ask?"

"Because you're sitting all the way over there." He finished with the dressing, returned it to the center of the table. "The food's not the only thing I'm wanting to get my hands on, you know."

She sipped at her wine, her eyes downcast as she said, "David, I've been thinking that it might be a good idea if we keep our distance. At least for a while."

"When were you thinking that?" he asked after several seconds passed, his tone sharper than he'd intended. "Before or after you kissed me ten minutes ago?"

Color stained her cheeks. "Before, actually."

"I see," he said, stabbing up a forkful of shredded and cubed greens. A sharp burst of bell pepper kept his mouth closed when he wanted to say a whole lot more.

"I'm not sure you do see," Avery was saying when her hesitation finally forced his attention away from his salad.

"Oh, well. Feel free to enlighten me then." He'd come here with high expectations, yes, and they'd grown higher the longer the kiss. Now he felt as if he and Avery were back in high school and that he was putting his foot in his mouth the way he'd always done when around her.

She set her wineglass on the table, moved her hands to her lap. "You were right earlier today. What you said. About us not being ready to sleep together."

This time he refused to look up, certain that she'd already made up her mind, closed herself off from the doors they'd only recently opened. He didn't want to see her shut down when minutes before she'd been ready to give him his dream.

Instead, he went after his salad with a vengeance until the tines of his fork wouldn't hold another lettuce shred and more than likely wouldn't fit in his mouth. "You're afraid I'm going to throw you across the table, is that it?"

She said nothing, and he thought for a moment that walking away and leaving her to her salad and her King Ranch Chicken would be the smartest thing to do. He was getting close to taking things too personally when this dinner was simply a date with no promises made. He shouldn't be having this much trouble remembering that.

Her continuing silence, however, finally drew his gaze from his bowl to her face. And the purely prurient grin lifting the corners of her mouth hit him like a fist to the solar plexus. It was a full ten seconds before he could breathe.

"No, David." She leaned forward, both wrists now resting on the table's edge, her blue eyes uncannily bright, the tone of her voice suggestive. "I'm afraid I'll be the one to throw you across the table."

He dropped his fork against the edge of his bowl. Avery's lashes drifted down to hide her eyes, her voice going soft as she said, "I know. I've avoided you for ten months and now I want you to take me to bed. What an about-face, huh?"

Oh, yeah. A big one he wouldn't have seen coming had he been looking through the Hubble. And here he'd been determined to take things slow, not wanting to lose the ground that had taken him so long to gain.

He sat back in his chair and considered his dinner partner intently. "Well...I'm not about to complain."

"God, it's so hard to talk about." She laughed as she shoved her hair from her face. It fell back in big blond waves he wanted to feel sweep over his skin. "It's as if since my mother brought us together Saturday morning, nothing about my life has been the same."

He watched as she picked up her fork and toyed with her salad, finally taking a bite as if eating would keep her from having to speak. He followed her lead, pushing cucumbers here, tomatoes there, not the least bit surprised to find his appetite for the food long gone.

Finally he reached for his wine. "Strange how one moment in a lifetime can change everything, isn't it?"

Her expression grew solemn. "That's what happened to you, isn't it? It was that night beneath the bleachers."

He nodded, because he couldn't deny his actions had started the chain of events that had brought them full circle. It wasn't something he'd ever planned to get into with her, but now that she'd brought up the subject he wasn't going to avoid the truth of their connection.

The oven's timer buzzed, and Avery pushed back from the table, appearing relieved to have the interruption. She set the casserole dish bubbling with cheese, green chilies, corn tortillas and chicken on the table. The smells set his stomach to rumbling, yet he didn't move a muscle. He simply waited for Avery to make up her mind.

He saw her indecision in the way she took too long turning off the oven and pulling the hot mitts from her hands, the way she was slow to grab the wine bottle off the countertop and refill both glasses. By the time she returned to the table, David's gut was tied in knots—knots that tightened and throbbed and tangled beyond repair when she picked up her place setting and moved to sit in the chair at his side.

For a long, tense moment, neither of them said a word. David sat with his shoulders back, his hands gripping the railings that joined the top of his chair to the seat. Avery spread her napkin in her lap, smoothing it out repeatedly until not a wrinkle remained.

He listened to her shallow in-and-out breaths and shifted to face her. He watched the throb of her pulse in the soft hollow of her throat, longed to place his lips to the spot and feel the heavy beat. Suppressing a groan, he released his grip on the chair back and flexed his fingers. This evening was going to become a big fat disaster if they couldn't deal with the heat of this simmering tension.

And so he reached toward her and lifted her chin with the long edge of one index finger. Then he leaned forward and lightly brushed his lips to hers. It took the willpower of the saint he'd never been not to increase the pressure of his mouth, especially when she strained toward him seeking more.

But he set her back, dropped his hand and smiled. "See? No table-throwing. No ripping off of clothes." Her grin teased him, tempted him, as did her sense of good humor in the face of an awkward moment.

"If you can keep your hands to yourself, then so can I," she announced. And, at that, she reached for the serving spoon and dished up the casserole.

Once she sat back, however, he moved his left hand to her thigh. "I didn't say anything about keeping my hands to myself."

One eyebrow arched, she fought a grin. "And I'm supposed to be able to calmly sit and eat when you're touching me?"

Oh, but he was on the verge of hardening where he sat. Knowing the way she wanted him, feeling the heat of her body in the palm of his hand…yeah, it was too much. He moved his arm to rest along the back of her chair instead. "Is this better?"

"Honestly, no. I'd rather you touch me. But practically speaking, yes." She cast him a quick sideways glance and reached for her fork. "This way you're not so much of a distraction, but are still near enough for me to feed you."

Before he could object, she offered him a chunk of creamy, cheesy chicken. He opened his mouth and died. "Mmm."

"You like?" she asked before feeding herself from the same dish, the same fork.

He watched her lips close, watched her pull the fork free, watched her eyes twinkle and her grin light up her face. "What's not to like?" he asked gruffly.

She turned to the side, hooked her heels over the chair's low railing and set the plate of food on her knees. Her shins pressed the outside of his thigh.

He shifted even closer. "I didn't know if you were more of a steak-and-baked-potato kind of guy," she said.

"I'm pretty much just a food kind of guy," he admitted.

"Ah, that's the best kind."

"How's that?"

She fed him another bite, her chin raised, her nose lifted, her gaze on his mouth as he chewed. He amazed himself by not choking or pulling her into his lap.

"A guy who won't turn up his nose at a meal makes cooking for him a lot more fun."

"You cook for a lot of guys then?"

She laughed, shook her head. "You're one of a very few. I was actually thinking how much my mother loved cooking for my father."

"Hmm." He reached for the distraction of his wineglass.

"Oh, God. That didn't come out right at all." Grinning, she waved the fork back and forth. "I wasn't comparing my cooking for you to my mother cooking for my father."

He raised a brow. "That's good to know," he said, and hearing her laughter was worth any conversation or any comparison he had to endure.

"I mean, considering this is only our first date,

it would be fairly presumptuous of me to think we would be headed for thirty years of wedded bliss.''

"Uh, right." He cleared his throat.

"Poor David." She swirled the fork through the food on her plate. "Are you about ready to start gnawing off your leg?"

"I'm getting there," he lied.

"I'm sorry. I didn't mean to sound as if I were setting a trap. Please tell me you know that."

Thing was, if she wanted to trap him, she wouldn't even have to try. It was her mother, not the subject of marriage, that he wasn't wanting to talk about. "Don't worry about it. I figure if you'd been serious about trapping me, then we'd both be naked by now."

"Very funny," she said, before shoving a bite of food at his face.

He opened his mouth and took it, but held her hand while he did. He rubbed his thumb into her palm, wrapped his fingers around her wrist just tightly enough to let her know the truth of how much he *did* want to drag her across the table and strip her bare.

Her eyes flashed in response. He released her, and she pulled the fork from his mouth and moved it to her own, where she licked the tines clean. He simply sat and stared. It was the least he could do, the most he could do. Hell, it was all he could do unless he wanted to risk his fantasy becoming a very real reality before she was ready.

But while he was mentally clearing the table, making room to climb on top, Avery was busy moving on. Shrugging, she turned her attention back to the plate of casserole balanced on her knees. "I do worry about my mother, though. I suppose I shouldn't. She told me that I shouldn't. But it's hard to see her alone after all the years she had with Daddy."

"I'm pretty sure your mom's doing okay," he said, reaching again for his wine.

"I know she's doing okay. I just wonder at times if she'd be doing better if Daddy were still around." Avery returned the half-empty plate to the table, then leaned a shoulder against the back of her chair and sipped at her wine. "School's out in another couple of weeks. She won't have the daily routine of kids and classes to keep her busy during the summer."

"Trust me. Those few weeks off are only long enough to get done what we don't have time to do the rest of the year," he said, looking down into his wineglass and avoiding her gaze.

"I know," she said, her voice growing pensive. "But Mom's always taught summer school in the past. This year she waited until the last possible minute to make her decision, and now she has this block of free time looming ahead. That's what concerns me more than anything.''

He shifted uncomfortably in his chair. "Avery, I don't mean to be insensitive here, but your mother is an adult. If she's decided not to teach summer school, I'm sure she has a good reason.''

"I don't know—"

"Avery, listen." He hated cutting her off, but this had been bugging him for a while now, this hold Avery seemed to have on her mother's apron strings. "Letting her do her thing while you do yours would do both of you a lot of good."

"Is there an echo in here or are you channeling my mother?''

He couldn't help it when one corner of his mouth twisted into a warped smile. "Has she been sneaking out behind your back again?''

"As a matter of fact…'' She swirled the wine in her glass, staring into her drink for a moment before looking up and meeting his eyes squarely. "As a matter of fact, yes. Though that's none of your business.''

"True." He nodded. "The catch-twenty-two of being a casual observer who lives in proximity to the both of you."

"And what exactly have you observed since you've been here, Mr. Marks?'' she asked with a teasing sarcasm.

ALISON KENT   335

It was her eyes, however, that told him she wasn't teasing at all. He took a deep breath and set his wineglass back on the table, twirling it by the stem. "That you work too much. That you rarely go out and when you do it's usually with Suzannah."

"You say that like it's a bad thing."

"It could be." He glanced in her direction then. "If you're using your mother as an excuse. Or as a crutch."

"That's not it at all," she said too hurriedly. "It's just that being here, should she need anything, is important to me."

He wanted to press harder, to ask whether it was mother or daughter most likely to need the other. But he didn't. Her pensive expression told him he'd made his point. "Well, like I said, she'll have her calendar filled before you turn around."

"I supposed you're right," Avery said with a sigh as a smile settled over her face. "Especially now that she's catching up with old friends. The timing of this Leslie coming back into Mom's life couldn't be more perfect."

Or more obviously the reason Suzannah *wasn't* teaching summer school this year. He cleared his throat. "So you haven't met Leslie yet, right?"

Avery shook her head and glanced at him quizzically. "Mom only mentioned her to me on Saturday morning. Why do you ask?"

Her. David groaned. This secret wasn't his to tell. It was Suzannah's. But he really hated for Avery to spend the next five days expecting her mother to show up for dinner this weekend with an old female friend in tow.

He took a long swallow of wine then said, "Look, Avery. Here's the thing. You need to know that Leslie is a him, not a her."

Avery blinked once, twice and then her eyes widened. He reached for the glass of wine she held in shaking hands, pried it free and returned it to the table. "A man? Leslie is a man? My mother is seeing a man?"

He nodded, decided to go for broke. "A man for whom your mother holds a great deal of, uh, affection."

"Affection?" Avery snorted. "What the hell is that supposed to mean, affection? You think she's having an affair?"

"That's not what I said."

"But it's what you think."

In the minute David took to reply, Avery was out of her chair, arms crossed tightly over her chest as she paced the floor of red-and-white kitchen tiles.

"Your mother has been alone for five years, Avery."

"My mother loves my father."

He ground his jaw, refusing to grab her and shake her out of the past and into the very real present. "No one is saying that she doesn't. But your father is gone, and your mother is very much alive."

Avery stopped in front of the sink, closing her eyes and hugging her arms to her middle as if she feared falling apart. He pushed out of his chair and went to her, refusing to back away even when she turned her head.

"Look at me, Avery." He waited patiently until she did, until she opened her eyes and brought her chin up defiantly. Only then did he place his hands on her shoulders and squeeze. "Your mother is a beautiful, vibrant woman. Don't tell me you've never seen the way men look at her."

Avery kept her lips pressed tightly together.

"Fine. Don't tell me anything. I'll tell you." If not for her stubborn refusal to face the truth, he would've been gentler. But her unwillingness to open her eyes and see, truly *see* those around her had gone on years too long.

"There's an assistant principal at the junior high who can't keep from smiling when he sees her. There's a maintenance worker who brings her flowers every Monday. There's a school-board member, a widower, who times his frequent arrivals on campus with your mother's. And he always has fresh coffee and breakfast from *your* bakery when he does.''

Avery's eyes widened like saucers. ''Robert Brown? He's taking those muffins to my mother? She doesn't even like blueberry.''

''She eats them. I've seen her. They sit in a corner of the faculty lounge and giggle like they're thirteen years old.'' When he felt her shoulders slump, he worked to massage away the rest of the tension. And then he wrapped her up in his arms and pulled her to his chest.

''It's just so hard to imagine,'' she said, her voice muffled by the fabric of his shirt. ''I didn't think she'd ever get over losing Daddy.''

''Maybe you're the one who's never gotten over it.''

She shook her head where it rested against him. ''No, I'm doing okay. I miss him, yes. But the memories now are good ones, and the hurt isn't quite as bad.''

He took a deep breath. ''That wasn't what I was saying.''

Avery pulled back far enough to look up. Her blue eyes were bright but blessedly dry. ''I don't get it.''

He stroked a hand down her hair. ''Maybe you've never gotten over the idea of your mother not having your father. Maybe you can't see her as a woman who might still respond to a man who finds her attractive.''

''Well,'' she said, the corner of her mouth crooking upward. ''I don't often think of my mother and sex at the same time.''

David chuckled. ''I'm sure Suzannah appreciates that.''

Rubbing her fingertips over her temples, Avery stepped back and out of David's embrace. ''Leslie. A man. How stupid of me not to notice the lack of pronouns. That's the sort of sneaky thing that happens when one's mother is an English teacher.''

''I think that's what happens when one's mother is afraid of her daughter's reaction to the new man in her life,'' David offered softly as Avery returned to the table.

''Why would she be afraid?''

''Because she doesn't want you to be hurt that she's moving on with her life.''

''So what do I do now?'' she asked, pouring wine into her glass until it reached the brim.

He wasn't quite depraved enough to suggest she strip and join him on the table, so he simply asked, ''Start planning Saturday's menu?''

She snorted. ''Oh, well, thanks for that.''

He waited until she'd taken a long swallow before moving in behind her and nuzzling her neck.

"Then why don't we pop in a DVD and cuddle on your couch."

"Cuddle?" she asked, arching her neck to give him better access.

"Yeah, cuddle. Make out," he growled as he tasted her skin.

She turned in his arms. "You want popcorn?"

"Nope. I just want you." He leaned down to show her exactly how much...rolling his eyes as she slipped free and, laughing, headed for the living room.

All he could do was follow. And so he did.

CHAPTER SEVEN

AVERY PUTTERED from the kitchen to the dining table and back, certain she'd never manage to get everything as perfect as she needed to and wondering why she even felt the need.

Impressing David or her mother was hardly necessary, but this Leslie who was coming…if he truly *was* a he and was more to her mother than a friend, well, a good first impression just seemed worth the effort.

Since Monday evening and the bug David had put in her ear about Suzannah being more than a widowed mother, Avery hadn't stopped processing all the possible clues she'd missed that her mother had moved on with her life.

She supposed it was a good thing one of them had. She'd obviously failed to. She was thirty-three years old and still lived at home, she mused with a bit of a laugh, as she opened the oven to peer at the bubbling lasagna.

Yes, she had her own place, but it was still in the house she'd grown up in. Until confronted with both her mother and David's subtle finger-pointing that she was having issues getting beyond the past, she'd never even considered why she was so comfortable living where she did.

Now it was growing too obvious. She *did* fear stepping outside of her safe boundaries. When she had, the results had not been what she'd expected, or what she'd wanted to have to live the rest of her life facing down. Like the chance she'd taken with Johnny that had cost David so dearly.

Yet if she hadn't been so stupidly reckless that long-ago night, she might not be here now, anticipating David's arrival even more than that of her mother and Leslie. What had begun as a horrific disaster might just possibly have very positive and long-term consequences.

And if that wasn't a reason to move out of the past into the present, she didn't know what was.

Speaking of the present…dinner was five minutes from being ready, which barely gave her time to make a quick trip to her vanity and touch up her makeup and hair.

But the doorbell rang before she made it across the living room to the apartment's short hallway. She ran her ring fingers beneath both eyes to clear away smudges, finger-combed her bangs and fluffed up her hair.

A deep breath, a wide smile, butterflies on the back burner and she pulled open the door.

David stepped inside and quickly shoved it closed behind him. "Are they here yet?"

She shook her head. "They should be here any min—"

Taking hold of her shoulders, he spun her around and backed her into the door. His eyes glittered sharply, the heat in them enough to sizzle her panties right off. "I never thought tonight would get here. I'm sick of middle-of-the-night phone calls and catching you coming and going."

"I thought you enjoyed passing me on the staircase," she teased, drawing a shallow breath and prepared to say more. But then his mouth came down, driving away all her intentions of keeping her feelings in check. As it was, she couldn't manage her growing arousal or get enough of his mouth.

He pressed his body to hers; she wrapped her arms around his waist and pulled him as close as she could. He fit in ways she'd never known a man had of aligning and settling into a woman. His mouth explored hers deftly yet gently.

He made clear how much he wanted her with the sounds that rolled from his belly to his throat and with all the ways he touched her, his hands moving from her shoulders to her ribs, and then around to her belly where he hesitated before sliding his palms upward to rest beneath her breasts.

It wasn't enough. She wanted so much more. She adored the show of respect but right now, what she wanted from him was the clothes-ripping, table-throwing, promised wild ride into oblivion—

A knock on the door sent David into reverse. He'd backed five feet across the living room before she'd even taken a step. The startled animal expression on his face had her giggling like a schoolgirl.

And then she did her best to keep her own face straight as she took another deep breath and opened the door.

DAVID ONCE AGAIN found himself sitting opposite Avery at her dining room table.

This time, however, her reserve wasn't about avoiding her conflicted feelings for him—which he didn't think were as conflicted as they'd once been—but about how to react to the truth of the new man in Suzannah's life.

Funny how after no more than a week of intense kisses and phone conversations in the wee hours, when Avery was up already and he should've been in bed, that he was able to read her moods, to tell where she was coming from.

But they had a long evening ahead to get through,

and it was going to require a big fat jump-start for this party to make it from here to there considering Suzannah and Leslie were carrying the bulk of the conversation while Avery mostly nodded and smiled.

Since David's plans for Avery wouldn't fit into any socially acceptable dinner discussion, he launched into the next best thing. "You much of a baseball fan, Les?" he asked, watching Avery's eyes roll back in their sockets.

"No. No sports talk. Please," she begged, though she did so with an honest laugh.

This time it was Suzannah's eyes rolling, which caused Leslie to glance from mother to daughter before looking to David for help. He feigned ignorance and shrugged.

Leslie cleared his throat. "I take it the ladies here aren't much on sports?"

"And living in West Texas at that. It's gotta be some kind of sin," David said with only a half effort at a straight face since at long last everyone was talking. "The excitement spurred on by Friday-night high school football is contagious beyond belief. You hang around long enough, you'll see."

"It is only contagious to those who have not been inoculated," Suzannah said sagely. "And usually those are the same ones who do not teach at the districts in question and have to battle the sports-over-education mentality.''

''And to a lesser extent,'' Avery went on, ''it's a relief, when the season is over, to those providing doughnuts for the booster meetings and cakes for celebrating all the wins and cookies for the pep rallies and—''

Leslie waved a hand and, laughing, cut Avery off. ''Okay, okay. I surrender. Sports will forever be off-limits when I'm around either of you two ladies.''

David tossed his napkin to the side of his empty plate. ''Well, hell. I see where I rate around here.''

Gray eyes twinkling behind round, wire-rimmed glasses, Leslie leaned to the side, raised his hand to hide his mouth and spoke in David's direction. ''I'm considering season tickets for the fall Tornadoes schedule. We'll have to finagle a guys' night out. Maybe two or three.''

''Season tickets.'' Avery glanced from Leslie to her mother, her gaze skating over David only briefly before returning to the older man. ''Does that mean you'll be in Tatem more often from now on?''

''Actually,'' Leslie began, hedging a bit as he pulled his glasses from his face. While he crossed his legs and cleaned both lenses with the corners of his napkin, he cleared his throat and continued.

"Yes. I took an editorial position this week with the Brewster County Press."

Suzannah fairly beamed, her elbows on the edge of the table, her chin resting on her laced hands. "As if they would've let you get away once you stepped foot inside the door and offered your services."

"Roaming the world has become tedious," he replied, his expression as besotted as hers.

"Oh, I don't know." Avery laughed, though David sensed a hint of the reaction being forced rather than genuine. "I'd like to give it a try. Then again, traveling outside of Texas sounds good to me."

"Then you should. And I think this summer would be the perfect time for the two of you to get started." Leslie fought a smile. The corners of his eyes crinkled all the way to the dark gray of his temples. "Maybe you could talk David here into showing you the West Coast. Especially since he has a good eight weeks off coming up, am I right?"

David grinned. No matter that somehow he was going to end up paying for this one, he could've hugged the older man for planting the seed. Showing Avery the world was the least of what he longed to do.

Avery reached for her glass of red wine, her hand amazingly steady, before turning an expression of friendly accusation on her mother. "I think my mother may have misled you as to the nature of my involvement with David.''

"To tell you the truth, she hasn't said anything leading me to believe one thing or another. If I've spoken out of turn, the fault is my own and I apologize,'' Leslie replied, and David watched a flurry of emotions cross Avery's face.

"And even though I know you were teasing,'' Suzannah said to her daughter, "I forgive you anyway for your uncharitable thoughts. Gossiping about you to Leslie, indeed.''

Avery laughed then, shaking her head at her mother's dramatic display. "Well, you did tell me the two of you had been discussing your children.''

"Your mother has been a model of propriety, Avery.'' Leslie returned his glasses to his face. "I know you have no reason to trust me, but I ask that you do when I tell you that she hasn't compromised your confidentiality.''

"Oh, I know.'' Avery sat back, appearing caught off guard by Leslie's humbleness. "It's just my job as a daughter to give her a hard time.''

"And you do your job so well, sweetie,'' Suzannah said, causing Avery to laugh with a hint of relief, and causing David to chuckle. God, but he was enjoying himself.

Being here in this company, experiencing this

warmth, this teasing, and having it all with Avery...yeah, this was good, he thought, swallowing against the tightness in his chest. This was very, very good. And he found himself smiling as he turned his attention back to Leslie, who was speaking.

"Actually, I made my comment based on observing the two of you throughout dinner," the older man said to Avery. "Thirty-five years reporting for the *New York Times* has given me a fairly extensive education in reading people."

This time Avery's mouth quirked as she swirled her wine and stared into the glass. "And what have you read into this situation?"

Leslie glanced from Avery to Suzannah. His affection was obvious even to David. "Much more than I'm sure you want to hear me wax over ineloquently."

"Oh, no. I do want to hear. Very much so," Avery said, sipping her wine and considering the man her mother had brought into her home.

"Okay, but you have been warned," Leslie said with a laugh, his eyes twinkling as he settled back, hands clasped in his lap. He looked thoughtfully around the table. "Here the four of us sit. Two generations. Old friends becoming reacquainted after years of living unconnected lives. We bring worlds of experience and expectations with us. Yet, in the end, we're all wanting the same things. Fine food and drink, stimulating conversation, the warmth of companionship and, if we're lucky, of a partnership.''

Again Leslie glanced at each of them in turn. ''And, in what seems to be our shared case here, we've come to find those things by looking to the most unexpected places. I truly believe that to everything there is a season. Suzannah and I happen to be approaching the winter of our years. But I fully intend to stick around and show her the beauty of spring.''

David found himself held fast, but not by what the older man was saying. It was the rapt attention on the faces of both Avery and her mother that grabbed him by the throat. It was as if they were hearing a prophet speak. As if they'd cut out their hearts and pasted them to their sleeves.

He kept his attention on Avery's face; she must have sensed his intensity because her lashes drifted down, and when she next looked up she stared at him with an expression of longing that left him amazed. He'd known her for so long yet until this past week, he had barely known her at all.

He'd held on to his fantasy of the girl she'd been from the time he'd left Tatem until he'd returned ten months ago. But he'd arrived to find a woman he didn't want to live without.

All he had left to do was convince her that they were meant to be.

"LET ME HELP YOU clean up before we go," Suzannah said, once David and Leslie had headed out into the living room and left the women to the kitchen. Suzannah and Leslie had plans to continue their evening by driving to the cinema in Alpine.

"No way. You're cutting it close as it is." Avery refused to be responsible for her mother missing out on a minute of her, uh, date.

Suzannah shrugged. "If we're late, we're late. There will always be another feature."

Avery wasn't buying her mother's casual nonchalance. Not for a minute. She crossed her arms, blocking the path to the kitchen should Suzannah try to slip away to do the dishes as some sort of penance for the deception name Leslie.

"Mom, please go and enjoy your night out. I've met Leslie. I approve. He's a wonderfully insightful man, and quite cute to boot! I refuse to stand in the way of the rest of your evening together."

Suzannah laced her fingers and held her hands at her waist. The look she gave Avery conveyed both repentance and concern. "I am sorry, sweetie. I should have been up-front in telling you about Leslie."

"Considering how adamant I've been about keeping Daddy's memory alive, it's no wonder you didn't."

"I had hoped that meeting him without having formed expectations would give you a chance to see him for who he really is. And to see how happy he makes me." Suzannah asked, "Avery, are you pouting?"

"Of course not." Pouting? No. About to cry? She feared exactly that. Her emotions were all over the map. Tonight had been a series of highs and lows as she'd considered how often she'd rejected a challenge, refused an adventure because she didn't want to open herself up.

"You look miffed."

"I'm not miffed. I'm…frustrated, I suppose. I've been so wrapped up in keeping the status quo. I thought having me around after Daddy's death would make things easier on you."

"And it did. It has. You're my daughter. I love you being here where I can be reminded daily of my greatest accomplishment." Suzannah took Avery's hands in her own, stroking her thumbs over the backs, bringing Avery to the verge of tears.

"Oh, Mom."

"Shh, sweetie. Let me finish." Suzannah took a deep breath. "What I don't love is wondering if you've given up living your life to the fullest out of a sense of responsibility to me. I haven't stopped living my life at all.''

''I know.''

''I see the friends I want to, take the trips I want to. The only status quo being kept is your own.'' Suzannah then lifted the brow that had inspired compliance in decades of students.

''I think it's time you let the past go and stepped into the future.''

CHAPTER EIGHT

LISTENING TO LESLIE and Suzannah's laughter as they made their way down the staircase, David closed Avery's front door and turned toward her.

She wasn't there. She'd been standing beside him until moments ago, having seen her mother and Leslie to the door. The second the older couple stepped from the apartment onto the landing, Avery had obviously flown the coop.

He barely restrained himself from rolling his eyes. Such typical Avery behavior, backing away when the heat was on. And more often than not, backing into the kitchen. It was as if she found whatever comfort she needed in food.

Not in eating, but in the preparation and the presentation. The familiar routine. The expectation of having things go her way and turn out exactly as planned.

He'd wondered why of all the things she could've done with her life that she'd chosen to open a bakery. In the light of her food fetish, the business made sense. Avery Rice was a creature of habit, one at home in her element, one who had done everything in her power to secure her safe harbor—a harbor she was about to have buffeted to the ground.

He headed for the kitchen, where he heard her banging around, and stopped in the doorway to watch as she flipped on the switch for the garbage disposal and began to shove a perfectly good and barely half-eaten loaf of French bread down the drain.

The motor ground and whirred, chugging hard as the bread became nothing more than wet floury goo. Undaunted, Avery continued to feed the loaf to the unforgiving blades. It was time for an intervention.

David crossed the kitchen and flipped down the disposal's switch. The motor halted mid-grind. Avery looked up, her eyes wildly bright and red rimmed though as dry as the proverbial bone.

"What do you think you're doing?" she demanded, her anger palpable though he didn't know the source.

"You have something against leftovers?" he asked, using his height to advantage as he towered above her.

"No, I'm just cleaning up." Mouth clamped shut, she waited for him to move his hand from the switch. When he didn't, she tossed the rest of the loaf into the sink and returned to the table for the casserole dish of lasagna.

David moved to intercept the food before it suffered the same grinding fate. "Avery, destroying the rest of dinner isn't going to make anything better."

A dark blond brow went up. "Who said I'm trying to make anything better? Unless you consider cleaning up this mess making things better."

It was the way she said the word *mess* that got to him. She wasn't talking about the leftover food or the dirty dishes at all. She could've ground the salad, the lasagna, hell, even the wine and salad dressing into oblivion, and nothing would change. She would still be caught up trying to fix what she thought was broken, to put her insular world back to rights.

She needed to understand that time had moved on without her. Or perhaps that was exactly what was going on. The very reason she was bent on destruction. God, but he hated seeing her hurt.

He reached up and tucked her hair behind her ear. "Avery, listen to me. I ate way too much and I need about twenty minutes on the couch before I can move. Then I'll help you with the dishes."

"I don't need help with the dishes."

"Maybe not. But I need to help you with them." He took hold of her arm just above the elbow, yet he didn't move until she made up her own mind to follow. They headed for the living room, and when she tried to sit in her overstuffed chair covered with blue-and-white mattress ticking, he guided her onto the matching loveseat and into his lap.

He snuggled back into the corner and took her with him, his legs extended and hers nicely draped over his. He liked the weight of her, liked it a lot. With one arm around her back, the other resting above her knees, he decided he could sit like this for a very long time and be a happy man.

Having a happy woman, though, would be even better. And to get there they were going to have to talk, no matter how much he enjoyed digesting in silence. With his eyes closed. And too often with his mouth open while he snored.

"Avery?"

"Humph."

Not quite a full snort. He supposed that was a good sign. "Talk to me."

"About what?" She settled farther down into his lap.

Another good sign. "Dinner went well, don't you think?"

"I suppose," she said, her tone not as petulant as before but still pensive.

"What did you think of Leslie?"

She hesitated for a moment, pushing her hair

back from her face. "I thought you would've given me an I-told-you-so by now."

"Gloating's not really my style."

She cast him a sideways glance. "What is your style, David? Just your average sneaky bastard type?"

"You think I'm sneaky?" He gave himself the benefit of the doubt and left out the bastard part.

"I think you have an agenda, yes."

Well, yeah. He did. He wouldn't be here otherwise. "That's a pretty broad observation. I actually have several."

"So you admit it?"

"Sure. Why not?" He shrugged, resting an elbow on the loveseat's padded arm and playing with the ends of her hair. He was going to die if he didn't get to feel her hair on his skin—and soon. "Doesn't everyone have one or two? You included?"

This time she shifted away in order to face him straight on. "And, Mr. Know-It-All, I suppose my agendas are obvious to you."

He shook his head, feeling his pulse pick up speed as he took this conversation deeper. "Only the one that's kept you in Tatem all these years."

Her expression blanked. "And that one would be, what?"

"Staying connected to your past, though I'm not

sure of the why," he added, then waited, expecting her to jump up and show him to the door.

When she didn't, he began breathing normally again. He wanted so much from her, with her, yet knew he couldn't force what she wasn't ready to face.

"Where did you go when you left Tatem?" was what she finally asked.

"El Paso, why?" And why did he think she'd known that?

"Was it easier for you there than it had been when you'd come back to school here, you know," she added with a hitch of her shoulder, "after your suspension?"

That suspension had been the hardest thing he'd ever had to face in his eighteen years. He'd never fit in; that was true enough. But school had always been a breeze. It was returning with a new reputation that had put stars in his eyes.

Yeah, he'd been cool. But he still hadn't had Avery. "Easier? In a lot of ways, yeah. I blended. Didn't stand out as a brain, or as the troublemaker that had my father moving us out of Tatem in the end."

"But did you hate it?" she asked, yet what he heard was, *But did you hate me?* She was still caught up in their senior year because of what she thought she'd caused to happen to him. Damn, but why hadn't he seen that?

He moved his hand from her hair to the back of her neck where he began to massage. "Avery?"

She stiffened. Her gaze slid away. This time he wasn't going to let her go until he said what he needed to say.

"It was my choice that night. My choice, to go after Johnny. I could've gone for help."

She frowned, looked back at him, softly asked, "Why didn't you? You wouldn't have been hurt. Or suspended. You could've stayed in Tatem."

"You think Johnny wouldn't have gone after what he'd wanted if I'd ran?" He tried to keep the emotion from his voice, but his words came out strangled. "Do you think I could've lived with myself if I'd been too late getting back?"

"But I went with him—"

"No," he said, cutting her off as tears welled in her eyes. "It was not your fault, do you hear me? Nothing that happened that night was your fault."

"But if I hadn't gone. If I'd told him no." She closed her eyes, bowed her head. "I should have told him no."

He wasn't going to argue that. But he wasn't going to let her accept responsibility for what he'd had to do. "Avery, you need to let it go. It's been over and done now for fifteen years. Hell, I'm the one whose life was upended and I've gotten over it."

"Have you?" she asked, moving her far hand to his chest and resting it there in the center where his heart had started to thud.

"Sure." He tossed off the answer, sure of nothing but the way her touch was causing his blood to stir. "Why would you think I hadn't?"

"Because you're here. In Tatem. A tiny dot on only the most thorough road atlas." She offered him a sadly wry smile. "Not a lot to see and do here. Even Mom and Leslie had to go to Alpine, for God's sake, to have a decent night out."

"I didn't come back because I was looking for a decent night out." He moved one hand to cup the back of her head, the other to cover hers on his chest. He watched her eyes widen, felt his own heartbeat thunder into their hands.

This was it. A moment fifteen years and ten months in coming. "I came back for you."

For a moment, he thought she believed him, then the sad tinge to her smile deepened. "I don't know why you would."

He wanted to growl with frustration. "Are you still thinking I was serious? That day in your kitchen when I told you you'd ruined my life?"

She shrugged, twisted her mouth into a grimace. "No. I know you weren't serious. But I've wondered so long about how things might've been. It's strange, but that moment and all the 'what ifs' that followed have been hard to let go.''

"The 'what ifs' don't matter, Avery. Nothing matters but here and now.''

"Give me time?'' she asked so hesitantly that his aggravation stirred.

Time was one thing he wasn't going to let her have.

"I can't,'' he said, before he pulled her toward him and ground his mouth to hers.

He poured all that he was feeling—the irritation and the desire—into the kiss, giving no quarter as he demanded she respond. He was desperate for her to respond.

And finally she did, tossing off her reticence, her hesitation, the uncertainty of her mood as she matched each stroke of his tongue, scooting around until she straddled his lap and wrapped his neck in her arms.

He'd never known a woman so mercurial yet so free with her passion when stirred. Tiny whimpers spilled from her mouth to his, and he felt the vibration of the sound all through her body.

He spread his legs and she shimmied even closer, then released him, her arms moving from around his neck to her blouse's first button. Her eyes went glassy with desire.

It took the strength of Atlas for David to stop her from undressing and offering him heaven.

"Avery, wait."

Her expression grew cold. "I'm beginning to think you're a tease, David Marks. How many times now have you stopped me from jumping your bones?"

"Trust me," he said with a less-than-steady growl. "You jumping my bones is the stuff of fantasies."

"So...what, then?" She backed off his lap, got to her feet and looked down. "The reality's too much for you?"

He managed to work himself up to a standing position without his erection snapping in half. Stifling a groan wasn't as easy. And so he didn't even try, though he toned down the sound from the werewolf howl he felt like letting go.

"Here's the reality, Avery. My reality," he said once he stood in front of her. "I love you. I want you. But I don't want a one-night stand. Or a cheap roll in the hay." God, what a liar! At this point his body was ready for either of those.

He stepped closer; she backed toward the door. "What I want is for you to come to me because you want me. Not because you're all revved up and need what I can give you. And not because you feel you owe me, or think sleeping with me will be a twisted way to make amends for the past.''

''I didn't say—''

He cut her off ruthlessly. ''I want you to come to me because I'm the only man you want. The only man you need. If that's the case, then I'll be at my place. I think you know where it is.''

CHAPTER NINE

BY THE TIME Avery knocked on David's door, her palms were slick with sweat. This was the first trip she'd made to the third floor since he'd lived here. She couldn't name another time in her life when she'd ever been this nervous.

Not even that night beneath the bleachers when she'd narrowly escaped certain rape.

He was right. None of that mattered now. All that mattered was climbing the staircase without falling on her backside and letting David know how she had spent the past fifteen years holding on to the past because that was where she could find him.

God, how she loved him. She hadn't carried a torch all this time, no. But the kindling for this fire had been laid so very long ago when he'd put his life on the line to save her from a harm that could've been irreparable. Now she was ready to strike the match.

The climb seemed to take forever. She supposed the fact that she was trying to keep David from hearing her had a lot to do with her snail's pace.

And not wanting him to hear her was really dumb since she was coming up with the intent of crawling into his bed.

Ugh, but this love business was so confusing.

Finally she was there, and she took a deep breath before she knocked once, twice, figuring if he was already asleep she didn't want to wake him and two knocks should be enough even if she hadn't knocked hard and maybe she should just forget it and go back—

The door opened. David stood there wearing ragged gray sweat shorts and a faded navy T-shirt with a Penn State logo. The shirt barely stretched over his chest or his biceps and the only thing she could think to say was, "When did you go to Penn State?"

He laughed cautiously, stepping back and gesturing her inside. She entered, watching as his expression ran the gamut from relief to pleasure to an emotion much more intense. One that seemed to mirror her own sense of her heart being unable to contain all she felt.

"I didn't go to Penn State. I went to University of Texas in El Paso." He could have gone to Harvard. To MIT. To any of several bastions of higher education.

"David, here's the thing," she said quickly, turning to face him without taking in a single detail of his apartment, knowing she had to get this out before she lost her nerve and scurried back downstairs. She felt so much safer when on the second floor than she did facing him now.

"The thing?" he echoed, closing the door while his gaze remained on her face.

"Yes. The thing." She twisted her hands at her waist. "It's killing me that I never lifted a single finger to intervene when things for you started going so badly downhill—"

And that was all she got out because he was there and his arms were around her and his mouth was there seeking out hers. The force of his kiss left her unable to breathe. He wrapped himself around her until she wasn't sure a shadow could squeeze between their bodies.

She wasn't truly aware that her feet had left the floor until she felt the back of her knees hit the edge of his sofa seconds before he followed her down to the cushions. His weight above her felt simply like another part of herself, and she pulled him down to cover her.

He shifted to the side; she urged him back, loving the bulk of his body, the press of his strength that took her deeper into the cushions. His chest was firm, the one shoulder pinning her rounded and hard. Their legs tangled, as did their arms, a hand stroking a hip, a shoulder blade, fingers twining together.

His mouth warmed her skin when he trailed kisses from her ear along her jaw to her chin. She nudged him, wanting his lips on hers, his tongue on hers, but he made her wait, nipping at the edges of her mouth just enough to make her want to hit him, and hard.

And so she did, smacking a hand as close to his bottom as she could manage. He chuckled, the sound rolling through her like thunder in the air, and then the lightning followed as he aligned their bodies hips to hips.

Bracing himself on his forearms, he kissed her the way she'd wanted, but he kissed her even more. Deeper and stronger yet with a tenderness she had never thought to feel. His tongue stroked along the length of hers until she swore she felt sparks pop and sizzle over her skin.

She squirmed beneath him, not seeking her freedom, simply wanting to touch him, to get him out of his clothes, to shed her own. She couldn't wait to feel his skin, his strength, his beautifully hard body in all the places that mattered.

Right now she felt him most of all in her heart. The beauty he showed her body paled in comparison to the flood of emotion bringing tears to her eyes as he began to move, sliding down her body until his mouth hovered over her chest.

He raised his gaze then, his heavy-lidded eyes asking permission for more things than she knew to imagine. She nodded. She wanted them all, wanted him, David, and willingly surrendered.

The expression on his face darkened intensely. He slid farther down the length of her body, took hold of her shirt hem and raised it slowly, his tongue circling her navel as he bared her belly's skin.

Blowing warm breath over the dampness he'd left, he made his way back up, taking her shirt with him. Once the hem reached her breasts, she grabbed hold and pulled it over her head. David slipped an arm behind her, releasing the clasp of her bra before returning to slowly uncover her.

The room's cool air breathed across her skin. Her nipples grew taut in anticipation as she waited for his touch.

"Do you know how beautiful you are?" he said, before swirling the barest tip of his tongue around one hard peak then moving to the other.

She arched her back. She didn't want to talk. She only wanted to feel. "Shh."

He chuckled against her skin. "Not much of a talker, huh?"

"Oh, I can talk," she whispered breathlessly,

gasping as he sucked harder. "I just can't walk and chew gum at the same time."

David raised to one elbow and stripped off his shirt. In the next second, she found herself breathless, faced with the broad expanse of his bare chest and shoulders instead of only teasing glimpses.

"Do you know how beautiful you are?" she asked, overwhelmed, swept away, by nothing more than looking at him like this.

His face solemn, he lowered himself to kiss her, his mouth opening to hers as he made the skin-to-skin contact she'd been dying for. He was warm, so incredibly warm. She shivered, feeling gooseflesh prickle her skin, feeling so much more, the smooth resilience of his bare flesh as she ran her hands all over him.

He lingered to kiss her, nipping, sucking, nibbling along her jaw, her neck, her collarbone to her shoulder, yet she was greedy for more. Heat built deep in her belly, between her legs, growing itchy and insistent. She swore she was going to scream.

She settled with slapping him on the backside. "You're taking way too long."

"Ah, darlin'. Judging by that love pat, I'd say I'm taking just long enough," he said softly, his tone starting her to shivering all over again.

But finally he moved, sliding down her body, kissing his way around and beneath her breasts without paying the least bit of attention to the taut peaks of her nipples in spite of the way she arched upward and begged him to do. He just continued on his way to unbutton the waistband of her pants.

Once he'd released the button and slid the zipper down, he raised up to his knees and stopped, staring at her with an expression she wasn't sure she could name. It was almost as if he wasn't sure he should continue—which was ridiculous.

Making love to him, with him, was the fulfillment she'd been looking forever to find.

She pushed up to her elbows. "What's wrong?"

David's gaze swept her from belly to breast before settling on her face. His voice was a gruff tremor when he asked, "Why are you here?"

She longed to be flip, to continue their teasing banter of earlier but knew playtime was long gone. The next few moments could possibly be the most important of her life and deserved her full honesty. Yet she wasn't sure she could give it. She was too lost to trust what she might say.

"I can't talk now. I really can't talk now," she pleaded, lifting her hips and urging him to finish stripping her of her clothes. "Please, David. We'll talk. I promise. But later. Later."

He wasn't happy about it. She was certain he wanted to hear of her feelings, yet she feared she would say anything to get her way. And that would hardly be fair.

He gave in at last, pulling both pants and panties from her legs. She lay bare before him, and his chest heaved with his effort to breathe. He muttered a curse as he shucked off the rest of his clothes, and then it was Avery's turn to struggle and gasp.

She'd thought him beautiful before. Now she was without words to describe the gorgeous perfection of David's body. She wanted to cry, moved to tears by the sweet and tender emotion of wanting him.

He returned to her then, settling his weight fully, his sheathed erection probing between her thighs. She opened for him, adjusting the angle of her hips, the position of her legs, shifting and squirming until he found her entrance and pushed slowly inside.

She cried out softly as he filled her, panting sharply in order to hold on. His gaze remained locked with hers, and she saw him waging the same battle for control. His jaw popped, his pulse throbbed in his temple. And just as she saw his eyes grow damp and redden, he buried his face in the crook of her shoulder and began to move.

She held him tightly, her heels pressed to his hips, her hands roaming his back in loving strokes. Her heart was so full, so full, and when joyous tears fell from her eyes she knew she could hold back no longer.

As David loved her, she loved him back. Their bodies moved together. The completion they reached came as one. She cried his name. He groaned in response, his hands beneath her bottom holding her tight for his finishing strokes.

And then she shuddered and collapsed, knowing that she had reached her future and would never return to the past.

EARLY THE NEXT MORNING, having come awake to an empty bed, David dressed and left the house. In the end, he and Avery had never talked. They'd done nothing more than move from couch to bed, where they'd spoken only with their bodies.

It had been a hell of a bad way to wake up, finding the side of the bed that she'd warmed all night ice-cold. Her scent remained on his pillows, in his sheets and blankets. He hadn't even stopped to make a pot of coffee. He'd just gotten the hell out of Dodge.

Now, for the first time in fifteen years, he stood beneath the bleachers on the scruffy grass field behind Tatem High. The field wasn't in a whole lot better shape now than it had been then. Such was the reality of the West Texas heat.

The bleachers, however, were new. They were still constructed of metal rather than the heavy-duty concrete found in larger school districts, but the

wooden seats had been replaced with the same gal-
vanized aluminum as the frames.

With the school year winding down and summer
on the way, the grounds had been manicured to
within an inch of their life for the upcoming grad-
uation ceremony. He didn't know why, when the
dry heat baked graduates and attendees alike, the
powers that be insisted on the tradition of sending
seniors off into the big bad world with the setting
sun at their back.

He could appreciate the symbolism, just not the
temperature. And damn if he didn't wish that he'd
been able to graduate with his classmates from Tatem High.

No wonder Avery was hesitant to have anything
to do with him. She'd finally bedded Tatem's bad
boy and now she could get on with the rest of her
life. This sure as hell wasn't the full circle David
had hoped to complete when he'd returned last year
to the town in which he'd grown up.

Having now taught in that same environment, he
better understood his father's decision to move
them away from the rural area to one more urban,
one where David wouldn't stand out as either a
prodigy or the troublemaker he'd become. Once in
El Paso, he'd easily blended into the crowd; he'd
run up against kids a hell of a lot smarter as well

as a hell of a lot meaner. The experience had put Tatem into perspective.

Yet he'd never gotten over Avery Rice.

And here he stood, wondering what he was going to do now that it looked like she didn't return his feelings. Move out of her house for one thing, he grumbled, hands stuffed in his pockets as he kicked at dry clods of dirt that went *poof* when he did.

He knew Yvette Lapp had a garage apartment for rent, except Yvette worked at Avery's bakery and renting from her instead of Suzannah wouldn't be a whole lot better. Since he obviously wouldn't be showing Avery the West Coast this summer, moving while he had the time wouldn't be a bad idea. Yeah. That's what he'd do this next week. See about finding a place.

Packing wouldn't take him much time at all since he'd never done more than a cursory move-in. He'd certainly never settled in, as if he'd been waiting to do so until he knew how things would go down between him and Avery. Judging by the past few days, they'd pretty much gone down like crap, he admitted, just as he heard the rumble of a diesel engine.

He looked up in time to watch Avery pull her big black Dodge Ram to a stop, and was hit with the incongruity of this woman driving this truck. Yes, it made perfect West Texas sense, but it was the only thought that came to mind that he could manage. Everything else was a blur.

When she cut the engine, he thought his heart had stopped as well. He couldn't feel a single beat. And then he could feel nothing else, the pounding ringing in his ears as she climbed down from the monster, slammed the door and headed his way as if she'd known exactly where she'd find him.

"What are you doing here?" he asked when she stopped only a few feet away.

"I could ask you the same question," she said, her hands shoved into the pockets of her denim shorts.

He shrugged. He wasn't going to let her get to him. Not today. Not after last night. "Visiting old haunts. You know, remembering the good ol' days."

"You do seem to be getting the hang of small-town life again."

"What do you mean?"

"You left your front door unlocked. I came back to bring you breakfast in bed." She inclined her head, gesturing toward her truck. The smile on her face was as soft and gentle as any he'd ever seen. "I have coffee and hot croissants."

He swallowed hard as he looked away, glancing toward the football field where he'd chased after her and made such a fool of himself. He was done with that. His days of being a fool were over. "Why are you here, Avery?"

"Oh, David. I came here for you. To be with you. To love with you." Her voice broke and, as he turned toward her, her eyes grew wet. He watched as her throat seemed to choke off her ability to breathe. "You've been a part of my life for so long. Even the years that I didn't see you…you were still there. In my heart. I just never knew why."

"And now you do?" he asked, his tone rough, harsh, as if he were bracing himself for a blow.

She delivered it softly. "I love you, David. The boy you used to be got under my skin. But the man you are now has shown me the beauty of being alive. I want to be with you as long as you'll have me."

God. Now he was the one unable to draw a single breath. He opened his arms, and then she was there, holding him, loving him. And he said the only words his heart allowed him to say.

"Forever, Avery. Forever."

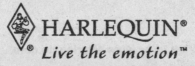

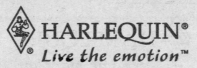

Forrester Square

LEGACIES · LIES · LOVE ·

The mystery and excitement
continues in May 2004 with…

COME FLY WITH ME
by
JILL SHALVIS

Longing for a child of
her own, single day-care
owner Katherine Kinard
decides to visit a sperm
bank. But fate intervenes
en route when she meets
Alaskan pilot Nick Spencer.
He quickly offers marriage
and a ready-made family…
but what about love?

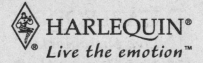

HARLEQUIN®
Live the emotion™

**Visit the Forrester Square web site
at www.forrestersquare.com**

FSQCFWM

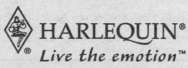

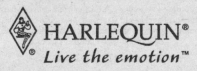